By the same author

BRIAN MOORE

The Feast of Lupercal

GRANADA
London Toronto Sydney New York

Published by Granada Publishing Limited in 1983

ISBN 0 586 05784 6

First published in Great Britain by
André Deutsch Limited 1958
Copyright © Brian Moore 1958

The Feast of Lupercal has previously been published
under the title *A Moment of Love*

Granada Publishing Limited
Frogmore, St Albans, Herts AL2 2NF
and
36 Golden Square, London W1R 4AH
515 Madison Avenue, New York, NY 10022, USA
117 York Street, Sydney, NSW 2000, Australia
60 International Boulevard, Rexdale, Ontario, R9W 6J2, Canada
61 Beach Road, Auckland, New Zealand

Printed and bound in Great Britain by
Cox and Wyman Ltd, Reading
Set in Plantin

To my mother

Chapter One

Diarmuid Devine, BA (Junior and Senior English), stood at his desk sizing his books into a pile. He hooked his cane under the armhole of his academic gown and walked to the door. In ten years of teaching, he had learned to calculate each forty-minute class period without reference to his watch. Time was up. The bell would ring. He looked back at the boys, warning them to silence. Then he left the room.

At that moment, in a small cubbyhole off the entrance hall of Ardath College, the hall porter pushed a key into the switch block and pressed it down. An electric bell, deafeningly loud, screamed out into corridors, crying unheard in empty dormitories, echoing across wet playing fields to die in the faraway mists over Belfast Lough.

In the silence that followed, the long grey façade of Ardath appeared to shake. Boys of all ages crowded corridors and stairs as though the buildings were on fire. Priests, wearing black soutanes, appeared at doors and turnings, swishing canes to restore order, harrying stragglers in transit from classroom to classroom. It was ten minutes to three. All were eager to finish the day.

Mr Devine had avoided this rush. He took the back stairs down to the main corridor. A minute to step into Masters' Lavatory and pump ship . . . then over to Senior I, for the last period. *Macbeth*, it was. And their compositions to be collected . . .

Entering the lavatory, Mr Devine reviewed the row of half doors. No feet protruded. He chose the second stall and shut himself in, glad of a moment's peace. But he had no luck. The corridor door banged open and someone moved into the wash-basin area. A priest? He heard the Someone whistle a few bars of *The Rose of Tralee*. That was a favourite of Frank Turley, who taught geography.

The door banged a second time. A voice spoke. This time, he had no trouble identifying Young Connolly, a junior teacher of mathematics.

'That you, Frank?'

'Hello there.'

'I thought I saw you popping in,' Young Connolly said. 'You're the very man I was looking for.'

Mr Devine, enclosed in his stall, stared at the wall. He wondered if he should cough, or something. But then he'd have to speak to them. And if there was one thing he hated, it was being forced to carry on a conversation in the act of pumping ship.

He heard Turley turn on the water tap.

'Say, Frank,' Young Connolly said in a confidential voice, 'have you heard anything about a party at Heron's place tonight?'

'Not me,' Turley said.

Mr Devine nodded his head. *He* knew. Tim Heron, one of the senior lay masters, was having a party that night to announce his daughter's engagement to a young doctor called Carty. Mr Devine knew why Connolly had not been invited. Connolly used to have a notion of the girl. It would hardly have been tactful to invite him on such an occasion.

'So they didn't ask you either?' Young Connolly said.

'Why should they? I've never been thick with Heron,' Turley replied.

'Well, they might have asked me,' Connolly's voice was indignant. 'After all, I'm supposed to be going around with Mary.'

In his stall, Mr Devine was shocked. So poor Connolly didn't know yet. Oh, poor chap! He supposed old Tim Heron hadn't the heart to tell Connolly about the daughter getting engaged to someone else. He felt damn sorry for Young Connolly.

'Well, who else has been invited?' Turley asked.

'Devine, for one.'

'Well, why don't you ask Devine?'

'Och, that old woman!' Young Connolly said.

Mr Devine pressed his lips together and stared at the lavatory bowl. Old woman? What on earth . . .? He was relieved to hear Frank Turley stick up for him.

'I don't know what you mean,' Turley said. 'I've always found Dev a very decent skin. Why *don't* you ask him?'

'How can I ask him?' Young Connolly said in a disgusted voice. 'Sure, he'd think I was angling for an invitation. He might even tell Heron I was asking. And that's the last thing I want.'

'Well, you can always explain why you want to know,' Turley said. 'Dev's very discreet.'

'Explain? Och, he wouldn't know what I was talking about. How can you expect the likes of Dev to understand what a fellow feels about a girl?'

Mr Devine heard Turley laugh: a short amused chuckle. He stared at the lavatory bowl, buttoning, his face hot. He no longer dared to stir, in case they heard him. He prayed they would go away. If they found him now, he could not look them in the face. He had never been so mortified in his life.

'Well, ask Tony Moloney then, if you don't want to ask Dev,' Turley said. 'Tony would know, he knows all the dirt.'

'My God, I never thought of that,' Young Connolly said. 'Where is Tony, this forty?'

'Over in Junior III,' Turley said.

'I'll nip over now.'

'You'll be late,' Turley said.

'Ah, to hell, I'm no bloody robot. Let them wait!'

Mr Devine heard the door bang. A moment later Turley's feet passed in front of his stall. He prayed that Turley would not . . .

But the door banged a second time. He could come out now. It was all right. He waited to make absolutely sure Frank Turley had gone before he emerged from his stall. His face was flushed. He was very upset.

He was a tall man, yet did not seem so: not youthful, yet somehow young; a man whose appearance suggested some painful uncertainty. He wore the jacket and waistcoat of a business suit, but his trousers were sag-kneed flannels. His black brogues clashed with loud Argyle socks. The military bravura of his large moustache was denied by weak eyes, circled with ill-fitting spectacles. Similarly, his hair, worn long and untidy behind the ears, thinning to a sandy shoal of his freckled brow, offset the Victorian respectability of waistcoat, gold watch chain and signet ring.

He made straight for the wash-basin in a hurried ritual of hand-washing, hand-shaking, and hand-drying, all the time staring shamefaced at his image in the mirror opposite. Young Connolly had been upset, of course. Probably sick with suspicion that Mary Heron might be ditching him. So there was some excuse for his making an unkind remark. But Frank Turley had laughed at it, as if it were a well-known fact that Devine was – odd.

Still, he had no time to think about it now. He was late for class. He pushed the door open and ran, a stitch in his side, his footsteps loud on the terrazzo flooring. Late, late. And listen to them up there. Raising the roof.

He reached the staircase and went up, two at a time. A look-out's voice warned: 'Dev!' Feet thumped on bare boards as boys rushed to their places. Desks banged shut. The noise died to whispers as Mr Devine entered the classroom. He laid cane and books on his desk and then, his right hand tugging the collar of his gown in the manner of prosecuting counsel, he surveyed the class with a familiar magistral challenge. The whispers ceased. He turned his back on them in contempt and stared at the blackboard. He waited. When the silence was complete, he spoke:

10

'Daly. Clean that board.'

A back-seat boy, dirty-faced and troublesome, went to the blackboard and wiped it clean in a swirl of chalk dust. Mr Devine sat down.

'McAvitty. Collect the compositions.'

Essays, written the night before, were brought to his desk.

Four boys had not submitted work. Two had excuses written by parents. These, Mr Devine accepted. He asked the other two boys for their reasons.

'Please, sir, I had so many exercises to do, I couldn't finish them all.'

'Me too, sir.'

The class pondered the odds. Yesterday, a junior boy had offered this old and true excuse. Mr Devine had questioned the boy on each piece of homework and had remarked that, this time, the set tasks did seem excessive. He had been an Ardath boy himself and he knew the work was sometimes very heavy. But now, hearing the same excuse one day later in a senior class, Mr Devine realized it had become usable currency. If he accepted it again, he would be imposed on.

He stepped down from his desk, picking up his long thin cane. With practised gentleness he raised Frankie Deegan's arm to shoulder level. Then, sighting along the cane, like a matador about to administer the kill, he reared back and brought the cane whistling down, striking the ridge of the boy's palm. Deegan doubled over in pain. At Ardath, stoicism is regarded as folly. Stoics made a master think he had missed.

'Other hand,' Mr Devine ordered.

The class watched Deegan extend his left arm. On the whole, they were glad Dev had not accepted the excuse. If he had, they would have wasted their time writing essays last night.

Again, Mr Devine sighted and struck. Deegan, both palms tucked under his armpits, went crippled to his seat.

McAleer, the second offender, stood out. Mr Devine punished, McAleer registered suffering, and the class opened the blue-bound *Macbeths* at Act Two, Scene One.

'Now,' Mr Devine said. 'Sullivan will be Banquo; O'Hare, Fleance; and Deegan, if he has recovered from his fearful torment, will read Macbeth.'

Satisfied, the class relaxed its vigilance. In half an hour the school day would be over. Day boys would go home and the boarders would have two free hours before supper and the long study period.

But Mr Devine could not relax . . . *That old woman!* Since when was thirty-seven considered old? Surely Young Connolly didn't mean he was a pansy, or anything of that sort? No, he did not think Connolly had meant that. It was more that he was some ninny, incapable of getting a girl. And to think I felt sorry for *him*, Mr Devine thought indignantly. And Frank Turley laughed as if everyone knew I was a fool. Frank's older than me and married, Mr Devine recalled. Still, I never thought Frank felt that way about me.

He stared at the wooden partition, behind the back row of the class. It was a shock, dammit, to find out you were a laughing-stock. And unfair, Mr Devine thought. Unfair. What's so great about marriage, I'd like to know? Look at my sister Josie, she got married and now she's miserable. Stuck out in Dungannon with a dozen in-laws on top of her. Which of us is better off, I ask you?

Their father, his and Josie's, had died fourteen years ago. Their poor mother followed him to the grave one year later. He and Josie had been left all alone. Josie got married and he moved to digs. So no one could say he was one of those fellows who'd been tied to his mother's apron strings, now could they? He had lived in digs for thirteen years, ten of them in his present place. He was quite comfortable, thank you.

As for girls, well, he had never been a ladies' man. He

was not ugly, no, nor too shy, no, but he never had much luck with girls. It was the education in Ireland, dammit, he had said it many a time. He had been a boarder at this very school, shut off from girls until he was almost a grown man. And when he looked at the dirty, ill-kempt lumps of lads before him now, it was hard to believe that they were, many of them, sons of professional men, well-to-do publicans and farmers. They looked like slum boys, every blessed one of them. Ardath cared little for appearances or social graces. No wonder these boys weren't fit to go out with girls when they left school. It was a matter of ignorance, pure and simple.

There was a sudden pause in the reading. He became aware of the eyes that watched him.

'Well, what is it?'

'Lady Macbeth, sir, who'll read Lady Macbeth?'

'As guilty as her lord and master, she was,' Mr Devine said. 'Guiltier, according to most authorities. Well, then, who better than Deegan's fellow culprit? McAleer, you'll be Lady Macbeth.'

McAleer, still nursing his paining palms, had ceased to take any interest in the class. He had been flippered, after all. That should be enough for one forty. Now, in great confusion, he searched for the place to start. Someone whispered a cue. He began, in monotone:

'That which hath made them drunk hath made me bold . . . What hath quenched them . . . hath given me fire . . .'

As for thinking about women, Mr Devine said to himself, I'm perfectly normal, God help me. But how am I supposed to tell them that, short of making a damn fool of myself, like Connolly, spilling out my private affairs in the jakes, of all places. I have as many sinful thoughts as any one of the fellows, I'll bet my shirt. Still, there's no sense letting them anger me. Forget it.

He sat up straight at his desk and turned his attention to the text. Aha, I missed that favourite with the examiners.

'One moment, gentlemen. On the page just read, top of the page, mark this passage: "Is this a dagger which I see before me?" Commit it to memory. It is often set in Senior when *Macbeth* is the text. I will ask Deegan to read it once more and then I will explain the meaning.'

'Is this a dagger which I see before me?' asked Deegan-Macbeth.

When the soliloquy finished, Mr Devine began to speak. He could remember that question was asked in '36, in '39, and again in '49 and '53. He phrased his explanation on the points usually raised. The class listened attentively. Dev was known to be a great hand in amateur theatricals. He was also good at anticipating examiners' questions. His classes got good marks. But the boys did not listen because of that. They listened because at Ardath a master did not tell a thing twice. In a week's time he might ask them to explain it back to him.

And at last, the last bell rang. Mr Devine, as always, was the first master to catch the bus which took them from the suburb of Glengormley to the centre of Belfast. He lived midway between the school and the city, in a quiet avenue once prosperous, now failing. Its small front gardens had a naked, communal look, occasioned by the wartime removal of their iron railings for use in making tanks. The railings had not been replaced, the avenue had not recovered. Dusty squares of lawn, enclosed by low stone parapets, lay like neglected empty pools in front of the houses. It was an avenue whose first owners had moved to new areas, making way for widows on annuities, salesmen on commission and policemen pensioned off. Most of the houses took in boarders and some had converted their basements into flats for single gentlemen.

Mr Devine lived in such a flat. He let himself in now, entering a dark hallway, off which were his sitting room, his bedroom and a small lavatory and closet. At the end of the hall a flight of carpeted stairs rose to his landlady's kitchen. He went up those stairs at least three times a day; to shave, to breakfast and to supper. He ate his meals in his landlady's dining room, but did not sit in her living room. Mrs Dempsey was careful of the proprieties.

Taking off his raincoat and hat, Mr Devine went into his den. The fire was drawing and it was not dark yet. A late afternoon sun shone through the iron-barred basement windows, beyond which he could see the back garden with washing on a long line. He was very fond of this room. The makeshift bookshelves which rose dustily towards the ceiling had been his own idea. He himself had worn the armchair to its present faithful submission: his carelessness with pipes and teacups was responsible for the mosaic of dark rings which inlaid the round mahogany table. His old periodicals stacked along the far wall had yellowed with the wallpapers to a common brownish blur. The heavy sideboard and portable gramophone were old and familiar. They had come from his parents' home.

Above the fireplace, ranged along the wall, like a display in a photographer's window, were his souvenirs, glass fronts regularly dusted, black frames shining. School groups, row upon row of boys with masters, arms akimbo, in the middle. Snapshots of university days, Dear Old National, some of the young men in the pictures now dead, some far away in the Foreign Missions. Centred over the fire in the place of honour was a large wedding photograph. A bearded man, his moustaches curved like buffalo horns, his hand pressing flat on a white stiff shirt; a lady in white silk brocade, her face set in a coy, long-held smile. On their best behaviour, his unknown young father, his smiling mother. Stiffly standing, unnaturally posed, they patiently awaited their long-ago photographer as though guessing the curious immortality of that moment. In tribute to his parents, Mr Devine had hung a silver shield above the wedding picture.

It had been won first ten years ago by an amateur drama group, when his name, as producer's assistant, had been left off the programme. The group had won the award for five years running. Each time, despite apologies, his name had somehow not been included. The others made up for this oversight by presenting Mr Devine with the shield. *In perpetua.*

He sat down, opened the little firebox door and poked the coal about. Then he read his post. A subscription to the *Spectator* to be renewed, a move in a chess game he was playing with a man in Manchester, a life insurance company's calender. Nothing else. As he put the chess move in his waistcoat pocket, a voice called from the kitchen above.

'Are you there, Mr Devine?'

'Yes, Mrs Dempsey.'

'The water's hot, will I fill up the bath now?'

'All right.'

The kitchen door shut. Familiarly irritated at this hurrying-up of his twice-weekly bath, Mr Devine went into his bedroom to change. It was a small room. The bed was one he had slept on since he was a boy. The dresser and chair also came from his parents' home. Over the bed was a memory of boyhood, a large coloured map of Ireland, red-pencilled with records of his walking tours. He took off his mis-matched trousers and jacket, put on his warm padded dressing gown over the long white combinations and slopped in slippers up the basement stairs, stopping to knock on the kitchen door before entering Mrs Dempsey's terrain. As usual, when he went for his bath, he met no one. Mrs Dempsey had two growing girls. She made sure that the way was clear.

On the second floor of the house Mr Devine entered the foggy steam of an old-fashioned bathroom. He locked the door, tested the water, and considered washing his hair. Was there any truth in that yarn about too much hair washing inducing baldness? It must be a hereditary thing. His father at fifty went as bald as an egg.

16

He thought of his father. Remembered that his father did not like to duck his head when he was swimming. Remembered Portstewart; he had been a boy of ten at the time; his father had swum to sea with a strong, slow breast stroke, leaving him behind on the beach. He had wept – his daddy was swimming away forever! To Scotland . . .

Saddened, Mr Devine remembered the last time he had seen his father. Lying on the big double bed in a brown cashmere shroud, his hands like a waxwork, clenched around rosary beads, his feet at attention in white cashmere stockings . . . And the small ugly details, remembered after all these years . . . The tapes at the back of the shroud had not been tied because his father was so heavy to lift. The unseen back was naked. The feet stayed together because the undertaker's man had fastened them with tape. A small missal had been propped under the chin to help death's stiffness to close the mouth forever. Mass cards fell like leaves on the bed, for many people knew his father. The elder Devine had been principal of a big public elementary school in a town not too big for everyone to know the head teacher. Yes, more knew Daddy than will ever know me, Mr Devine thought sadly. And remember him as I do. *The Tempest* we did in Junior III today brought him back to mind. *Full fathom five they father lies, of his bones are coral made*. Beautiful thing, that, under the water, the white skeleton. *Nothing of him that doth fade* . . . In Rome, Trelawney had that line inscribed on Shelley's tomb. I must find out how much those boys know of Shelley's biography. It has been asked, once or twice.

Slowly Mr Devine unbuttoned his combinations. His body was unpublic, skin never sunned, contrasting strongly with the lines of demarcation at wrists and neck. It was as though his head and hands, exposed to rain and wind, did not fit this hidden body, white as a farmer's belly. Now, as he lowered its whiteness carefully into the water, it suffused a painful pink. Catching his breath, he rested in the steaming, scalding heat.

But even his father was not really remembered by people nowadays. How many people ever thought of his father on any given day? Even Josie and I rarely think of him, Mr Devine realized. Aye, a fellow is easily forgotten when he shuffles off this coil. Children help; now take Old Tim Heron I'm going to see tonight – never has two shillings to rub together, every month stretched to meet the next, but he's a *pater familias*, dammit; his boy Eamon will carry on the name and his daughters will mingle his blood with other families. Moses and the bulrushes. They'd have drowned me. Male.

Standing in the tub, soaping his buttocks, he dropped his chin to stare. *Deo gratias*, he could still see it; he had not put on a pot yet. Unused though it was. But dammit, he chided himself, there is no sense in being morbid, no sense thinking things like that. And it was all bunkum, this business of carrying on your line. Take genius, it did not transmit. For example . . .

But he could not think of an example, offhand. He stepped out onto the rubber mat, wiped the steamy mirror and put on his spectacles, inspecting his stranger face. His hair was getting just a wee bit thin on top. He remembered when it used to stick up like a whin bush. He tousled it, trying to remake that whin bush. But it was no use. *Sic transit* crowning *gloria*. Oh, well, he was not such a bad-looking cuss; he had seen worse in his day. He bowed to himself and gave his moustaches a military twirl. After all, he was off to a party that very night. There would be lots of girls there, you would imagine.

Decent and comforted, he unlocked the door. Had he pulled out the bath plug? He listened. Yes, he could hear a last cupful swirl around the waste hole. He glanced at the bath and something about it – long, white, recumbent – put him in mind of a cemetery plinth. Dammit, he was in a very morbid frame of mind today! The water was all gone now. As the last drops sucked through the waste hole, they made a strange, half-human gasp. He shut the bathroom door and went downstairs to his own place.

Chapter Two

A damp night wind, blowing along the Cavehill Road, almost took Mr Devine's hat with it as he entered the street where Tim Heron lived. It was a street of small, red brick houses, their bay windows thrust out to repel the stranger; a street whose back-yard laundry lines offered an intimate census of the inhabitants. Children, now in bed, had fought all day long up and down its pavements, laying waste the tiny front gardens with the litter of their presence; chalked walls, overturned tricycles, sagging, abandoned prams. It was quiet now: the yells, the shouted refusals, the adult bicker done. Here, people went to bed early, rose early, and had a tiring day.

But inside at Number Six, all this had been changed. The house was *en fête*. A bright orange glow spilled into the street from the lamp in the narrow hall. And at the opened front door, lips taut in a little-used smile, Timothy Stanislaus Heron, MA, greeted each newcomer, helping off with the coats.

'Dev! Come in, come in. Throw your coat over there some place, like a good man. And listen, come here, I want a word with you.'

Tonight, Tim Heron was wearing his best and doing his damnedest to be sociable. But it was a poor performance in a role he had not studied. All his life, his constant fear had been that he would be overlooked, his constant preoccupation the seeking out of fancied insults. At sixty, he bore the signs of it; he could not look happy. His bony body was warped by tics and tremblings of suppressed rage, his electric-blue eyes flickered to and fro in search of a sneak attack. His hand constantly calmed his brow, smoothing his grey, waved hairs, each of which lay single on his skull as though drawn on in pencil.

'Have you heard the good news?' he said.

'No, Tim, what would that be?'

'Young Gerry has just bought a house on the Somerton Road.'

'Oho!' said Mr Devine. 'Well, Tim, he must be a man of means, this new member of your family. Somerton Road, indeed.'

'Ah, he's a great lad,' Tim Heron said. 'A great lad.'

'Well, he's getting a great wee girl,' Mr Devine said.

'True. True. Ah, the young people nowadays are lucky. Times have changed, eh, Dev? Who ever heard of a young fellow just out of medical school setting up in that style in our day?'

In our day? Mr Devine looked bleakly at his host. Tim Heron had got him the job at Ardath years ago. And often invited him to his house. They were friends of long standing, no question of that. But what the blazes did Tim mean, *in our day?* He's nearly twice as old as me, Mr Devine decided.

Still, there was no sense offending him. Let it pass.

'True enough,' he said. 'True enough.'

'Well, good luck to them, is what I say,' Tim Heron said. 'And by the same token, what about a drink, Dev? Here I am, keeping you at the door when you could be in the heat.'

'That's all right, Tim. Quite all right.'

'Aye, well, everyone is not as considerate as you,' Tim Heron said, his whitish lips pulled down at their edges as one of his sudden angers seized him. He put his face close and Mr Devine saw the large Adam's apple jiggle in Tim's scrawny throat. 'The President never came, Dev. Never came.'

'Oh, I wouldn't take offence at that, Tim,' Mr Devine said hastily. 'Sure, he never was a social man.'

'But I asked him specially,' Tim said, his right eye blinking in rage. 'You'd think when the senior lay staff member asked him as a special favour, you'd think he'd have the politeness to attend.'

'He'll send Father McSwiney instead. He's getting too doddery to come himself, poor old fellow.'

'Do you think so?' Tim Heron paused to consider this compromise. 'Aye, you might be right, Dev.'

'Sure, you'll be better off with Father Mac,' Mr Devine said. 'He's a more sociable man.'

'Aye.' Tim Heron nodded his head and smoothed his thin hair once more. 'Father Mac will be President himself before long, Dev, mark my words.'

'True enough,' Mr Devine said, smiling. He saw that his remark had pleased Old Tim, had soothed another rage to rest.

'Aye.' Cheered, Tim Heron patted Mr Devine on his shoulder, urging him inside. 'In you go now, Dev, and join the party.'

'Right, Tim.'

Entering the parlour, Mr Devine stopped to say good night to young Eamon, Tim's only boy, and a senior student at Ardath. He exchanged good evenings with Mrs Sullivan – a friend of his sister's before his sister moved to Dungannon. At the far end of the room male backs shielded a table with drinks on it. I wonder who I know, Mr Devine asked himself. Someone to have a yarn with, a jorum of whisky, a little company. Who?

But he paused. After all, if he got stuck in with a bunch of fellows, he would spend the evening among his own sex. He thought uneasily of Young Connolly's remark in the jakes. What about talking to a woman for a change?

There were three ladies sitting in the window seat. One was a grandmother, one was forty, and one was a nice-looking girl. Who is she, I wonder? Nervous, pretending not to be doing it, he edged towards them. The girl looked up. Immediately, Mr Devine sighted an imaginary old friend at the other end of the room. He waved and smiled at this imaginary figure. The girl looked away and the women's talk resumed.

Now, if I had a plate of biscuits, I could go up and offer them something. But there were no biscuits in sight. I could offer them a drink. What would you ladies like to drink? Or, could I get anybody anything to drink? Yes, that was the note. Decided, he turned to face the ladies.

'And then she said that Peggy said they weren't going to get the house at all.'

'Go on! Well, then, that explains why Meta didn't speak to Peg and I, last Sunday, when we met her coming out of Lisbreen, after eleven Mass.'

And the good-looking girl said: 'Oh, she and Peg had an awful row, didn't you know? You know the trick she has of fingering everything and asking the price. Well, she went to Peg's house one day and she was no sooner in the door than she . . .'

They hadn't noticed him at all. Character-assassins, every blessed one of them. That was a thing he couldn't help noticing about women, they always had the bad word for one another. Men had far more sense, at least they shut up when they didn't like a person. And anyway, Mr Devine thought, what man in his right mind would want to listen to women's chat? Look at this room. Every man in it was talking to another man, and the women were left by themselves. And no wonder. Well, he might as well join the lads and have a drink.

But just then a woman passed by, a tall woman he did not know. Nice looking. He smiled vaguely in her direction and immediately she turned and came up to him.

'Excuse me,' she said, in a confidential voice, 'but are you a friend of the young man?'

'I beg your pardon?'

'Young – Oh, what *is* his name, anyway? I'm awful at

23

names. *You know*. The young man who's just become engaged to Mary Heron.'

'Oh, I see what you mean.' Mr Devine tried a second smile. Nice figure she had, too. 'Yes,' he said. 'His name is Carty. Dr Gerry Carty.'

'Where is he now? Can you point him out to me?'

'Well, ah, I'm afraid I don't see him at the moment. I only met him once. I might not know him again.'

'I thought you were a friend of his,' she said, looking at Mr Devine as though she had caught him in a lie. 'Well, thank you, anyway.'

And she walked away. He was just going to follow her – after all, he must pay his own respects to the engaged couple – when an old lady came in the parlour door and said to the tall lady:

'Oh, Mrs Reddin, have you got a minute?'

Mrs . . . Might have known. Well, that settled it, once and for all. She was too tall anyway. He went back to the table where the drinks were. He saw Harry Sharkey and Dan Cavanaugh there. But the face that turned to welcome him was a face he did not welcome.

'Devine, my son, how are you?'

'Can't complain,' Mr Devine said, trying to catch Harry Sharkey's eye over his interceptor's shoulder. But Moloney took hold of him, drawing him towards the drinks. 'I'm stationed at the fountainhead,' he said. 'Would you say no to Scotch?'

'A little whisky would do nicely, thanks,' Mr Devine agreed. To tell the truth, he had no use for Tony Moloney; a conceited little Dublin cockerel, he thought him; the soul of vulgarity, so he was. But Moloney was a colleague at Ardath, a fellow had to live with him. No sense cutting a man dead, was there, just because you didn't like his manner?

'Have you met the bridegroom-to-be yet?' Tony Moloney asked.

'Mary's intended? No, I haven't seen him yet.'

Moloney looked around, curly forelock tumbling over his right eye. 'Young medico,' he said. 'The old father has a shop somewhere in the Glens of Antrim. Pots of dough and ignorant as all get out.'

Look who's talking, Mr Devine thought. But he did not say it.

'Mind you, it's a blessing for Old Heron,' Moloney said. 'That girl of his is a fearsome-lookin' scourge.'

Mr Devine cast shocked eyes at the other guests, praying that no one had overheard. 'Now, she's not bad-looking, Tony,' he muttered uneasily.

'Not bad? My God, you're no student of the form divine, then. Form Devine – do you get me?' Moloney laughed loudly. 'Didn't you see the legs of her, man?' he continued. 'Beef to the heels like a Mullingar heifer.'

'Oh?'

'You mean to tell me you never noticed the legs?' Moloney laughed again and hit Mr Devine a slap on the shoulder blades. 'You and young Ray Connolly both need glasses, so you do. I told Ray to look at her legs, and I thought he'd flatten me.'

'And no wonder. He was doing a line with her,' Mr Devine said indignantly.

'He must be blind then. Man, she has a rudder on her that would steer the *Queen Mary*.' Moloney coughed over his drink, his face red with his own amusement. 'Women and horses,' he said. 'Look from the hoofs up.'

'Somebody might hear you,' Mr Devine whispered. God save us, he thought, Old Tim is not fifty feet away. But wasn't it the height of Moloney to say a thing like that? Wasn't it, though? It wasn't safe to be around this fellow.

'Look, old man, I'll be back in a moment,' he said, putting down his drink and moving away before Moloney had time to catch hold of him. He hurried out in the front hall, but there was a flock of women chittering away there.

He saw a fellow going upstairs and decided to follow him. Anything was better than going back to the likes of Moloney. And come to think of it, there was a dig at himself in Moloney's remarks, implying he was too holy to look at a woman's legs.

Nothing but insults I'm getting today, Mr Devine thought. Young Connolly hinting that I'm not interested in women, Moloney thinking I'm too holy to have thoughts, and Old Heron implying that I'm the same generation as himself. All in one day!

But the fellow he followed upstairs had only come up for a leak. Mr Devine paused, irresolute, as the fellow entered the bathroom. Turning, he saw that he was on the threshold of the upstairs sitting room. It was a room the children must not play in, a room used only on special occasions. The best Mrs Heron owned adorned it; plush sofas, tottery highboys, brass fenders, silver trays. And as soon as he entered, Mr Devine saw his mistake. The bored, nervous faces turned in his direction, welcoming the diversion. There was no going back now. He had to enter.

Here were the old ones. Tim Heron's mother and his wife's father, an aged uncle, a solitary aunt. Five or six unmarried females, elderly, out of things. All of them dressed in their Sunday best, wondering what to do with themselves. For they had so looked forward to this party, and now, as usual, they were not enjoying it. They sat in a stiff oval on the sofas and chairs, trying to think of small, useless remarks. Unwanted, even by each other, they were the kind of relatives who must be invited to every function because, being the least noticed, they were quickest to take offence. Someone had given them glasses of sherry and there were a few small biscuits on a plate. All waited for supper, like children for a treat.

They were delighted to see Mr Devine . . . Oh yes, indeed. They all knew him, or knew of him; he taught at Ardath with Tim; yes, his mother was a Henry on her mother's side – his father passed away some years ago; every one of them had read the funeral report at the time. They were great readers of obituaries. They could, with their inexhaustible genealogical knowledge, have traced Mr Devine's family back for three generations; and most of them, seeing him enter, assembled the opening moves of this favourite game. They smiled up at him; he was not young enough to be rude to them, not old enough to be their familiar. A fine figure of a man, he would have made a lovely priest; well educated he was, and well spoken too. Ah, yes . . . The old ladies whispered among themselves like mice, placing him, turning to look at him again, showing coy smiles, bloodless lips, shining white false teeth . . . Ah, Mr Devine, how do you do? How do you do? You wouldn't know me, or my sister – this is my sister, Minnie – but we knew your father, rest his soul, and your mother too. She was a saint of God, Mrs Devine. Ah, yes. And do you know Mrs Clery? And Mrs Kane and Mr McGurk? . . . Aye, Mr McGurk said, hawking up the dottle in his throat. You teach at Ardath with Tim, eh? Ah, times have changed, I went to the old school myself, as a lad. It was only one house then, Priest's House, they called it, and it was in the country in those days. All around the Castle it was open fields. Aye, aye . . . And this is Miss Lacey . . . Oh yes, I know Mr Devine, but I'm sure he doesn't remember me, we met once in Mr McAlister's house. Oh yes, you don't know me, but oh my, ha ha, I feel I know you quite well, my little nephew is always talking about you. Mangan is his name, he's a grand little chap, yes. He's in his junior year at Ardath . . . And oh, Mr Devine, this is Tim's mother – you've met before? . . . Indeed, and how are you, Mr Devine? You're looking well. I declare, you bachelors get younger every day. Ah yes. Yes . . .

And when that had been said, there was nothing more to say. They sat waiting for *him* to say something – and after a few moments of silence, the old ladies turned to each other;

the mice-like whispering began, talk in tiny contrast to the laughter and liveliness from the floor below. Out of it, in this room, the old ones and maiden ladies waited for Mr Devine to bring some of the party to them. And when he could not, they wished that he would go, they could discuss him then, they could use him as a starting point to begin again that familiar conversational pilgrimage from the un-satisfying present to the familiar past. And soon, supper would come. A nice supper. They could discuss the meal. They waited, therefore, watching him, willing him away. And sensing this, Mr Devine sipped his sherry, said he must find the happy couple and congratulate them, ha, ha. They were downstairs, he was told. Yes, Miss Lacey had seen them, the picture of young love, in the back hall. Mr Devine thanked Miss Lacey and said he must see for himself. Ha, ha. Yes, indeed.

Well, that was a *faux pas*! Walked right into it. All those poor old things on the shelf. He remembered that his own mother had been like that before the end. Lonely and old. Old and useless. Nobody wanted to talk to them.

He stood in the shadows of the corridor, fingered by that warning. That was the fate of every man, to age, to die. *Tempus fugit, irreparabile tempus.* He wished he had never gone in there tonight. Added to all the other little digs of the day, it was an omen, was it not? Even this engagement party was an omen. He could remember Tim Heron's daughter as a little girl in a school pinafore. And next year she would be a mother, most likely. It was enough to make any fellow pause.

He leaned over the banister and looked down at the heads in the hall. A red, oiled head, snug on black shoulders, moved in triumphal progress to the parlour, while attend-ant heads bobbed in compliment. Mr Devine recognized Father Alphonsus McSwincy, Dean of Discipline at Ardath. Tim Heron will be happy now, he thought, he has an official representative from the college to grace the occasion. It didn't take much to make some people happy, did it? Ah, parties were all a cod, anyway, people putting themselves out to be nice to other people. As you would, said Christ, that men should do to you, do you also to them in like manner. Did He have parties in mind? Mr Devine wondered.

A door opened: a bedroom light shone in the corridor, dazzling him with its brightness. A young girl came out, switching off the light, starting in surprise when she saw him.

'Oh!'

'Excuse me,' he said, standing aside.

'No, no, it's just that I didn't expect to find someone outside the door. I almost walked into you.'

He could see her better now, without the light blinding him. She was wearing a blue party frock and high-heeled patent-leather shoes. Her hair was dark and cut short and there was something rebellious and boyish about her face. She was pale, she wore no rouge, and her eyes were large and dark. Who was she?

'Did I frighten you?' he asked.

'No, no. That's all right.'

The thing to do was let it go at that. Smile and move aside. But look here, he had promised himself he'd get out of the rut and now he'd met a girl. Offer her something, lemonade or something. Talk!

'Can I get you something to drink, perhaps?' he heard his stiff voice say.

'But they're downstairs, the drinks. I should know, I helped to lay the table.'

'Oh, are you a relation of the Herons?'

'I'm a niece. I'm staying here.'

Now, dammit, Mr Devine had never heard Tim Heron talk of a niece, let alone a niece that was staying at his house. And Old Tim was not one who kept his affairs private, quite the contrary. It was funny he had never mentioned this girl.

'I'm from Dublin,' she said. 'I'm going to do nursing here.'

'Oh?'

She laughed at the puzzle she had set him. 'My name is Una Clarke,' she said.

'Very, ah, very glad to meet you. My name's Devine.'

'And your first name?'

'Ah, it's, ah, Diarmuid.'

'Diarmuid Devine. I've heard of you – you're a master at Ardath, aren't you? They call you Dev.'

'Yes.'

'That's funny,' she said. 'I'd never have taken you for a schoolmaster.'

There is nothing more interesting than hearing what other people think of one: Mr Devine was greedy for more. 'Well, is that so? What *did* you think?'

'Oh, a doctor, maybe. Or a businessman.'

He was glad he had worn his best suit. He looked at her hands and saw they were slightly reddened. Chilblains? Any ring? She was too young, of course. But by jingo, here he was, flirting with a girl. It was pleasant, was it not? Very.

'Well . . .' he said. 'I don't suppose I'd have taken you for a nurse, come to think of it.'

'Well, I'm not a nurse yet. I'm trying to get into the Memorial, but they won't be taking anybody for a month yet. I'm just sort of waiting for interviews and all that rigmarole.'

So she had just arrived. That explained why he had not heard of her. But the Memorial was a Protestant hospital. He was still puzzling over this when she said: 'Look, I must go downstairs now, I have to help with the supper.'

She moved to pass. He grasped her elbow, detaining her. But the moment he touched her soft, bare skin, he was taken with embarrassment. What on earth had possessed him, what would she think of him? And, like an infection, his embarrassment was transmitted. He could see it reflected in her face. He let go of her arm at once, his mind stumbling with excuses: 'Ah, excuse me, I thought you were going to trip. I mean, perhaps I could go down and help you, ah, carry something for you?'

'If you'd like to . . .'

'I'd be delighted.' He almost shouted it.

He followed her downstairs, his face warm, wondering what in heaven's name had happened to him. He did not know. He had a terrible urge to slap Father McSwiney's back as he passed him in the hall. He must control himself, this meant nothing, nothing, her allowing him to help her. But she was a girl. A pretty girl.

He followed her into the darkness of the back hall and through to the kitchen, where three women, their hair disarranged, aprons over their party frocks, laboured, with much crossing and recrossing of the kitchen floor, with constant hurried injunctions and instructions to get what was to be a casual bit of supper for the guests.

'Where *were* you, Una?' Mrs Heron asked crossly. Then she saw Mr Devine. 'Oh, hello, Dev, you'll have to excuse – '

'Not at all, Maeve. I just wondered if I could carry something?'

'Oh, no, we can manage.'

'It's no trouble, really.'

Mrs Heron looked uncertainly at the food which was already prepared. Small sandwiches cut in triangles, sliced jam rolls, hot sausage rolls, a big silver tureen of trifle and plates of *petit fours* . . . 'Well,' she said, 'the trifle dish is a bit heavy. It needs to go in the dining room. Una will show you where.'

Mr Devine elevated the silver tureen like a monstance and Una collected plates of sandwiches. Through the dark back hall into the dining room, where a table, covered with virgin linen, waited . . . Mr Devine laid the tureen in the centre. Knives and forks he arranged, taking her orders like a schoolboy. Back to the kitchen for more good things, busy at this unaccustomed task and, he realized, happy, very happy at it.

When all was laid and ready and Mrs Heron herself had inspected and approved, the dining room doors were opened and the word was passed around. A little something to eat. The guests, leaving their drinks, came crowding to see, in ones and twos and fours and more, stopping to exclaim at the splendour that met their eyes. Father Alphonsus McSwiney, Ardath's official representative, Father Rowe, the Herons' parish priest, and Father Fullon, a curate friend of the bridegroom-to-be, put knowing heads around the hall door, greeting all with social smiles. Priestly, they took precedence, the ladies hurrying forward to tempt their appetites. A bit of this, Father, or can I get you some of the other? Just a nibble; it won't hurt you; oh, go on with you, Father, you're not in the least bit fat! Priestly, they tasted, complimented, and moved to the fireplace warmth. The other guests were served. And in the middle of it all, Mr Devine. Passing plates with the girl by his side, smiling at her and she at him. He had not enjoyed himself so much in years; he felt dashing and daring; he wanted to show her something of his reckless mood. So when someone told him Father Rowe needed sugar and cream, he turned to the girl and winked. 'Ladies first, where I come from,' he said. 'The clergy can wait their turn.'

She laughed. 'You're awful,' she said. 'But you're right, it won't hurt them, for a change.'

Now did you hear that? he said to himself. She has a bit of spunk in her, not like most girls, shocked if you say a word about the priests . . . Smiling to himself, he bent to offer sugar and cream to someone's aunt. What a damn fine party this was! It just went to show, a fellow could have more fun with a girl than with male company. A different sort of fun. Exciting.

Mrs Heron appeared before them in her usual fluster. She whispered to Una and Una nodded. Mrs Heron hurried back to the kitchen. Una handed Mr Devine her plate of cakes. 'I'll be back in a jiffy,' she said. 'I'm needed to help with tea.'

'You'll be back, though?' he insisted.

'Yes.'

She said 'Excuse me,' and passed some people and then he could not see her any more. He felt like a damn fool handing silly cakes around. He put the plate down and went through the connecting doors into the front parlour. Moloney, lonely among the whisky bottles, made a come-hither sign.

'Divine Devine, the model man, the guest every hostess desires.' A mocking smile loosened Moloney's features and he made a small, skipping bow. 'I saw you, I saw you, with the sugar and cream in your paw.'

Mr Devine smiled. That meant Moloney had seen the girl too. He might even tell the other masters tomorrow. *Dev was squiring a smashing-looking girl last night.* I hope he tells young Connolly.

'Will you have a wee sup of something stronger?' Moloney asked.

'Just a small one. Irish for preference.'

'Well, now,' Moloney said, pouring a large measure of Jameson, watering it lightly. 'Getting off your mark with the wee Clarke girl, were you?'

'Do you know her, Tony?'

'Do I know her?' Moloney raised his eyes to the ceiling. 'I know *of her*,' he said significantly. 'She used to be in Dublin. I didn't know she'd come here. Ah, well, Dublin's loss, as they say . . .'

'What, ah, what do you mean?'

'Tell me,' Moloney said. 'Do you fancy her?'

Mr Devine put up a warning hand, like a policeman stopping traffic. 'Whisht!' he muttered. 'Keep your voice down, man.'

Moloney danced closer, his unbuttoned checked jacket

flapping like gaudy wings around his narrow hips. 'Answer me. Isn't she a nice wee cuddle?'

'Now look here, Tony, I only met her a moment ago – '

'Hot stuff,' Moloney said. 'I have a pal up in Dublin used to take her sister out. He had a rare time of it.'

'Whisht!' Mr Devine implored, his frightened eyes skittering around the parlour.

Moloney winked. He opened his mouth, convict-style, and said, his lips barely moving: 'They must have sent this one to Belfast to get rid of her. She was mixed up with a married man the year she left school.'

Mr Devine, searching like a blind man, found the table and put his drink on it. His hands, clasping each other as if for comfort, met in a familiar gesture, thumb and forefinger twiddling the signet ring on the little finger of his left hand. He was more shocked than if he had heard this story about his own sister. For he would not have believed it of his sister. But Una Clarke was a stranger. Information about a stranger needs no defence. In the balance against nothing, it weighs complete. To think that he had been so taken with her. And now this. A heavy grief surprised him, as though someone close to him had just died. For once, he had hit it off with a girl from the very beginning, had not even tried a line on her, had told no lies, had felt she liked him. Young and pretty too. But wasn't that proof that something was wrong? It had been a great beginning: it was bound to fail.

'You look as if you don't believe me,' Moloney said.

'I, ah, I have no reason not to believe you.' He peered into the crowded dining room, hoping she would not come back just yet. And then, afterthought, urgent and sudden, made him say: 'But she's a Catholic, isn't she?'

'Catholic? Not on your life. Old Tim's a convert, didn't you know?'

Of course Tim was! It had happened a long time ago, must be thirty years, Mr Devine decided. But now it made sense, her talking of going into the Memorial Hospital.

34

Heron's other relations would be Protestants. That changed everything.

For in Mr Devine's world, Protestants were the hostile Establishment, leaders with Scots and English surnames, hard blunt businessmen who asked what school you went to and, on hearing your answer, refused the job. He feared them as a Spanish Protestant might fear cardinals: their power was great, their intolerance absolute. To them, Catholics were a hated minority, a minority who threatened their rule.

Mr Devine had heard it said, of course, that Ulster Protestants were atypical: in England, and even in Dublin, things were not quite so bad. There, Protestants were unbigoted pagans, enjoying a freedom which Catholics would never tolerate. To this world, to this pagan Protestantism, Una Clarke, a Dubliner, must surely belong. It changed everything. Everything. Among people like that an affair with a married man was possible. Anything was possible.

'She's only a kid, mind you,' Moloney said. 'But for a kid – ' He stopped speaking, his mouth frozen. 'Don't look now,' he muttered. 'Right behind you.'

'So here you are,' Una Clarke said. 'I wondered where you'd gone.'

'Oh, I was, ah, I was just having a – do you know Tony Moloney?'

'I haven't had the pleasure,' Moloney said, his face a disguise of welcoming innocence.

'You're a Dubliner,' she said.

'Ah, you caught the accent. You must be Dublin too.'

Dodging closer, Moloney offered a drink. He began to talk in a way Mr Devine envied, all warmth, all at ease. He made her laugh. And Mr Devine waited between them, touching the crest of his signet ring, pushing it back, pulling it into place again. Useless, unwanted, *de trop*. Might as well leave them to it.

'*Aren't* you, Dev?'

'I'm sorry, what was that?'

'Would you look at the modesty of the man?' Moloney said. 'I've just been telling Miss Clarke that you're a big cheese in local drama circles.'

'Oh, no. On the contrary.'

'He is, Miss Clarke, don't you heed him. He's the man behind the scenes, the man who keeps out of the limelight. He was a tower of strength in *Mulligan's Will*, a play we put on last year. Stage manager, he was. I had the leading role.'

'Did you?' she said, smiling at Moloney.

'Yes,' Moloney said. 'With Trinity Players.'

'Oh, that must be exciting. I'd love to be an actress. I've always been keen on the stage.'

Keen on the stage! Mr Devine's long face turned bleakly towards the stacked bottles on the table. We'd have that in common. But there it was: she was a Protestant. Besides, she was only twenty; she probably thought he was too old for her. He must be thankful for small mercies. He was lucky he had found out so soon. No good could come of it.

'It's a pity we couldn't do *Mulligan's Will* again,' Moloney said. 'I know the Dean is looking for a play for some charity affair.'

'Will you excuse me?' Mr Devine said to the girl. 'I must be running along.'

'So soon?'

'I, ah, I have some work to do.'

'Oh, I'm sorry you're leaving.' She did look sorry and, immediately, he was ready to renegue. But he had said he must go, so go he must. He smiled and repeated his good nights.

His coat was sodded under layers of others. He pulled and pushed the wobbling coat rack, hoping Tim Heron wouldn't discover him dodging off so soon. He had not even paid his respects to the engaged couple. Ah, well, his good wishes would not be missed. No more than those of the old people upstairs. Nobody cares, he thought sadly. I'll never be missed.

And he was not. No one called after him as he shut the front door. It was dark and cold in the street. The wind sent his hat brim patting gently against his forehead as he bent forward, hurrying to the Cavehill Road and the bus stop. It was cold. There was no bus. He slipped his hands through the vents of his raincoat pockets, finding the trousers pockets beneath, his fingers cradled against the warmth of his belly, as, pacing up and down, waiting for his bus, he remembered and defined the sensation of the evening. It reminded him of the first party he had ever gone to, the first time he had ever met a girl and spent the evening with her. And yet, it had all been ruined by a few unkind words. Moloney's slanders and Moloney's information. *Hot stuff*. *Protestant*. Three words to change everything. Remembering, he saw her face once more. A pale statue face, the lipstick adding the startling touch. Virgin white or whited sepulchre? It depended on what you knew about her. Protestant girls were fast.

Under the street lamp tiny black circles appeared on the pavement, dropping like insects from the night darkness above. The drops grew thicker, putting a chain-mail of wetness between the light and the pavement. Narrowing his eyes, Mr Devine saw two yellow eyes glow in the distance. Bright-lit, the bus drew near, the driver leaning forward to peer past his soft, flicking windshield wiper for the man waiting at the stop.

Now was the time to go back. Wave the bus on, run back to Heron's place, take off his coat and rejoin the party. She liked him, she was sorry to see him go. It was not every day a thing like this happened.

Far out in Belfast Lough, a ship foghorn lowed like an animal in pain. Warning: *Go back*. He should not have run away. She liked him. The foghorn lowed a second time: *Go back*.

But the bus driver had seen the man waiting. He drew in at the curb, the bus passengers jerking like marionettes in their seats as the bus stopped. The conductor waited for Mr Devine to board, his impatient finger on the communication buzzer. The foghorn, far away, lowed a third time. But the conductor was waiting. The bus had stopped for him. Mr Devine got on.

Chapter Three

Standing at the waiting room window in Priests' House next morning, Mr Devine watched two groups of boys at soccer practice in Big Field. The junior boys, barred from the use of the goal posts, had laid down piles of coats forming their own limits and now played defiantly across the seniors' game. In a moment the seniors would start a fight. Mr Devine turned away: it was his lunch hour, after all. None of his business.

On the wall opposite, the Virgin Mary in blue, white and golden robes conferred her blessing on the visitor, imitated with childish seriousness by the Infant on her knee. They had the sad look of divinities betrayed, their eyes a constant reproach for human waywardness. Mr Devine looked at those eyes and then looked at the rug. It was inconsiderate of Father McSwiney to keep him waiting.

As though aware of this resentful thought, the Dean of Discipline entered the room almost immediately. He was tall and elegant in a new black soutane, shoulder cape thrown back to reveal a silk underlining. He bobbed his oiled head in greeting and advanced, holding out a large white hand. Hand pumping, he forced his visitor backwards. 'Sorry to keep you, Dev. Sit down, sit you down.'

Mr Devine sat down. Father McSwiney excavated a packet of Player's Number Three from the folds of his black skirts. He offered them wordlessly, found a lighter, and then sat opposite Mr Devine, hands on his knees, his long skirts pulled wide.

'I suppose you haven't had your lunch yet, Dev? No? Well, I won't keep you long. I need your advice on a matter that's been worrying me.'

'Yes, Father?'

'It's this committee I'm on, to raise funds for the Foreign Missions. You see, we had a dance planned for next month, tickets printed, hall booked, and so forth. Now, at the last minute, we have to call it off because it conflicts with a big parish do. So, to make a long story short, I mentioned my dilemma to Tony Moloney and he suggested a play to me.'

'Oh, but Kevin Cooke's the man you must see about that,' Mr Devine said. 'He's our producer.'

'Well, now, I spoke to Kevin this morning. Kevin told me you're the man to see, Dev. You're the one the burden of work will fall on. A tower of strength, Kevin says.'

'Oh, I'm only stage manager,' Mr Devine said. But it was flattering to hear that Kevin had said that about him. He had only been a helper when he started with the group – painting scenery, giving a hand with the lights and props. And it was true that nowadays he was the organizer; he did all the dirty work, as Kevin called it. Dates and halls and tickets and all. And he even helped coach people in their parts, when Kevin was too busy.

'You're too modest, Dev,' the Dean said. 'Kevin left it entirely up to you. He says you'll have to do it, if it's to be done at all.'

'But we're rehearsing for the drama award, Father. Did Kevin say which play he had in mind for you?'

'He said you'd tell me the possibilities.'

Kevin had passed the hard job along as usual, Mr Devine thought. If I pick the wrong play, everyone will blame me. 'Well, we're rehearsing a good play at the moment, Father. The one for the award.'

Father McSwiney removed a wet cigarette from wet lips. 'What play is that?'

'*The Well of the Saints*.'

'Correct me if I'm wrong, Dev, but that's by Synge, is it not?'

'Yes, Father.'

'Well now, maybe that wouldn't be suitable. I was thinking more of a comedy.'

'I'm afraid we're no great shakes at comedy, Father.'

'*Mulligan's Will*,' Father McSwiney said. 'That was a comedy. You made a good fist of that, if I remember rightly.'

Mr Devine sat still. That was Moloney's suggestion, of course. Moloney was paying them back because he hadn't been included in the Synge play. To get back in the limelight, he was forcing them to do that old turnip again.

'Well, Dev?' the Dean asked, his voice cautious.

'It's a rotten play,' Mr Devine said. 'We only did it once. It's just a kitchen comedy.'

The Dean smiled. 'Kitchen?' he said. 'There's a kitchen in some of Synge's plays, if I remember rightly. And besides, there's a lot of people have no great opinion of your man Synge.'

'You couldn't compare Synge with drivel like *Mulligan's Will*, Father.'

'Oh, I'm not so sure,' the Dean said. '*The Playboy*, for instance. Now, there's a play didn't reflect much credit on the Irish race. And not true to life either, in my opinion.'

'Aye,' Mr Devine said uneasily. 'Still, *Mulligan's Will* is not in the same class.'

The Dean's large white face lost its smile. He looked at Mr Devine as though the latter were a junior pupil who had contradicted him. He wet his already wet lips and said: '*Mulligan's Will* should sell tickets. Your man Synge will not.'

My sainted foot! Mr Devine thought bitterly. Sure, everyone knows what sells tickets in a case like this. The clergy says buy, and the people buy. Charity, not choice.

'Besides,' the Dean said, 'you've done the *Will* before; it wouldn't be hard to polish it up.'

'It's not my decision, Father. I'd have to ask the others.'

But he felt he was losing ground. The Dean tossed his

41

objection aside with a flick of his oiled red head. 'They'll help us, I'm sure, Dev. Trinity is a Catholic group and this is a great cause. Now, there's the matter of a hall. I want to get a hall for you right away.'

'But I don't know if we're going to do the play yet, Father.'

'In any case, it won't hurt to be prepared. We'll have to get our bid in early. Fergus Deegan has promised to help us with a hall. He's a big man in the Knights – do you know him?'

'Yes, Father.'

'He knows you, he told me. And he'll be in Campbell's Coffee Shop at four this afternoon. He'll be looking out for you. Will that suit you?'

Uneasily, Mr Devine raised his eyes to meet the Dean's. All pretence of choice had been pushed aside. In his well-cut soutane, surrounded by the incense of priestly authority, Father McSwiney seemed an impossible opponent, remembered from childhood, twice as large as life. There was no hope of changing that authoritarian mind.

'Yes, Father,' he said.

'That's very decent of you, Dev. Well, I won't keep you any longer. You must be starving for your lunch.'

'That's all right, Father.'

The Dean rose, his smile restored, his hand once more offered in friendship. 'Thanks, Dev. Thanks very much indeed.'

Hand-shaken, back-slapped, a departing guest speeded, Mr Devine went aimlessly down the steps of Priests' House. This was Moloney's doing. Moloney was getting his own back for being left out of the Synge play. Not that there was any reason why he shouldn't be. He had been picked for *Mulligan's Will* only because of his Dublin accent, talentless wee braggart that he was!

But it was no use making Moloney the scapegoat. It was my own fault for letting the Dean force me, Mr Devine thought. Self-reproach returned as he turned into the double row of trees known as Priests' Walk. There were a dozen parish groups who'd have been glad to do a kitchen comedy for the Dean. But that wasn't good enough for him: he insisted on the only Catholic group devoted to doing something better.

Mr Devine walked on, his guilt turning inwards. Dammit, he was a grown man now, why should a priest still make him feel like a wee boy? Why should he be afraid of Father Mac? He should have refused point-blank, he should not have allowed himself to be bullied at his time of life. Well, he said to himself, the harm is not done yet. I won't go and see Fergus Deegan. I can change my mind, can't I? Deegan can wait in Campbell's till kingdom come, for all I care. I won't go.

He would not go. Just this once, he'd show them. He was sick of being bullied into things.

But at two minutes to four, his back to the formal ugliness of City Hall, Mr Devine waited to cross Donegall Square. He had already telephoned Kevin Cooke to ask which hall Kevin wanted, but Kevin had left it up to him: he was very busy, Kevin said, he couldn't come before rehearsals. But not too busy to get his name on the programme while I do all the work, Mr Devine thought. Still, Kevin was not a bad sort. He couldn't blame Kevin for what had happened.

The traffic lights were red. Behind him, Queen Victoria stared sightless at her unheeding Irish subjects. Below her stony plumpness, quick, violent flower sellers hawked colour in white tissue paper. Farther on, at pavement level, hoarse voices offered *Illustrated* and *Daily Mirror*. Pennies fell on paper piles and a torn news poster dragged along the street. It caught Mr Devine's shoe and he looked down to see:

CESAREWITCH RUNNERS
BERLIN TALK . . .

A weak green glare met the autumn sunlight. Sidestepping the news, Mr Devine crossed the street, bumped into a lady on the opposite pavement, touched his hat, hurried on. It was so crowded downtown these days, a person could hardly move. He would be late, and Deegan would be angry. Deegan was a big stick: men like Deegan did not like to be kept waiting.

At one minute past four, Mr Devine pushed open the door of Campbell's Coffee Shop, moving into a confusion of fresh baking smells; housewives picking over pastries; starched, uniformed girls stuffing white loaves into bags. Hat in hand, male in the unfamiliar, Mr Devine searched for Deegan. Surely he would sit where a person could see him? Or he might possibly be in the room on the second floor. Mr Devine climbed to the second floor. The fluorescent lights had failed and the occupants of tables near the large windows were black-paper cut-outs against the whitish background of City Hall, across the street. One of the cut-outs beckoned to him:

'Hello there, Dev!'

Blinking into the white window light, Mr Devine saw the other occupant of the table. Female, her face in profile, shadowed, invisible . . . The beckoner said in the unmistakable accents of Tony Moloney: 'Come and join us'.

Mr Devine did not move. Hat in hand, eyes growing used to the light, he stood, surmise becoming certainty, as he studied the girl's averted head.

'You remember Una, of course.'

'Yes, yes. How do you do, Miss Clarke?'

She looked at him now and smiled. Moloney rose and pulled an ugly chrome-and-red-leather chair out. 'Sit down for a minute, Dev.'

'Well, just for a moment. I'm looking for someone.'

She was wearing a black beret and a grey belted overcoat that did not seem to fit her. He knew many people would not think her beautiful at all. She was young and there was

44

something wild and unfinished about her, as though she were in her first year of nylon stockings and lipstick and not yet used to them. But when she looked at him, he was the awkward one: he felt clumsy, unworthy. He watched her fiddle with her gloves on the red-checkered tablecloth. He could not think of anything to say.

'Coffee or tea?' Moloney asked.

He looked. They were having coffee. 'Coffee will do nicely, thanks.'

Moloney said he would fetch it.

Mr Devine sat down and put his hat on the floor between his feet. Moloney was being uncommonly obliging, he noticed. But he did not think about it. He must not sit here like a dummy. She was waiting for him to talk.

'It's, ah, awfully nice running into you again, Miss Clarke. Quite a coincidence, isn't it?'

She looked past him at the counter where Moloney queued for coffee. Then – in a great hurry to get it out – she said:

'It wasn't coincidence, you know. Your friend Tony knew you'd be here.'

'Oh?'

She avoided his eye. 'Yes,' she said. 'I'm beginning to see a pattern in this. Last night he said he could get me a part in a play. Today, he phoned me and invited me to tea. He never mentioned it until we got here, but then he told me it depended on persuading you that I was suitable.'

'Oh? I don't see . . .'

'He said there's a part vacant, but that you don't know about it yet. I'm telling you this because I don't like this way of doing things. It seems sneaky, keeping you in the dark.'

Her frankness left Mr Devine . . . well, dammit, he never could have come out with a thing so honestly himself. His admiration for her was sudden and confused. Moloney must have lied to her, he thought. I'm only stage manager, it's

Kevin's job to choose the cast. If I were honest as she is, I'd enlighten her. But still – it wouldn't be difficult to ask Kevin to give her a part. He had never asked Kevin for any favours: Kevin could hardly refuse him. What part was vacant, by the way?

'I think it's better to be frank about these things,' she said. 'It makes it easier for everyone concerned. But Tony doesn't agree. That's why I decided to tell you now – while he's not here.'

'I see,' Mr Devine said. 'And very right too. Very decent of you to warn me, so to speak. Not that I, ah, ever would suspect you of collusion, of course.'

'*Shh!*' she said. 'Here he comes. Keep this between us, will you?'

'Yes. Absolutely.'

Moloney, curly forelock blinding his right eye, advanced with caution, clutching three mugs of frothy coffee. He slid them onto the red-checkered tablecloth. 'I ordered some cakes too. They'll bring them over.'

Mr Devine allowed himself to look at her. She was as embarrassed as he. Dammit, this girl couldn't be fast. That must be another of Moloney's fibs.

'Didn't expect to see you here, Dev,' Moloney said. 'This isn't one of your hang-outs, is it?'

'We're going to do a play for the Foreign Missions,' Mr Devine told him. 'I came here to arrange with Fergus Deegan about a hall.'

'What play do you have in mind?'

When Moloney said this – innocent, curious – Mr Devine looked quickly at the girl. Her worried eyes warned him: *Don't give me away.*

'*Mulligan's Will*,' he said. 'That's what Father McSwiney wants.'

Moloney could not conceal his pleasure. 'With me as Mulligan?'

'Aye.'

'And is Deegan here yet? Have you seen him yet?'

'Doesn't seem to be here,' Mr Devine said, watching with pleasure the worry this caused Moloney. He risked a side glance at the girl. She seemed secretly amused.

'Maybe Deegan's gone upstairs to the third floor,' Moloney said. 'There's tables up there, you know.'

'Maybe.'

'I'd better look.' Moloney rose from his chair and peered around the room. At that moment – emerging from the stairwell – a pink-and-white face, striped shirt, striped tie, dark pin-stripe suit. Moloney caught Mr Devine's arm. 'There he is, Dev. That's him, isn't it, coming up now?'

Mr Devine swivelled slowly in his chair. It was Deegan, all right, and Deegan had not seen them yet. A swift distaste overcame him. Why should he leave this girl to Moloney? Why should he go and talk about parish halls with a stuffed shirt like Deegan?

'Will I call him over?' Moloney asked anxiously. 'He hasn't seen us: he's going upstairs.'

'Why don't *you* go, Tony?' Mr Devine said, surprising himself. 'Tell him we want Saint Finbar's, Rosary Hall or Saint Iona's. And we'll need the hall six weeks from Monday next.'

'Me?' Moloney put his hand flat on his chest. 'Why me? You're the man he came to see.'

'Well, I just don't feel like seeing Deegan,' Mr Devine said.

'But what about Father Mac, Dev? What about the play?'

'I don't give a damn about the play,' Mr Devine said. 'You go, if you're so concerned.'

Mr Fergus Deegan's pin-striped rear had disappeared out of sight on the stairway. Moloney hesitated, his anxiety plain. 'Will I tell him we're doing *Mulligan's Will*?'

'Right,' said Mr Devine.

'Fair enough, Dev. I'll look after him for you.' Triumphant, his point won, Moloney dashed for the stairway,

47

hound's-tooth jacket billowing like a spinnaker behind the thin mast of his body. Mr Devine looked at the girl and, for the second time that afternoon, surprised himself: he winked at her.

'You had him worried stiff,' she said.

'Serve him right.'

'Do you not like him then?'

That was the kind of question Mr Devine feared. There was no sense making enemies, was there? You never knew when a remark would get back to a person. So he hedged. 'Don't *you* like him, Miss Clarke?'

'I asked you first.'

'Well, ah, I suppose he's not a bad fellow.'

'I only met him last night,' she said. 'So maybe it's unfair to judge him. Still, I can't help thinking there's something underhanded about him.'

'Do you?' Mr Devine smiled happily. 'As a matter of fact,' he said, 'I believe you're perfectly right, Miss Clarke. I've often had the same idea.'

'Don't call me Miss Clarke,' she said. 'You make me sound fifty. My name is Una.'

Mr Devine twisted his signet ring to and fro under the table, turning it as though it would grant some unspoken wish. 'By the way,' he said, 'what part did Tony say was vacant?'

'The daughter. The girl who played it last time is having a baby.'

'And have you – ah – have you had any acting experience, Una?'

'Only school plays. I'm twenty, you know. I'm afraid I haven't had experience in anything yet.'

'Well . . . It's a young girl's part . . . We might try you for it.'

After all, he reasoned, I could ring Kevin up and put it to him that it wouldn't mean any extra work, that I could coach her in the part myself. And, for once, they might give me the title of assistant producer, or something. Kevin wouldn't mind, he's not likely to care about a play that will run two nights in a church hall. But this girl was so honest, it was unfair not to warn her that Kevin would have the final say.

'I'll probably be hopeless in the part,' she murmured, folding and unfolding her gloves on the table.

A guilty confidence filled him: she was afraid of him; she had no idea how terrified of her he really was. Guiltily, he was glad of her shyness, her innocence. It made possible what he next proposed.

'I could teach you,' he said. 'I've seen a lot of acting in my day. I could give you special lessons.'

'But wouldn't that take up a lot of your time?'

'Oh, no,' he said, feeling his face warm as he thought of the idea. Alone with her, rehearsing. Protestant girl. Fast. Pretty. 'I'd like it,' he added.

For a moment he had the frightening feeling that she was going to touch him, perhaps even kiss him, in gratitude. But a waitress came between them and put four chocolate éclairs on the table.

'Yiz ast for these?' she accused, in flat Belfast tones.

'Yes.'

'Two shillin's.'

He paid. The moment had gone. It had probably only been one of his sinful, wild imaginings. He offered her a fat creamy éclair. And Moloney hurried over to the table.

'Deegan wants to know will the eighteenth of next month be okay? A Thursday. I told him I'd phone you. He doesn't know you're here. I hope he doesn't see you on his way out.'

Mr Devine stared at him, hardly listening. 'All right,' he said. 'Tell him the eighteenth will be all right.'

'Okay. And duck down when he passes this table,' Moloney warned, turning away, hurrying two at a time up the stairs.

Watching him go, Mr Devine realized that he had not got

49

long alone with her. He must try to arrange something before Moloney returned. He must not let this girl slip as he had let so many in the past.

'The, ah, the Gaiety Theatre crowd will be here next week,' he said. 'You must have seen them often, being a Dubliner?'

'MacLiammoir and that gang? Yes, I have. What play are they doing?'

'Shaw's *Saint Joan*. I hear it's a very good production.'

'I haven't seen it,' she said.

'Well, ah, would you like to go? I mean, I could get tickets.'

'I'd love to. Thank you very much.'

'Ah, Monday night, would that suit you?'

'Any night,' she said. 'I've nothing to do until I go into the Memorial.'

'Well, could I, ah, could I ring you up?' His voice had risen to a nervous half-shout.

'No, I'd better ring you,' she said. 'Are you in the phone book?'

'Yes.'

'I'll phone you the day after tomorrow then. Your first name is Diarmuid, isn't it?'

'Yes.'

She looked past him, her hand raised slightly in warning. Mr Devine, following her glance, saw Moloney and Fergus Deegan coming downstairs. They had not seen him. He huddled forward in his chair, staring out the window at some people queuing for a bus across the street. He heard Deegan's voice as the two men crossed the room and went downstairs to street level.

'All right now,' Una Clarke said. 'They've gone.'

'Good.'

He smiled at her and she at him. Then, embarrassed again, they both stared out the window, watching the people pass on the street below. They could not think of anything to say to each other. They were glad when Moloney appeared, pulling his chair out, straddling it back to front, glancing at them with quick suspicious eyes, wondering what was up.

'All settled,' Moloney announced. 'We're getting Rosary Hall. He seems a very decent scout, old Deegan.'

'Why wouldn't he be?' Mr Devine asked. 'We're doing *him* the favour.'

'Aye, true enough, Dev. True enough.' Moloney took a deep breath and paused. 'By the way, Dev, speaking of favours, I have a favour you might do for someone else.'

'Oh?'

'Yes. Did you know Peg Shea is going to have a baby next month?'

'Is that so?'

'I was wondering . . .' Moloney said softly . . . 'I was wondering what you would think of Una here, as a replacement?'

But Mr Devine and Una Clarke burst out laughing. Moloney was a little miffed. What the hell was so funny, what was old Dev so cocky about this afternoon? Showing off, so he was, for *her*. By God, she should know him like I do, Moloney thought contemptuously, the fella that wouldn't say boo to a dead duck, tripping over himself agreeing with everybody. What's the big joke, I wonder?

He did not have long to wonder. Mr Devine touched his moustache, smoothing it complacently.

'Well, Tony,' said he, 'as a matter of fact, we've already discussed the matter. I'm going to try Una out in the part.'

Chapter Four

When Mr Devine left the teashop that afternoon, he was filled with an outrageous joy. He smiled into the shocked faces of strangers, walked across Donegall Street against a red light and stopped to kick an apple core into the formal flowerbeds of City Hall. As he boarded his bus, the conductor decided he was lit up. Unheeding the conductor's warning glare, Mr Devine strap-hung, smiling, his lips forming soundless phrases as though he enjoyed a delightful, inaudible conversation.

This joyful recapitulation, this gladness which rendered him unsober, led him past his usual stop. Only when the bus met an unfamiliar incline and a row of shopfronts dragged by did he realize where he was. In a great hurry, pushing past his fellow strap-hangers, he made his way to the bus platform, where the conductor, glad to see the worst confirmed, let the drunk fella off. Stepping down, Mr Devine's smile failed. He was six stops past his destination.

It was dark now. The street lamps were lit and people were hurrying home to tea. A cold damp, the beginnings of fog, misted houses across the road. It was no night to dawdle. Mr Devine walked quickly, taking a short cut up the back street, hoping to avoid the rush-hour traffic.

Monday night, then, he would take her to the Opera House. He would get the tickets tomorrow. The best seats. Stalls. He would give Kevin Cooke a ring tonight and try to have Kevin and maybe Kathleen Boland come next Tuesday for a reading. Maybe he could run over the lines with Una first. That would be better. As for Moloney, by jingo, he had put Moloney's nose out of joint. And Deegan – he had not even bothered to see Deegan. All because she was sitting opposite me, he thought. It's astonishing the confidence she gave me; I was a different man. Serve Moloney right, with his dirty talk about her. Serve him right!

Still, he was not much better himself, was he? Other times, other girls, fled in pale reproach before him. In thought, if not in deed, he had been as bad as Moloney in his time. He was ashamed of the thoughts he had entertained about decent, ordinary girls he knew. He remembered a photograph he took of himself with a Brownie in another boy's back yard. In it, he wore a flowing bow tie and glared at the camera, trying to give himself a vicious, mad look, like the look of Baudelaire in a photograph he admired. He had added certain touches: a meerschaum pipe, a velvet smoking jacket, borrowed from a theatrical costumer. The purpose of the photograph had been to impress a pen pal, a girl he was corresponding with in England. He never met her, and he burned the photograph, without sending it. Yes, he had thought himself an Irish Baudelaire in his day, a man who'd been a hellish sinner but who'd come back to the Faith in the end. Diarmuid Devine: it was a poet's name. At twenty, he wrote poems that would make him blush today. Some of them he had long since burned. They were too sensual. And girls did not care for poetry, he found. They wanted a manly chap. So he bought a second pipe, a straight briar, only to learn it was not manliness they wanted either. They wanted fellows who were good dancers. The only way to become a good dancer was to dance a lot. And when a girl let him take her out once, enduring an evening of his mathematical shuffle and multiplying feet, there was never a second time. Dancers!

If you were not a good dancer, you had to have a good line. It made him wince, even now, to think of some of those lines. He remembered how Niall Coyne advised him to tell each girl that she reminded him of some film star. He told an Armagh girl she reminded him of Hedy Lamarr.

The girl burst into tears and said he was making fun of her. She wouldn't go out with him after that. And then someone advised him to tell girls he was a big noise in amateur theatricals and that the Gate was sending someone to look over his next production. So he told a girl he met at a dance that she had acting talent. She might even wind up in the West End of London or in New York, on Broadway, he said. She said she was on Broadway already. Broadway, Fall's Road, Belfast. And she ran around telling everyone the joke until he was a laughing-stock. Lines! The trouble was, none of us knew how to talk to girls at all, he thought. Lines!

By the time he finished his studies at University College, Dublin, he knew all about Baudelaire and Rimbaud and Verlaine and orgies. But he had never done more than kiss a girl. He, Jack Healey and Sean Rourke went on a blind date in Portrush one summer with three typists. They were going to do it, now or never. The girls were hot stuff, Jack said. They had a lot of drinks and his girl got drunk, so drunk that when he paid her admission into the Palais, she went off at the second dance with some fellow he had never seen. He felt like a fool. From then on, he decided to content himself with sinful thoughts. He'd had some shocking sinful thoughts in his day. Shocking!

And still do. I haven't changed, he thought. Even this afternoon, for a moment, a sinful thought came into my mind. About her and me, alone at rehearsals. But that was the only bad thought, and it would be the last, he vowed. This was different, this feeling he had for her. There was nothing sensual in it, it was a pure, sinless thing. He had not even thought of her as a woman, except for that moment. And that was the difference between love and lust, he remembered a missioner once saying. Love was pure. Love was respect. Well, he respected Una, so he did, it made him boil to think what Moloney had said about her. How dare he, damn his filthy tongue!

He had reached his avenue. It was quiet and dark. Under

a street lamp, two children played a chalk game. At the end of a row of houses, a man came out and looked at the night sky. The avenue's leafless trees groaned faintly in the night wind as he turned in at number eight. With the wind came the first drops of another shower. He was home just in time. No light shone from his place. No one waited for him. It was not natural, coming home to a dark den like this to lie alone till morning. And would any girl live here in a basement, with no place to cook, no bathroom even? Una would never stand for it.

Or for him. As he switched on the hall light, his face surprised him from the hallstand mirror. Disembodied, framed in that small rectangle, it stared: long, sad, bespectacled. The heavy moustache aged him, he realized. His face was another species from the handsome men who daily looked down on him from cigarette, shaving cream, and hair tonic advertisements. Wouldn't he look ridiculous on a cinema poster? It would have to be a comedy picture. And his clothes. Old flannels and his father's watch chain in his waistcoat. He looked middle-aged. A young man should wear a wrist watch, he decided. What must she have thought of me? A freak.

By the fire, he unlaced his shoes and took his slippers from the wooden box beside the coal scuttle. Was it any wonder he had no luck with girls? He was still young but he had slipped into old bachelor habits. This room, look at it. A museum of papers, books, pipes and pullovers. Not even a wireless in the place, let alone television. Nothing for a girl to amuse herself with, not even an illustrated magazine. And two old holy pictures on the wall. What would she think of him?

One picture was of the Divine Infant of Prague, His baby body robed in prelate's garb. Twenty years ago, an Irish Sweepstake winner gave devotion to the Divine Infant of Prague as the cause of a Derby victory. Mrs Devine, reading the story, sent out at once to purchase this picture and family prayers in the Devine household regularly implored a repetition of that good fortune. But the Infant never completed the double and one member of the household knew why. One member who sinned by secret, lustful thoughts. That member, years later, took the picture with him to his new digs out of some vague need for penance. But a Protestant girl could not be expected to understand all this. It must come down.

The second picture was a reproduction of *Ecce Homo*, an insipid seventeenth-century work by Guido Reni, which Mr Devine's father had greatly admired. In moments when his migraine headache troubled him, the elder Devine could be seen kneeling before the agonized face of his fellow sufferer. His son felt there was something absurd in comparing a migraine headache with the real pain a crown of thorns must cause. When his father died, the son remembered that unworthy thought. Migraine may have been very painful, after all. So he took the picture and hung it in his digs in pious memory. Now, looking for the first time in years at that effeminate, suffering face, he thought that his father's suffering made mock of this artistic agony. There was no point in keeping that picture up. It must come down. Now.

He unhooked the dusty picture from the wall. A whitish oval of wallpaper marked its former position. No matter. He pushed the picture behind a row of books on a lower shelf.

'Excuse me, Mr Devine.'

A thief caught robbing an altar, Mr Devine swung around, his dusty hands an evidence of guilt. Mrs Dempsey's eldest daughter, her wall-eye staring with the peculiar, inattentive look of the strabismic, waited by the door.

'Yes?'

'Mama says your supper is ready, will you have it now?'

'Yes. I'll be up in a moment.'

'O-kay.'

She turned away and went up the basement stairs. Did she see me, the skellyeyed wee sneak? Well, dammit, what odds if she did?

Chapter Five

In the faded gilt heaven of the circular ceiling, a crystal chandelier floated, misty sun in a cumulus of cigarette smoke. Below, careful hands lifted above the rabble of heads, holding whisky, gin-and-orange, sherries, up and over, thank you, your change, sir. Pound notes implored: two Irish and water, please, Miss, Scotch it was, Miss. Och, MacLiammoir's not what he used to be, but the girl who played Joan was smashing . . . And the bell warned first call, the elderly, black-clad barmaids ran on paining legs to the cash register. Thanks, sir, and you, sir? Gin and . . . just a minute! Their feet were killing, but they were used to it; in a minute the last act, glasses down, empties all over the place, the cigarette smoke clearing, clean up and home. A Power, did you say? Just a minute, a minute . . . And a sherry it was? Two sherries . . .

Mr Devine, change in hand, glasses held high, careful not to spill (excuse me, can I get by?), was making his second trip to the theatre bar in less than ten minutes. He had not thought that Una would drink at all, but here she was like any seasoned toper on her third of the evening. Of course, that didn't prove anything, did it? But still he had said to the barmaid: Go easy on the gin in that one, Miss, easy on the gin.

When he finally pushed his way back to the place where he'd left her, she was talking to a young fellow, a careless-looking young fellow in an expensive tweed hacking jacket and dark grey trousers.

'Dev, this is Ronnie Irwin,' she said. 'We went to school together in Dublin.'

'How do you do?' Irwin said, barely glancing at him.

'So you left Trinity?' Una asked. 'Why?'

'My father was transferred to this God-forsaken hole. Some bloody silly principle of loyalty was involved. Love me, love my dog. So to prove he loved Belfast, he made me transfer from Trinity to the excuse for a university this place provides. I suppose you're from Belfast, Mr Devine?'

Mr Devine felt an instant and powerful dislike for this young man. But all he said was: 'Yes, I was born here, I'm afraid. But I went to university in Dublin.'

'Trinity?' The young man brightened.

'No. National.'

'Oh.'

There was nothing more to say. Irwin put his hand on Una's arm. 'Look here, I'm with some people and someone is clutching a drink for me. But I must give you a ring, if you're staying in town.'

'Yes, do that, Ronnie . . . It's double four one double five.'

Irwin wrote the number down in a small morocco leather notebook and put the notebook back in his expensive tweed jacket.

'I like your coat,' Una said to him.

'Do you? Had it made up here. Well, good-bye, Una. Oh . . . good-bye, Mr Devine.'

Wordlessly, Mr Devine handed Una her gin-and-orange . . . She gave that snooty little bastard her telephone number, yet she wouldn't let me ring her up. He's a Protestant, of course, same as she is. And plenty of money, to judge from appearances.

But just then someone pushed into him from behind and he was in turn pushed against Una. He smelled her scent, his hand was less than an inch from her bare shoulder, his stomach and the side of his leg pressed rough serge against smooth party silk. He forced himself away. 'Excuse me, I'm sorry.'

'Wasn't Joan of Arc a wonderful person?' she said, ignoring their bodily contact.

'She has a lot of trouble ahead of her in the next act,' Mr Devine said gloomily.

'Yes, but it's worth it. Oh, I admire people like her. People who defy people and do what they think is right. Don't you?'

'Yes, I suppose so.'

The warning signal sounded. Second call. She put her arm in his as they went out of the bar. In the aisle, a priest passed, turning his head, making a little bow. Mr Devine said: 'Good evening, Father.'

'Good evening, Dev.'

'Who was that?' she asked.

'Father Creely. He teaches at Ardath.'

'Well, he'll know me if he sees me again,' she said.

Mr Devine swung around so quickly he almost gave himself a crick in the neck. But Father Creely had disappeared. What did she mean – why had Father Creely looked queerly at her? Uneasily, he remembered that this might not seem so innocent to the school authorities; it might not seem so innocent to Old Tim Heron, either. He had avoiding telling Old Tim about the play, et cetera. Old Tim was apt to be unreasonable, always ready to fly off the handle. Ah, well!

The lights dimmed. The third act began. He was thankful for the darkness.

In Rosary Hall, the stage lights had been turned on and three people sat on kitchen chairs in the wings. They and the actors wore overcoats, for it was very cold. Beyond the footlights the auditorium lay like a dark well, echoing and empty.

'All right, now,' Kevin Cooke said. 'We'll continue with that bit in the second act where the daughter tells Mulligan he's inherited a fortune.' He looked at the three seated judges. 'That'll give us a chance to hear Miss Clarke read some comedy lines.'

He pointed to Anthony Moloney, who stood at centre stage beside a thin woman who wore a fox furpiece collar. 'You and Mrs Hanlon carry on in your parts, to give her the feel of it.'

Moloney said, in a loud stage voice: 'D'ye hear somethin', Ma?'

'It's the win',' Mrs Hanlon said. 'Only the win'.'

Una Clarke, holding the script, began to read, 'Oh, Misther Mulligan, are you here?'

'Can't you see me, girl? Has every sowl in this house taken leave of their senses?'

'Oh, Misther, me da wants you down at the shop.'

Under the pretext of studying the script, Mr Devine watched his fellow judges. Dan Cavanaugh, one of the group's founders, looked pleased enough. But Kathleen Boland had a curl to her lip. She was an old hand, Kathleen, she had acted with the Abbey before she married and came to live in Belfast. She was hard to impress. The pity was, everyone took Kathleen's word on acting ability. Worried, Mr Devine looked at Una. She was clumsy in her reading and the accent was wrong. But what could they expect from a first reading? She was not nervous and her voice was strong. She could be taught.

A few minutes later, Kevin Cooke held up his hand. 'That'll do,' he said. 'Tony, will you take Miss Clarke out for a breath of air? I'll send for her in a moment.'

'Right you are, Kevin.'

When the hall door shut, Mr Devine turned anxiously to the judges. 'Well?'

'You'd have to coach her,' Kevin said. 'I've no time for beginners just now. What do you think yourself, Dev?'

'I think she'll do rightly. She has a good voice and she isn't shy.'

'Does that mean extra rehearsals for the rest of us?' Dan Cavanaugh asked.

'No, no,' Mr Devine said. 'I'll bring her up to the mark on my own.'

'Fair enough. What do you think, Kevin?'

Kevin pulled at the tip of his nose. 'It's Dev's idea. If he's willing to do the work, I've no objections.'

Mrs Hanlon sniffed and smiled. 'I agree. I have great faith in Dev.'

'Kathleen?'

Kathleen Boland, leaning back in her chair, blew a jet of cigarette smoke at the cold darkness above her. Her voice was surprised, drawling, theatrical. 'Hasn't anyone noticed that this girl has a *pronounced* Dublin accent?'

'I did notice a touch of brogue,' Dan Cavanaugh said.

'So did I,' Kevin Cooke agreed.

'Couldn't we get a local girl, Kevin?' Kathleen Boland asked. 'The point about this play is that there must be only one Dublin accent in it. And that's Moloney, as Mulligan. No offence to Dev, but he's a stage manager.'

Kevin Cooke looked at his fingernails before answering.

'Well, as a matter of fact, Dev has subbed for me several times when I've been busy.'

'Oh?' Kathleen looked significantly at Dan Cavanaugh and Mrs Hanlon. 'So that's the way of it, is it? First I heard of these goings on. Still, this girl is no great shakes. No looks, no experience and the wrong accent.'

'Now, hold on! Hold on!' Mr Devine's voice rose to a sudden, nervous shout. 'Do you not say she's pretty, at least? Let's be fair. What do Kevin and Dan say about her looks?'

'She's pretty enough,' Kevin said.

'Not bad,' Dan said.

Mrs Hanlon nodded. 'Young. But she's a nice wee thing.'

All three looked at old Dev, feeling sorry for him. Nobody wanted to be the one to turn his protégée down. It was up to Kathleen, they felt. After all, *she* raised the objection. But Kathleen, having caused the fuss, merely said: 'Well, I suppose it'd be hard to find someone else at such short notice. If Dev wants to try this girl out for a week or so, well and good. Why don't you do that, Dev, and then let us listen to the results? In the meantime, we'll all put on our thinking caps in case you don't succeed.'

'Fair enough,' Dan Cavanaugh said.

The others nodded. Mr Devine stood up and said he would step outside and tell Miss Clarke they'd give her a try. They watched his single progress among the dark rows of seats, waiting until the door shut, before Kathleen said:

'What do you make of that, boys and girls?'

'He seems very keen on getting this kid a part,' Kevin said.

'It's not only that, Kevin. Didn't you notice how hurt he was when I said she wasn't pretty?'

'Oh, nonsense,' Dan Cavanaugh objected. 'Dev's no ladies' man. And besides, he does all the donkey work around here and gets no credit for it. If he wants her in the play, let him have her, I say.'

'And why wouldn't he?' Mrs Hanlon said. 'He's a young fellow; it's perfectly normal that he'd be interested in a girl.'

Kevin shook his head. 'Poor old Dev. He's too good-natured, that's his trouble. Though I don't know why I'm calling him old. He's younger than I am.'

They laughed. Kevin was touchy about his age. 'You're Peter Pan,' Kathleen Boland told him. 'You'll never grow up.'

'Seriously, though,' Dan Cavanaugh said, 'I can't believe Dev has a crush on that kid.'

'And why not?' Kathleen wanted to know. 'Still waters run deep.'

And then they all began to talk about how cold it was in this hall because the hall door opened and they saw Dev coming back with Moloney and the girl.

The sexton came down the side aisle of the church shouldering his feather duster like a soldier carrying a rifle. His sour old face was set in a righteous scowl. 'You're early, Mr Devine. I haven't finished in here yet.'

'I'm sorry. I didn't know it was early. Maybe you'd let me have the key and I'll return it to you after we've finished. That, ah, that would save you the trouble of coming out to lock the hall up after us.'

'No.' The grey head shook in annoyance. Jealous of his privilege, he refused. 'Father Malahide doesn't like me to give them keys to anyone. You wait here and I'll get my coat.'

He listened to the teacher's further apology, giving no sign he had heard it. He went back up the aisle, opening the altar gate, and went into the sacristy. He put his duster in a closet and changed the water in the flower vases before putting on an old black raincoat that used to belong to Father Prout. Let the teacher wait, it wouldn't hurt him, some people had no consideration, stopping a man in the middle of his work. Every afternoon for the past week they had come stravaging up for their rehearsals, the pair of them. Once, they even came back at night. And each blessed time, he had to stop what he was doing to open the hall for them and lock up when they finished.

Buttoning his raincoat, the sexton went out by a side door. It was raining again, and that meant the church would be dirty after devotions . . . After he had just finished cleaning the aisles. Never done, he muttered angrily as he hurried around the back of the church and saw the pair of them waiting at the front door of Rosary Hall.

They were walking up and down. They stopped talking and watched as he unlocked the door. The teacher thanked him and they went in alone. The sexton saw the girl switch the lights on before he shut the door. A quare sort of rehearsal that is, he thought, just the two of them. It's that curate, Father Kennedy, that let them use the hall, your man, Father Kennedy, always making free with Church property. Oh, you're welcome, says he; never thinks of the trouble it give me, all kinds of codology, whist drives, lectures, plays. Sure, the people is sick of their diversions, they'd rather go to the pictures any day.

Back in the shelter of the sacristy, he took off his raincoat. No one here. Father Malahide was on sick calls this afternoon. Might as well have a draw. He put some hard plug in his hard palm and scraped a pipeful with a short blunt knife. He lit his short dirty pipe, blowing a plume of pungent blue toward the jumbled statues behind the door. He thought, as he sometimes did, of the work a sexton would have in a Prod church. It must be a part-time job with them. But he had never known a Protestant well enough to ask. Nor would he. He took a chalice and began to polish it.

In Rosary Hall, under a single light bulb, Mr Devine sat, overcoat collar up, chair tilted back, listening to Una say her lines. Despite the cold, she had taken off her belted tweed overcoat and now, in black jumper, green skirt, her stockings splashed with mud, she stood alone at the back of the stage between the stacks of scenery. She wore no powder, nor needed any. Once more, he was struck by the sculptured white beauty of her face, her lipstick like red crayon daubed on by an irreverent schoolboy. How could they not agree she was beautiful? It was Kathleen's jealousy, he decided. Kathleen would never again have that purity, that innocence.

But the doubt stayed with him. Did he see her as others did? Was love a granting of qualities which the loved one did not possess? And doubting, he began to appraise her as a stranger might. She had learned her lines well, but the emphasis was wrong. Her delivery was elocutionary and false. He held up a gloved hand.

'No, no, the daughter is afraid of Mulligan. To show that fear, manoeuvre behind the table as you speak. Now – start again!'

This was the seventh rehearsal and not any better than the third. Una could not get inside the part, and no wonder. For she was no ignorant, clumsy country girl; she was an exceptional girl, wasn't she? He was not sorry, in a way. It meant she would never make a career of acting. But he would have liked her to be a wee bit better, all the same.

Teacher, he silenced her once more. 'No, no, Mulligan is angry now. When he grabs you by the shoulders and shakes you, he realizes that he loves you. You must show your love for him in that response. Now, I'll read Mulligan's line again and you start your speech.'

He began to read it again, growling in Mulliganese. But halfway through, he looked up. She was standing at centre stage, her hands over her face, her dark head bent forward as though she were in pain. 'It's hopeless,' she said. 'Hopeless.'

'Try it once more.'

'I can't. I can't act to a blank wall. You sitting down there reading all the parts and me up here alone. I need someone acting, not reading.'

'Don't think of the other parts. Think of your own.'

'I can't. I *can't*.'

'Now, a little patience,' he said. 'Try it once more.'

'Oh, what's the use, Dev, what's the use? I'm no good. I'll never be any good.'

She bent her head again and he realized that she was crying. Awkwardly, he left his aisle seat and climbed the steps to the stage. He advanced, his gloved hands patting the air, like a conductor fading out music. But he did not dare to touch her. 'Now, now,' he said. 'That's not true, Una. It'll be better with the other actors. You'll see.'

'Well, *act* with me then, instead of sitting down there like a judge.'

'Ah . . . as a matter of fact, I've never actually acted in a play. I'm . . . ha, ha . . . the sort of man who stays behind the scenes.'

'But you know about acting. You're coaching me.'

'Well, I . . . ah . . . I just picked up a few tips, watching Kevin and the others. That's different from acting oneself.'

'Please!' she said. 'Just this once.'

'Well, all right,' Mr Devine said nervously. He put the script down. He remembered the lines but it was another matter to play them. He stepped closer to her and grasped her by the shoulders. 'What do you mean, girl?' he bellowed, shaking her so that when she began to recite, the physical truth of the shaking produced a certain reality in her delivery. She's right, he thought, it has to be acted out. And as he shook her, listening to her lines, he thought suddenly how he would never, in real life, maul her; how he would be all gentleness, all tenderness, She was light under his hands and he almost lifted her off her feet. Small, light, lovely. But still Mulligan, still acting, he threw her aside.

'I'm ruined,' he shouted. 'Ruined!'

'You're not, you're not.' She ran towards him, her face flushed with the excitement of make-believe. He felt her arms about him.

'I love you, Louis, I love you,' she whispered and put her face up for the kiss indicated in the script. But Mr Devine pulled away. 'No, no,' he said.

'You love me too,' she said. 'You love me, Louis Mulligan.'

Mulligan must press her to him and kiss her again. Dammit, he couldn't. It might not be acting any more, it might be something else entirely. But she was waiting. If she was acting, she had a life to her that he had not believed possible. Reluctantly, he took her in his arms. He forgot the line.

'Say, "I love you,"' she whispered.

'I love you. Yes, that's the line. Sorry. Go on from there.'

'I love you,' she said. 'I want to marry you, so I do.'

Mr Devine stood stock-still. Was that the line? Yes, it was. 'That's better,' he said. 'Now, do you think you can carry on alone?'

The sexton, having given the paten a quick polishing with a rag, put it back in the cupboard which held the sacred vessels. He locked the cupboard and put the lights out before he left the sacristy. It was night outside. He hurried along the outside wall of the church with a quick glance at the presbytery. There was a light in Father Malahide's study. The sexton, thinking of his supper, came around the other side of the church and saw the lights in the Rosary Hall. Still there, bad cess to them. After six, it was. Well, he was not going to leave his supper for the likes of them. No fear. Go in now and tell them to finish. Then, lock up and go home.

He pushed the heavy front door of the hall, and as he entered the vestibule, with its notices advertising rosary crusades and parish dances, he heard voices on the stage beyond. Quietly, he opened the inner door and stood at the back of the hall, watching them.

The girl had her arms around him. The teacher said:

'It's not true. I love you, so I do.'

It's a play, all right, the sexton decided. But acted very natural. The teacher is good.

'Love,' said the girl. 'Sure, you don't know what love is.'

'Neither do you. It's only my money you want,' the teacher said. He turned away and the sexton saw his face. Tormented. He's a grand actor, so he is, the sexton decided.

The girl tried to kiss him then. But the teacher held up his hand. 'All right,' he said, in his own voice. 'That was good.'

'Do you think so, Dev? Honestly?'

'Much better. Shall we do the next bit?'

No bloody fear, they wouldn't. He walked up the main aisle, his boots noisy on the wooden floor. The teacher looked down into the darkened hall. 'Who's that?'

'It's me, sir. It's after six.'

'Is it? Oh, I'm sorry. I suppose you want to close up?'

The sexton switched the stage lights off as the teacher helped the girl on with her coat. 'Would you like to go out and have some supper?' he heard the teacher say. The girl said that would be lovely.

Are they codding me, or what? the sexton wondered.

Quare rehearsals these is, him and her alone in this place, acting out love stuff. He hurried forward to hold the door open for them as they reached the vestibule. He looked at the girl as she passed. Nice legs she has on her, God forgive me!

'Thank you,' she said, smiling at him.

'Not at all, Miss.'

When Mr Devine paused in the open doorway and put his hand in his pocket, the sexton's hopes rose. But he took out not money, but a handkerchief with which he wiped his glasses. The sexton stared and saw that the teacher's eyes were watery. What was the matter with him? Had he some bad news? At the threshold, he paused, and the sexton saw him stumble like a grieving man.

The sexton paid no heed to the fact that the teacher was upset. Plenty of people were upset, the sexton had seen too many funerals to worry about that. But there was something quare about the teacher. Aye, that's it, the sexton said to himself. I knew I seen a change in him. He used to have a moustache, Mr Devine did. He must have shaved it off.

In the dining room of the Midland Hotel the atmosphere was soberly prosperous. Well-to-do Unionist businessmen dined there with their wives. The waiters who guarded the expanse of white linen and silver were long in service, confident, assured. One of them, a tiny pad of paper cradled in his hand, waited with poised pencil for the order.

Mr Devine said they would have Chicken Maryland.

'Right, sir, and a wee portion of Brussels sprouts, maybe?'

Yes, that would do. And would he ask the wine steward to come over?

'Yes, sir. Right away, sir.' He handed a tiny sheet of paper to a busboy. He smiled at the young lady and withdrew.

Mr Devine did not know anything about wine, but surely

it was the thing for an occasion like this. After all, he'd never taken her out to dinner before. He had never been on the Continent, but wine was romantic: you read about lovers drinking wine in restaurants in Paris. It was the kind of thing impressed a girl, the kind of thing that young fellow, Irwin, would do to make a showing. Well, he could afford it as well as any young Trinity blaggard. He was careful of his money: he could let go on an occasional splurge any time he wanted to. But what wine would he order? What was right?

He welcomed this worry about wine: it was less disturbing than remembering what had just happened. An hour ago, on the stage, all the things he had been afraid to think – all those things had been said. Said in make-believe, of course, play-acted by the pair of them. But he had held her: he had even kissed her. And nothing had happened. If she had been in love with him, she'd have been embarrassed. So she couldn't be in love with him: she had no idea how he felt. I should have told her, he thought. I should have had the courage to speak up. But the caretaker came in, and then it was too late. Too late.

'What's wrong, Dev? You're very silent tonight. Is something worrying you?'

'No, no.'

'Are you sure?'

He raised his eyes, alarmed. 'What, ah, what do you mean, Una?'

'Maybe it's my own guilty conscience,' she said. 'You see, there's something I've been dying to ask you. But I've been afraid.'

Apprehension made him hold his breath. So she *had* noticed: she was going to bring it out in the open. At once, he was afraid, he'd have given anything not to discuss it. For surely she'd say it was hopeless, surely she'd say they'd better stop it now. He joined his hands under the table, his fingers twisting his signet ring, twisting it, unable to stop. Waiting.

'It's about me,' she said. 'Ever since I met you, I've been

70

wondering if you knew. Tony Moloney knows, I think. Perhaps he told you.'

'What?' Mr Devine stared at her, his face confused, his mind stumbling. How did we get on to Moloney . . . what . . .?

'I was in a bit of trouble back in Dublin,' she said. 'I've been dying to know if you knew about it? Do you?'

'Oh?' Disappointment made him slack. She had not noticed, after all. It was that story about her and the married man. 'No,' he said. 'What story was that?'

'About me and a man. Are you sure Moloney didn't mention it?'

'First I heard of it,' Mr Devine said quickly.

'Well, I think I'd better tell you about it,' she said. 'I'd rather you heard it from me than from someone else.' She bent her head, hiding her face from him, uselessly rearranging her place setting as she talked. 'Last summer, when I was on holiday in Greystones, I fell in love with a man. He's an accountant, a friend of my cousin's. The trouble is, he's married.'

Mr Devine pressed hard on his ring, as though trying to break its golden circle. It did not break.

'I didn't know he was married at first,' she said. 'His wife was away in England, and he never mentioned her. I made a fool of myself, I was in love for the first time, I suppose. I thought he was too. He *said* he was. It got quite serious.'

Serious? Was she implying . . . Oh God, it didn't even bear thinking about, what she was implying; it was too disgusting, a married man pawing all over her. And her, she should be ashamed, telling him about it, as if it were nothing at all.

'He should be shot, so he should!' Mr Devine said in a sudden, nervous half-shout.

'It wasn't all his fault, Dev. When I found out he was married, I was too mixed up to have sense. I went on

71

seeing him in Dublin after his wife came back from England. He promised me he'd divorce her.'

He sat still, his anger bled pale by fear. Divorce. If that fellow could get a divorce, if she could still marry the fellow – then this was not just the luxury of confessing old sins. It was still on. He must turn her away from this bloody accountant.

'Fat chance he'll get a divorce,' he said. 'I know these married philanderers.'

'A month or two ago, I'd have hit you for saying that, Dev. But you're right. He didn't get the divorce. His wife found out about us, and came to see my mother. She raised an awful stink. So I was sent to Belfast to get me away from Michael.'

Michael was his name, then. I'll Michael him, Mr Devine thought savagely. 'Does your Uncle Tim know about this?' he asked.

'Yes, worse luck. He's awfully strait-laced, being Cath – Well, anyway, he and mother are very close. My father is dead, you know. It was Uncle Tim suggested I come and stay in Belfast until the Memorial's ready to take me.'

'I see.'

'I was hoping nobody here would know about it,' she said. 'But Moloney mentioned it in a sneaky way, the night I met him at Uncle Tim's party.'

Mr Devine sighed and looked across the room at the other diners. These people ate and talked and waiters served them. They behaved as if nothing at all had happened. As if everything were normal. Beside him, he heard Una's voice. 'It's a terrible mess, Dev. It's not fair to bore you with it.'

'But I'm not bored. I mean, on the contrary. It will all blow over, you know. These things do.'

'I wish it were as easy as that, Dev. Maybe I'm still in love with Michael. I'm just not sure.'

Thank God she did not look at him when she said it. He

took off his spectacles and wiped them determinedly with his thumb, 'I, ah, I hope for your sake . . . I mean, it would be better for you, if you weren't. I'm sure this man is not sincere in his feelings for you.'

'How can you say that? You've never even met him.'

Mr Devine readjusted his spectacles, screening his face with his hand. 'I – ah – I mean, if he were sincere, he would be prepared to leave his wife. I mean, he should risk anything.'

'Do you really think so?' He heard sudden hope in her voice. 'Oh, Dev, I think you've put your finger on it. That's what's worried me all along. I'm the one who's taken all the risks in this thing.'

'Of course. If he, ah, if he stayed with his wife, he must have, ah, preferred her, mustn't he?'

'Perhaps. He says not. But he certainly hasn't shown any courage. He's just like a lot of Irishmen I know. He pretends to be a wild Celt but he's frightened to do anything his neighbours wouldn't approve of.'

'Yes,' Mr Devine said, confused. He did not quite get the drift of this, but at least they were getting off that cursed accountant and on to general principles. 'As a matter of fact,' he added, 'I was just thinking that in my case – '

'So we agree then,' she interrupted. 'That's one of the things I like about you, Dev. You're honest. You'd stand by your principles.'

'Yes, Una. You see, if it were me – '

'Of course, you're older than me,' she said, 'You've had more experience of life. With boys my own age, it's the other way around. I feel older than them. I can't talk to them.'

He put the black thought aside. *Experience*. Did she mean . . .? What else could she mean? He said: 'Men mature more slowly. Now, take me, for instance – '

'Oh, you're mature, all right,' she said. 'But let's not talk about love, any more. It's such a hopeless affair, this story I've told you.'

'I, ah, I found it interesting. I mean, I was sorry that you'd had such an unhappy experience; but you're young, you'll forget it. Everyone has problems in love, I imagine. Even me.'

'Yes. And that's why I mustn't talk any more about myself, Dev. You'd only feel sorry for me, and make me feel sorry for myself, and then I'd spend all night wondering if Michael still loves me, or ever did love me. And that would be bad. You see what I mean, don't you?'

'Yes. Oh, yes,' he said, unhappily.

'So let's change the subject. Do you like dances?'

'Dances?'

'You don't?'

'Well, yes,' he said. 'Yes I do. But I'm, ah, I have rubber soles on my shoes at the moment. It makes it a bit awkward.'

'I didn't mean we were going to a dance tonight,' she said in an irritated voice. 'As a matter of fact, I thought of going to the pictures. That's what I always do when I feel depressed.'

'Oh? Perhaps we could; I mean, perhaps you would let me take you.'

'Well, there's a Gregory Peck film on. I like him, do you?'

'*Mmm*,' Mr Devine said.

'You don't like him. I can see it in your face.'

'Oh, no, nonsense. I'd like to go.'

'Good.' She sat up very straight in her chair, as though everything had been settled. 'We can go to a dance some other night,' she said. 'If you still want to?'

There was nothing left to do but to lie. Girls liked men who liked to dance. So he assured her that he would like it. Very much.

'And you must let me pay for the pictures tonight,' she said. 'We're friends, after all. And it was my idea.'

'Nonsense,' he said. 'I, ah, I may not look very affluent, but I'm not poor. Ha, ha.'

'All right, then. Let's eat and go. I'm starved.'

She began to taste her food. But Mr Devine let his knife and fork lie unused, his mind turning back to what had been said, to the story she had told. If she was still half in love with that fellow, what chance had he? What chance, when she had not even allowed him to mention his feelings? When was it she turned the conversation aside, where was it she stopped him? She could not have foreseen what he was going to say. *Or could she?*

'Wine, sir?'

He opened the leather-bound wine list. Red with meat, was that it? What would she like. He looked at her across the table, she was so lovely, so young, it couldn't be true, could it? And he thought of himself, and how he must look to her. Dowdy, ugly, inadequate. Even with his moustache shaved off, he must seem much older than the boys she knew. Older and shabbier than that Irwin fellow, for instance. He must get some new clothes. Yes, better not risk asking her feelings on the subject; just as well he had not been able to bring it up. Let it wait. Wait.

Chapter Six

Next morning at ten o'clock, a college servant came to Junior IV and said Mr Devine was wanted on the telephone. This was unheard of. College rules expressly forbade staff members to receive private phone calls during class hours. It must be an emergency. But what? Mr Devine set his boys a task and hurried downstairs to the porter's lodge.

Old John Harbinson, seated beneath the school clock, his large red hands folded in the lap of his white apron, nodded civilly as Mr Devine entered. The receiver on the wall telephone dangled from its long cord; waiting. Mr Devine hoisted it up.

'Mr Devine speaking.'

'Dev? Oh, I thought I'd never get you. It's Una.'

Involuntarily, he hunched his shoulders, cupping his hand around the mouthpiece. Old John was deaf, but dammit, he was not five feet away.

'Yes,' he whispered. 'What is it?'

'Can you talk?'

'I'm teaching a class. Perhaps I can ring you back?'

'No, I had to say it was an emergency to get hold of you. So listen, and I'll tell you quickly.'

Mr Devine peered anxiously at Old John, seeing the porter's face in profile. There was about it a torpor, a serenity which surrounds the deaf.

'It's about the play,' she said. 'I never mentioned to Uncle Tim that I was rehearsing for it. I thought I'd wait until we were sure I was getting the part.'

'Yes?'

'Well, last night when I got home from the pictures, he and Aunt Maeve were waiting for me with faces like doom, wanting to know where I'd been. You'd have thought it was four o'clock in the morning to hear them.'

'Yes, yes,' Mr Devine said in a hoarse, impatient voice.

'So I said I'd been out with you, thinking that would set their minds at rest. But it had the opposite effect. They nearly had a fit! They told me I must stop seeing you, I mustn't take part in this play, and I don't know what else.'

'But why?'

'Oh, they're terrified that people here might find out about my dreadful past. I didn't dare tell you knew already. You know how suspicious Uncle Tim is. He puts the worst construction on every blessed thing.'

'Yes,' Mr Devine said miserably. Tim would put the worst construction on it, all right. That was why he hadn't mentioned this business to Tim. He had thought it wiser not to.

'Anyway, he said he was going to have a word with you today,' her voice continued. 'So I thought I'd warn you.'

'I see.'

'He says you're a friend of his, you'll take me out of the play if he asks you to. You won't do that, will you, Dev?'

'Well, no. Of course not.'

'That's what I wanted to be sure of. He has no authority over me, remember that.'

'Yes, Una.' Mr Devine, letting her name slip, peered back at Old John. My God, what if there's an extension on this phone some place? What if the President or the Dean is listening in?

'So we'll pay no attention to him, will we, Dev?'

'Of course not.'

A finger poked his shoulder. Old John, hoar face puckered in concern, pointed to the wall clock. He held out his hands, palms upwards, as though to indicate he had no choice. Then he sat down and turned the key in the switch

77

block. The electric bell, deafening, unbearable, made the room tremble. Dulled by sound, Mr Devine leaned against the wall, clutching the receiver.

'What? Can't – '

'Wait.'

At last the key was removed. In the silence, Mr Devine's voice was loud as a shout. 'Una? Hello, Una?'

'I'm here. What was that noise? Is the place on fire?'

'No. It was just the class bell.'

'Anyway, I must go,' she said. 'I'll see you this afternoon.'

'All right.'

The finger touched him again. He replaced the receiver and turned to meet Old John's hand-waving apologies. 'Sorry about the bell, Mr Devine, sir, very sorry. But I have my orders, sir, nothing must interfere with the bell.'

'Yes.'

'I beg pardon, sir, interrupting you, sir, I mean your tellyphone call, sir.'

'That's all right. Thank you, John.'

That must be part of being deaf, Mr Devine thought, the way he repeats everything twice. You have to use sign language on him.

But he had no time to think about deaf men, he was late already. He fled along the corridor to Junior IV; but when he entered the classroom, Mr Turley was already installed and writing out a physics problem on the blackboard. Tiptoeing in (sorry, Turley), Mr Devine collected his books and cane and fled to Senior II, which was already in a state of noisy disorder. He caned two boys who had been out of their seats, wrote a compound sentence on the blackboard and told the class to parse and analyze it. He must keep them busy. He must have time to think.

Sitting at his desk, distractedly bending his cane into a circle around his head, he joined the handle and tip at his chin. He was unaware of the odd picture he presented and his pupils, seeing the look in his eye, did not risk a giggle. For Old Dev was not himself these days. He would turn on you as soon as look at you.

This was true. For a fortnight he had been edgy and abstracted. Normally, he guided his speech and actions as a conductor leads an orchestra: his school conduct followed a set pattern, designed to evoke the proper response from pupils, colleagues, priests. Certain things were expected of the staff in a Catholic college. Certain standards were implied. A man like himself risked censure by taking a twenty-year-old Protestant girl out to public restaurants, by coaching her without her family's permission. It was all perfectly innocent, of course, but it would not look innocent to the authorities. Man was born sinful, he must avoid the occasions of sin. The men who ran Ardath did not believe in words of honour, they did not consider human intention a match for the devil's lures. No, force must be met by force. Occasions of sin must be rigorously guarded against, was that not clear? Then why did he, a teacher of boys, show such a bad example? The authorities would say he had courted an occasion of sin; he had risked giving scandal. He had not guessed at his danger, he realized now. For the past fortnight he had lived in a vacuum: the inward-turning world of a man in love.

He let his cane spring free and caught it once more, bending it to shape an oval frame for his face. He should have warned Tim Heron that he was coaching Tim's niece. It looked now as if he had been concealing it for some dubious motive, did it not? Be sure your sin will find you out, as the Temperance posters said. Well, Tim had found him out. And Tim was teaching a class not a hundred yards away this very minute. It was enough to give a fellow the shudders.

Supposing Tim Heron took the whole matter to the President, what would Dr Keogh say? Most irregular. This young person sounds highly unsuitable, Mr Devine. But,

Dr Keogh, unsuitable or not, I am in love with her. Is it my fault that she's a Protestant? All I can say truly is that I love her, that I am at an age when a man should be married and that I believe we would be very happy together. I am trying to be truthful, Dr Keogh.

He let the cane spring free once more. Materialistic values, self-love, neglecting your duty as a Catholic . . . Oh, he could hear Dr Keogh's answer, plain enough. Mixed marriage, danger to the faith of any subsequent issue, et cetera. But still, there was no sense crossing bridges until you came to them. Perhaps he was exaggerating. Perhaps Tim Heron had no notion of mentioning this thing to anyone. And if he does mention it, isn't there a perfectly straightforward answer? Tell him my interest was only in securing a suitable person to play in a charity affair arranged by the Dean of Discipline of this college. What could Tim say to that? Nothing. And it was not untrue, either. There was no sense in saying anything else. No sense stirring up trouble.

And that brought to mind a question he had once seen in a general knowledge test for senior boys. Appropriate, it was. He rapped his cane on the desk, calling them to attention.

'One moment. Which of you can convert the following verse into a well-known adage?'

They waited, wary, as he recited:

> If somnolescent on the ground you view
> Some huge exemplar of the canine crew,
> Beware with fierce and unrelenting blows
> To interrupt the quadruped's repose.

He watched them fret. A boy put up his hand.

'Well?'

'*Let sleeping dogs lie*, sir.'

'Correct,' Mr Devine said. And that was what he would do. Tim Heron always went home for lunch. No chance of seeing him in the refectory, therefore, and it would be easy enough to dodge him during class time. Una would come for her lesson this afternoon, as usual. *Let sleeping dogs . . .* Yes.

The refectory at Ardath was enormous, bare and cold; like some unhappy misalliance of the blueprints for an aircraft hangar and concert hall. It had been built in a period of materials shortage, and as its priority had been low, it had never been completed. Some effort had been made to ignore the steel girders of the ceiling by hanging large, unskilful copies of works by Tiepolo, Titian and Domenichino on the walls beneath; works which provoked in the ecclesiastical memory a sense of former munificence, having been purchased more than a century ago in Rome at three times their real value. A more recent memory was provided by a wooden platform at the far end of the refectory. It had been built with the halfhearted intention of using the hall as a forum for school debates and religious plays. Now, elevated above the heads of the student rabble, it contained two sacrosanct tables, covered with white linen, at which staff members dined. This motif of hierarchy was emphasized by life-size oil paintings of four robed and solemn Irish bishops who stared down from the platform, challenging the wickedness of any boy who dared look up.

At noon that day, when Mr Devine entered the refectory, a zoological chatter arose from the long wooden trestle tables which spread in prison rows from entrance door to staff platform. The day's reading had not yet started and the boarders were taking full advantage of the short liberty of speech. College servants, wearing long whitish aprons, moved up and down, ladling potato stew. On the staff platform, the clerics, seated in order of rank, had finished their soup and waited meat. At the lay table, four tardy masters gobbled Scotch broth. There was no sign of Tim Heron.

Mr Devine sat down at the unoccupied end of the lay table, placing a book beside him to indicate that he was in a reading mood. As his broth was served, the student chatter stilled. Father McSwiney, Dean of Discipline, had entered the refectory. He ascended the lectern and opened a calf-bound volume of *The Life of Father Damien*. Elbow digs warned the unwary. The Dean surveyed the refectory, staring out over the students' heads like a sailor searching for land. Then, although the room was quiet, he hammered the lectern, crying: 'Silence!'

He waited. His eyes closed in pain as a crashing chute of dishes dropped to oblivion in the kitchens beyond. 'Silence!' he shouted. 'Any boy I see talking will report to my study after the meal.'

He looked for mutiny. Dean of Discipline. The boarders sat as still as if they were being photographed.

'The defacing of desks, of walls and toilets, in fact the wanton destruction of school property, has become an open scandal. Why? Some of you seem to have the mistaken impression that you can leave your mark on this college by wood carving.'

At the clerical table there were a few smiles, acknowledging the Dean's sally. But Mr Devine looked at the President. Father McSwiney had not observed protocol. He had not asked the President's permission to speak. I wonder did the old boy notice? Mr Devine said to himself.

He did. He stood up shakily, freezing the clerical smiles. The Dean turned.

'Yes, Dr Keogh?'

The Very Reverend Daniel Keogh, MA, DD, was five feet tall, with a head so large it insulted the rest of him. His soutane – shoulders frosted by dandruff, seat and elbows polished to a shiny glaze – presented a perfect contrast to the Dean's clerical elegance. A halo of grey stubble circled his skull, spreading like a skin disease down his cheeks to meet at the point of his receding chin. Uncompromising steel spectacles were held together at the bridge of his chilly, beaked nose by a soiled piece of flesh-coloured adhesive tape. He was said to have been a brilliant lecturer in his day and had served in the Irish College in Rome and at Maynooth. However, he was old. His head nodded from some unspecified affliction. He was believed to be absent-minded and slightly deaf. His critics, including the Dean, felt it high time he retired.

'Thank you, Father McSwiney,' he said. He raised his head, peering at the steel girders as though a text was written there. Then, in a soothing voice, he began:

'*Harmp! Harmp!* There is a saying which comes to mind, a saying I once heard from an uncle of mine, although at the time, being of tender years – yes, it must have been shortly before my confirmation – I did not fully realize its import. It was said to me when, in my uncle's garden, I had carefully, with a rather blunt instrument, carved my own initials on a wooden gate. Alas, I was of your number, gentlemen.'

The President wrinkled his nose, nudging his spectacles back to the ridge.

'My uncle said to me on that long ago day, "My boy, *le nom d'un fou se trouve partout*". Now, lamentably ignorant as I was of the French language at that time, I was puzzled and at a loss. I was obliged to ask him for a translation. But he refused me, saying I must discover its meaning for myself. Curiosity led me to write it down. Curiosity led me to trace the saying to a French sage. *Fou!* Yes, that word is, I feel, strangely onomatopoeic, is it not? It is indeed. And since learning its meaning, I have confined my signature to paper and at the proper time Not only that, but I have been careful in the matter of appending my name or initials to any document the validity of which left any question for doubt. Some of you who have seen a report card will know what I mean. That is all, gentlemen. Those of you who do not have instruction in the French tongue will doubtless be led, as I was, to further elucidation and edification. And now, I trust that Father McSwiney, who drew this matter to my attention, will honour us with yet another reading from the life of Father Damien of Molokai, whose name is carved indestructibly in the immortal role of honour of the soldiers of Almighty God!'

Mr Devine looked at his colleagues for comment. But Moloney and Young Connolly were discussing Ireland's chances in the Rugby finals. Turley (geography) and Cavan (history) had begun something geopolitical which was developing into a row. That left Geohegan, the gym master, a man of no standing whatsoever, whose effrontery in daring to eat with his betters was the subject of a petition threatened triannually by most of the lay staff. Mr Devine, who did not like to hurt any man's feelings, never had the heart to put Geohegan in his place and as a result, Geohegan sought his company, with the tenacity of a poor relation. Now, catching his eye, the gym master began a long and boring recital about his youngest child's illness.

A platter of stew was placed before them. 'Problem, find the meat,' Mr Devine said. Geohegan laughed. Aye, that was about the height of it, find the meat, eh? Did the other fellows hear what Dev said? The others ignored him. Meekly, he turned back to Mr Devine, imploring friendship. Mr Devine inquired about Mr Geohegan's eldest boy, who was in the civil service. Geohegan gratefully explained.

Finally, dessert, an unknown brown pudding, made its appearance. Mr Devine picked up his spoon to test it, and heard an unwelcome voice say:

'Can I have a word with you in private?'

Mr Devine put down his spoon at once. 'Yes, Tim,' he said.

'Eat your pudding first. I'll wait for you in the corridor.'

Mr Devine looked with distaste at the brown mess. He no longer felt any hunger.

'Will you not stay and have a cup of tea, Mr Heron?' Mr Goehegan inquired humbly.

Tim Heron looked at the games master as though he had spoken in Swahili. Then he asked: 'Do you want tea, Dev?'

'No, no.'

'Come on, then.'

'Just coming, Tim.'

Tim Heron stepped down from the platform, walking quickly among the long rows of boys. As he passed the lectern, the Dean, reading aloud, looked up. Mr Devine passed. Again the Dean looked up. The reading continued. Heron reached the refectory door first, opening it quietly. It banged shut behind him, just as Mr Devine reached it. Everyone looked at him. He hurried into the quiet of the corridor where Heron waited, his back to a window, the points of his wing collar awry, his face haggard and grey as though he had left home without shaving.

'We can't talk here,' he said abruptly. 'Come with me.'

He strode off down the corridor, with Mr Devine at his heels. He stopped outside the door of the masters' cloakroom, looked left and right, and then guided Mr Devine inside with a quick sweep of his arm.

The cloakroom was warm and steamy with the heat from a leaky radiator under the window. Tim Heron looked down the row of olive-green lockers to make sure no one else was there. Then he shut the door with a bang.

'I suppose you know why I want you?' he asked.

'I – ah – ' Mr Devine's hopeful smile died of cold at the sight of Tim Heron's face. 'No,' he said. 'What was it, Tim?'

'It's about my niece. I gather you and she are going out together.'

'Well, ah, I'd hardly say that, Tim. I'm coaching her for a try-out in a play for Father McSwiney. A play we're putting on to help the Foreign Missions.'

'It's the first I've heard of it,' Heron said, his right eye beginning its familiar blink of rage.

'Didn't Una tell you, Tim?'

'She did not.'

'Well, I don't know why she didn't,' Mr Devine said weakly. Dammit, what else can I say? he reasoned. I have to find out what's angering him. But he felt as though he had committed sacrilege. How could he face Una, after letting her down?

'She didn't, I tell you,' Tim Heron said, trembling in front of Mr Devine as though he could not control himself. 'You had her out to dinner in the Midland Hotel last night, hadn't you?'

'Well, yes, as a matter of fact, I had. She'd rehearsed so hard all week, I thought she needed a little treat.'

'A little treat? What are you up to, Dev? I'd remind you that girl is only just turned twenty. She's still a child.'

Now *that's* unfair, Mr Devine decided. You'd think I was a corrupter of youth, or something. Dammit, that was not friendly of Tim to say a thing like that. He liked Tim, he was obliged to Tim, he counted him as a good friend, Tim had got him this job; but dammit, no man had the right to insult a fellow like that. No man. Still, Tim was upset. Tim always lost his temper easily.

'I, ah, I didn't mean any harm, Tim. Certainly not. I was just trying to be nice.'

'Nice? Do you know the girl's background? That's my sister's girl; she is not a Catholic, did you know that?'

'Yes.'

'And between ourselves – let it not go any further – that wee girl is not as obedient as she might be. She's going into the Memorial Hospital in a couple of weeks, thank God. I can tell you I'll be glad when someone else has the looking after of her.'

'Oh?'

Tim Heron's suspicious eyes fled to the door and returned to their accusing, angry inspection of Mr Devine's face. 'I always thought you were a friend of mine,' he said. 'I thought you were a decent fellow.'

'Well, now, Tim, there's no call for you thinking otherwise.'

'Maybe. Maybe. I want her taken out of this play, do you hear? At once.'

'Well, ah, what harm is there in her acting in a play, Tim?'

'Never mind what harm. I'm the judge of that. I want you to leave her out, do you hear me, Dev?'

'Well, ah, it would be very inconvenient, Tim. Father McSwiney is very keen to have the play put on on time. If we take her out, we'll have to find someone else.'

'Well, find someone else, then!'

'I, ah, I can't do that, Tim. It wouldn't be fair to her, now would it?'

'Fair? Who's talking about fair? I'm warning you, Dev, and I won't warn you twice. You take that girl out of your play or I'll do something about it.'

'Do what?' Mr Devine's voice trailed away at the implications of this.

'Never mind. You'll see.'

Tim Heron whirled, his ragged gown twisting on his shoulders. He hurried, warped and trembling with rage, down the row of lockers to the door. 'Mark my words,' he cried. 'You'll regret it.'

'No, hold your horses, Tim, just a minute – '

But the cloakroom door shut like a slap in his face. The gust of its closing dragged a stray scrap of exercise paper slowly across the room. Mr Devine stared at the paper, watching it come to rest against one of the olive-green lockers. His eyes were stinging. To think . . . to think Tim would speak to him like that.

He blinked and removed his glasses. He drew his sleeve across his eyes. He found his handkerchief and blew his nose noisily. Then, eyes still smarting, he heard the bell ring, signalling the end of break. He put his glasses on and went out to face the school.

Chapter Seven

It was useless to look at his watch again: he had looked at it a few minutes ago. But he did. It was ten past five. No sense waiting any longer. But he did not move. There was no hope she would come now, it was far too late. But he peered from the doorway of Rosary Hall, watching each bus arrive and depart.

The sky cast a harsh, strange light as the afternoon died in a storm threat. Spatters of rain began to appear on the pavement. They grew thicker, beating on the corrugated iron roof of the hall with a noise like operatic thunder. For sure now, she would not come. But he waited.

Night fought its way up the street, isolating the street lamps, the rain died to infrequent gutter splashings. Shipyard workers came home from Queen's Island in straggles, throwing out snatches of talk about football and the dogs. Six o'clock. Blinds were drawn in front parlours. People were eating their supper. What was the sense of waiting? His feet were cold and the shoulders of his raincoat were wet through. But a wee bit longer wouldn't make any difference. He paced a sentry beat outside the hall, watching another bus discharge its load on the corner. A woman got off, lowering a child to the pavement. She reached back to receive her parcels from the bus conductor. A tall, thin old man in a raincoat and a bowler hopped down, a copy of the *Belfast Telegraph* under his arm. The bus conductor touched the communication buzzer and the bus started again. And then, at the last moment, she rushed downstairs, jumping off, stumbling slightly, splashing her stockings in the gutter.

He ran across the street: she ran towards him and,

running, they met, his hands catching the elbows of her grey tweed coat.

'Oh, you're here after all,' she said. 'I was sure you'd have gone.'

'No.'

'I'm awfully sorry. I telephoned your digs and your landlady said you'd gone. So I came on down, late and all.'

'Yes, yes.'

'What time is it, Dev?'

'After six.'

'Oh, that's awful. And I can only stay a few minutes. We won't really have time for a rehearsal.'

'Oh?'

'Let's have a cup of tea instead. Do you want to?'

'Yes, yes.' Hastily, he took her arm and they began to walk towards the teashop on the corner. The rain began again, a brutal shower that stung the pavements and sent people hurrying to doorways. They ran again, Mr Devine making an extra effort to reach the teashop door before her. As he jerked the handle, a little bell rang shrill and a fat woman looked up from the cash register.

Una's hair was plastered to her cheekbones, her tweed coat was sodden. When Mr Devine closed the door and took his hat off, a brimful of water dribbled to the floor. They smiled at each other.

'We're like something the tide washed up,' she said.

He did not hear. Mopping his neck with a dry handkerchief, he looked around for a quiet place to sit. At the end of the room there was a small alcove, guarded by gingham curtains. He drew the curtains aside, revealing two backroom tables and rickety chairs. He took their coats and put them on a coat rack. Returning, parting the gingham curtains, he saw Una bend her head, lifting the dark, wet hair at the base of her neck, showing the white young nape. He paused, looking down at her. How young she was!

'That's better,' she said. 'What a downpour.'

90

'Wasn't it just?' He sat down opposite her, offering his uncertain smile. What could she see in him, a girl like this? How could she possibly care for him?

'What a day it's been,' she said. 'I gather you and Uncle Tim had words.'

'Yes. Yes, we did.'

'Did you tell him off, I hope?'

'Yes, I, ah, told him it was out of the question. He wanted me to drop you from the play.'

'Good for you.'

Mr Devine looked down at the empty chair beside him. Had he really told Tim Heron off? Hadn't it been the other way around? But still, he had refused to drop her. Yes, he had refused Tim, after all.

On the chair, abandoned, lay a copy of the *Daily Sketch*.

WIN A GREYHOUND
YOUR CHANCE TO
MAKE A FORTUNE

Photographs of greyhounds with alert animal eyes searched for prey among the headlines . . . Things were coming to a head. Tim Heron had warned him he would make trouble. He, in turn, should warn Una. This mess must be cleared up: he must tell her he loved her, he must bring it out in the open. But the moment did not seem propitious. Not yet.

'He's got no rights over me,' she said. 'And as long as you're not worried, I intend to go on as if nothing had happened.'

'Me? *I'm* not worried.'

'Are you sure, Dev? I had to listen to a long lecture from Uncle Tim on how I might ruin your career.'

'But that's nonsense.'

'*He* doesn't think so. He seems to think Catholics shouldn't go out with Protestant girls. Honestly, you'd think we were having an affair, the way he went on.'

Mr Devine looked at the tablecloth, too embarrassed to pretend he had not heard.

'Anyway, I don't want to make trouble for you,' she said. 'I'll drop out of this play. It's not that important.'

'Not at all – I mean, I wouldn't hear of it.'

The curtains parted and a middle-aged waitress entered, ridiculous in a milkmaid's smock, two menu cards thrust in front of her like loaded revolvers.

'Do youse want two teas?'

'No. Just a cup of tea. I've no time to eat anything,' Una said.

'Two cups of tea, please, Miss.'

The waitress snatched back the menu cards, letting the curtain fall on her displeasure. Wasting her time, they were, with their fourpenny cups of tea.

'I'm late already,' Una said. 'But I had to come for a minute, to find out how you felt.'

'Yes. I see.'

'So we'll go on with the rehearsals then?'

'Yes,' he said.

'How many more can we have before the general rehearsals start?'

'I should think about six,' he said. 'If we work every afternoon, I mean.'

The waitress returned, slopping two teacups on the table. Una immediately put milk in hers. 'I really haven't time to drink this,' she said. 'I promised to be back at half-past six. And with Uncle Tim in the mood he's in, I'd rather not be late.'

'Yes,' Mr Devine said unhappily. 'Yes, of course.'

Now was the time to tell her: he must show her his interest was in her as much as in the play. If there was to be a row about his friendship with her, he must know how she felt. But as he tried to gather up courage to say it, Una stood up and put her gloves on. 'Look, I really must run,' she said.

'I'll go with you.'

'No, finish your tea, Dev. I'd rather go back alone.'

'Well, ah . . .'

Not finding words, he went to get her coat instead. When he parted the curtains coming back, the coat held like a cloak in his hands, she was stooping over the table, hurriedly drinking the tea. She looked up and, in that brief moment, Mr Devine saw that she saw: his face showed it all, the worry, the fear, the disappointment at her leaving.

'What's wrong?' she said.

'Nothing, ah, nothing at all.'

She put her arms in the coat. Then, as he let go of the material, she turned suddenly and put her gloved hands on his shoulders. Stretching up, she kissed him on the cheek. 'Thanks, Dev,' she said. 'Now I must run.'

The curtains fell slack together. She was gone. He heard the little bell ring as she opened the teashop door, he heard the small slam of the door as it closed behind her. His hand went to his face, touching his cheek. There, where the tip of my moustache used to be. The trouble ahead, the certain trouble would be worth it now. For he had not needed to tell her, he had not needed to make any declaration. She knew. She knew he loved her.

Half-past six. Three frightened boarders heard the supper bell as they followed Father Creely up the stairs in Priests' House. In the priests' corridor, he told them to wait and, as soon as he went into the Dean's study, they gathered around a radiator, trying to warm their hands. Flippers hurt less when your hands were hot. They did not speak to each other: what was the use? They watched the Dean's door.

It had happened in the showers behind the gym, and Father Creely had hardly given them a minute to get their clothes on and follow him. So the three boys were only half dry, their wet hair slicked down, their dirty clothes sticking to their skins. They were junior boys, fourteen-year-olds, from the Glens of Antrim. That was why Corny had been telling the other two when Father Creely sneaked up and overheard them. They always told each other everything. They were all Cushendall boys together.

They did not have long to wait. Father Creely put his head around the Dean's door and said: 'Come in'.

Corny Coogan went in first. It was his fault, in a way. Jimmy Devlin and Phil Glover followed. Inside Father McSwiney's study it was nice and warm. A big fire was burning in the grate. There was no sign of Father Mac at first, and they were hoping he wasn't there.

But he was. He rose up out of a big armchair. He was not wearing his soutane, in fact, he had his coat off and was in his black waistcoat with his shirtsleeves rolled up. You could see his muscles. He went over to his cupboard and opened it. Everybody knew what was kept there. Canes. He picked one out now and swished it up and down like a golf club. He put it back and took out a longer one. Thin. It made a noise like a whip over a horse's back. He put the long thin cane on his desk. He was ready.

The three boys looked over at Father Creely. 'Old Faith and Morals,' the boarders called him. He was standing, his back to the fire, his thumbs hooked into his black waistcoat.

The Dean said: 'Father Creely tells me you boys were colloguing in the showers. Is that right?'

Six sick eyes watched him. Three prayed as one that one would answer. But no one spoke.

'Where are your tongues?' the Dean said. 'What cat's got them now? Not so full of chat, are we? Well, I give you permission, my lads. Talk all you want.'

Father Creely gave a wee laugh. 'I think Coogan had the most to say, Father.'

'Coogan!' the Dean shouted. 'Speak up!'

'I'm sorry, Father,' Corny got out. 'We never meant any harm.'

'No, Father,' Jimmy Devlin said.

Wee Phil Glover was too frightened to speak. But he nodded his head that he was sorry too.

'Sorry, are ye? I'll sorry ye. Sorry, is it? Aye, take my word for it, you'll be sorry in a minute.'

He picked up the cane. Then he put it down again. 'Coogan', he said. 'I believe you were repeating a conversation you overheard between two masters. Right or wrong?'

'Yes, Father, but I never meant any – '

'Malicious slander, that's what you meant. Sneaking under windows, listening to your elders, giving scandal to two other boys. Am I right?'

'Oh, no, Father. I never did, Father.'

'Telling me a lie is a mortal sin. I cannot punish mortal sins. Only God can do that. Father Creely will hear your confessions at eight o'clock tonight. All of you. You would not like to die tonight with mortal sins on your souls, would you?'

'No, Father.'

'I cannot punish mortal sins, as I said. But I can discourage you from tale-bearing in the future. I can give you a reminder that when you leave this room, you will not repeat these slanderous remarks to anyone. Anyone, do you hear?'

Anxiously, they nodded.

'Make no mistake,' the Dean said. 'If I hear this tale has been repeated in any shape or form' – he hit the table with the cane – 'I will hold each and every one of you accountable. I will make an example of the three of you, do you hear?'

He looked at each boy in turn, letting the threat sink in. Then he beckoned to Corny Coogan, pronouncing the phrase which every Ardath boy knew. 'Right, now, Coogan. Time for your medicine.'

Corny stuck out his right hand, as bold as he could. You had to hold it straight for Father Mac. If you trembled, he'd double the dose. Corny's outstretched hand was not high enough up. Father Mac's cane touched it, light as a feather, raising the hand to the proper position. Corny closed his eyes. He could hear the whistle of it before it hit him. A terrible flipper, right on the tips of his fingers, making them swell as if they would burst. He bent double with the pain.

'Stand up,' Father McSwiney ordered. But Corny could not. So Father Mac shifted his stance a little and brought the cane down hard across the back of Corny's bare legs. Corny jumped.

'Other hand.'

Left hand now. The cane whistled down. Corny was tough, but he was crying. Even though he had been warned, he doubled up again. Father Mac, without hesitation, began flogging him across the rump, telling him to hurry up and get his hand out. The other boys counted. Six on each, he got, not counting the skelps Father Mac laid on his legs and bum. Father Mac was panting now, like a man threshing corn.

'Next boy!'

The three were weeping when it was over. Father Mac threw down the cane. 'That's just a sample, mind you,' he said. 'Just a sample. If I hear one word of this slander against the masters, each one of you will be back in this room. And woe betide you then. Now, go to the study hall and wait until confessions. No supper. And you'll talk to no one until you've made your peace with God.'

He picked up the cane again. As they went through the door, one, two, three, he gave them a last cut across the legs. Afterwards, he shut the door and dropped the cane on his desk. He looked a lot calmer now, a little tired. He accepted a cigarette from Father Creely's case.

'Mind you, it was pure accident, my overhearing them.' Father Creely said. 'I just happened to look in, in case any boys were smoking, and I heard Coogan say he had been hiding in the masters' cloakroom for a dare. When I heard him mention Devine and Heron, I thought I'd better listen to it all.'

'A good thing you did,' the Dean said, sitting down. 'Somebody has to keep their ears open in this college. You never know what these little ruffians will be up to next.'

'It seems they had quite an argument,' Father Creely said. 'Devine and Heron, I mean.'

'Old Tim's very fond of Devine,' the Dean said. 'Always backing him up and so forth. Quite pally, in fact. Not that Devine is a hard fellow to get along with. Always very obliging, I've found him.'

'*Cherchez la femme*,' Father Creely said, smiling. 'Heron has a niece, it seems. Some row about Devine putting her in a play.'

'A play?' The Dean looked up. 'Hold on a minute. Could that be the Foreign Missions play?'

'I don't know,' Father Creely said. 'Why?'

'Nothing. Why didn't he want her in the play?'

'According to what Coogan heard, he said something about her being a Protestant.'

'What's her name, this girl?'

'Una something. That's the name they used.'

'Hold on, now.' The Dean smacked his large hand on the armrest of the chair. 'Una? I met her at Heron's place a couple of weeks ago. Nice-looking wee thing, from Dublin. Heron didn't say much about her, come to think of it.'

'D'you know, I believe it's the same one I saw Devine squiring to the theatre last week,' Father Creely said. 'At the Opera House, I met them. They were coming out of the bar.'

'Speaking of which,' the Dean said, 'will you have a small one?'

'Thanks, Father, I think I will.'

'But what could be upsetting Heron?' the Dean said, as he poured two stiff whiskies. 'Sure, Devine's a harmless enough lad. What age is he, Devine?'

'Middle thirties, I'd say,' Father Creely guessed. 'But maybe not so harmless, Father.' He smiled in his superior

97

way, as he said it. After all, he had done parish work and the Dean had not. He was more versed in human frailty than the Dean.

'That could be,' the Dean said. 'Still, I hope there's nothing to worry about. After all, a reflection on any member of the staff is a reflection on the whole college.'

'True enough,' Father Creely agreed. 'But I think those three lads you had in tonight won't give you any more trouble. You put the heart across them, Father.'

'Aye,' the Dean said. 'I don't believe in letting them away with the like of that.'

'You're quite right. Well, I must be pushing along, Father.'

'Is it that late? So it is. Well, thanks for bringing it to my attention.'

'Not at all,' Father Creely said. 'The least I could do.'

The Dean looked up from the fire, his large white face fixed in a friendly smile. 'As I see it, there's no sense bothering Dr Keogh with this, is there? Poor old soul, he has enough to worry him. Ah, there's a man too holy for this world.'

'Isn't he though?' Father Creely agreed. Their eyes met in complete understanding. 'Thanks for the drink, Father,' Father Creely said.

'Not at all, Father.'

A good sort, Creely, the Dean said to himself. Alone in the quiet study, he leaned forward and looked at the fire, watching the banked slack as the flames licked up from the coals beneath. Somewhere, hidden in the slack, a lump of coal was not burning properly. The Dean sighed. He thought of his own position: it was unfortunate that a man who had drive and administrative talents should be forced to take a back seat because some old fellow would not step down. I could make this college twenty times more efficient, the Dean thought, I could do wonders, if . . .

He looked at the fire. Somewhere in there was an old dead

coal which prevented the fire from functioning properly. The Dean picked up a poker.

Devine and Heron had been friends for years, had they not? Heron was the senior master, a quarrelsome, easily insulted old hand. If he didn't want his niece in the play, he could make it difficult for Devine. He might even force Devine to abandon the whole thing. And that wouldn't do, it wouldn't do at all. Hadn't the Dean promised Monsignor Sullivan that the play would be performed? Monsignor Sullivan had been grateful, he had personally sent a note of thanks to the Dean for his initiative in finding a substitute for the cancelled dance. The Monsignor was a good man to know, he was close to the powers that be. His recommendation could decide who would be next President of Ardath. So it wouldn't suit at all if the play were to be cancelled. No.

Very well. The thing to do was call old Heron in and find out what his objections were. And then perhaps a little influence could be used behind the scenes to have that wee girl dropped without Dev's being any the wiser. In fact, if it were properly managed, it could be a grand slam. Yes.

The Dean foresaw congratulations at the next committee meeting of the Foreign Missions Fund. Monsignor Sullivan could be told the ins and outs of the affair. Very wise of you, Father McSwiney. Very wise. I trust the President is pleased at the way you managed it.

No, the Dean would say, as a matter of fact, I hardly felt I should bother him, poor old Dr Keogh. Such a holy man, otherworldly, and he's getting on, you know, things like this upset him.

The Monsignor would not fall into error by comment. But he would note it. He would remember it. Remove the dead coal and the fire will burn.

Ah, God forgive me, the Dean said to himself. Am I too ambitious? But no, that was not true, was it? Anybody with any brains in his head would be irritated at the doddery way Dr Keogh kept putting off necessary improvements. Like the college chapel: it was a disgrace the way nothing had been done about it. And increasing staff, and the standard of marks received in Junior and Senior Leaving. The College had slipped quite a bit these past few years. And it was Dr Keogh's fault. Old-fashioned; not enough emphasis on the sciences; two Latin periods a day, in this day and age. No, a younger man, a man with push, a man with more organizing ability, could make the college a proud place. A proud place. Everyone thought so. Everyone.

The Dean began to probe the damp, smoking mass of slack. The poker touched something hard and dry. An old dead coal. One quick little push sufficed to knock it down to the hot bed of flames. The slack loosened, the fire puffed up a mass of yellow smoke. In half a minute, the fire was blazing wonderfully. Smiling, the Dean leaned back in his armchair and reached for his drink of whisky.

Chapter Eight

Mr Martin McDade was wakened by the record-player starting up a slow fox-trot. He bounded up from his studio bed and in jigtime he had run the electric razor around his pink smooth face. He dressed, as always, to dance: blue double-breasted, fresh from the dry cleaner's; elevator shoes; clean white shirt. Closing the door on his bedroom disarray, he entered his office at a fast walk, clipping on his blue bow tie, rubbing a little tonic over his pink skull, reversing his breast-pocket hankie so that the clean points showed. Then, *piano*, he opened the office door and peeked out at the ballroom. It was Craig, with a new pupil. Nine-o'clock lesson? That was early, even for a Saturday morning.

Craig was one of his regular girls, so she had her own key. But still an' all, she should have warned him. He found his rimless bifocals and looked more closely at the slow fox-trotters. Ah, the new fella. He put on his smile, his face becoming sentimental as an old cuddly doll's, a bit dented, perhaps, but clean and artificial as his large white teeth. He opened the door, letting it frame him like a grand arch. Behind him on the office wall were the triumphs of his career. All-Ireland Tango Championship, 1929. Harvest Moon Annual, 1934–38. Grand First Prize: Ballroom, 1941. Old-time Champion, 1947. Yes, he had not competed for a few years now, but at sixty, he could still show the younger fellows a thing or two. He was one of the All-time Stylists.

When Miss Craig saw him in his office door, she stopped her pupil at once. Mr McDade noticed that she had on a low-necked jumper and a tight skirt. That was against the rules. He liked all his girls in afternoon frocks for daytime

101

classes and formal, of course, for evening. That's a cheeky big thing, that Craig, he said to himself. She thinks she owns my place.

'Early birds?' he called merrily, stepping out on light, fairy feet. 'Well now, some people is gluttons for learning, as the sayin' goes. Good for you, good for you.'

The pupil looked put off. Men his age often were; you'd think they were ashamed of learning something which was good clean sport. This one was tall, a new fella, started private lessons the day before yesterday.

'Slow fox you're working on, I see. Ah, that's a lovely dance. You have to get the reverse turn right, yes, the reverse is the whole thing in a nutshell, Mr . . .?'

'Mr Devine,' Craig cued.

'Aye, to be sure, Mr Devine. We met the other day.' Mr McDade smiled his cuddly smile. 'Put the music on again, Miss Craig.'

While Miss Craig adjusted the record-player, Mr McDade winked at the pupil. 'Watch the old dog,' he said. 'I'll show you how *I* do it.'

The first bars of the slow fox-trot repeated themselves as the orchestra took up the beat. Mr McDade, featherlight, put his little pink hand in the approved position on Miss Craig's back. His plump, double-breasted tummy laid on close, and his left hand moved hers like the rudder of a state barge. Gracefully, he led off, slow tempo, two slow, reverse, reverse turn and double reverse. Gliding across the floor with sweeping twists, five-foot master of her five feet eight. His hand moved in tiny pressure, guiding her, steering her deftly towards the music's blare.

'Why'n't you tell me you had a lesson?'

'You weren't here last night, Mr McDade. This fella wants singles all morning.'

'I hope it's nat – ' Mr McDade said primly. You could never be too careful, running a respectable business.

'What d'you take me for?' Miss Craig said in a flat Ulster

102

voice completely divorced from her professional cooing. 'Anyway, I'm not workin' all morning, no fear. I'll take him till half-ten, and you can get another girl to finish.'

'I'll get Erskine, then. But the fella won't last all morning.'

'He will,' Miss Craig said. 'He's like a madman. Says he must learn it all in a day or two.'

'Dada-dada-Dum-da-da-da-DI-da!' Mr McDade hummed loudly as he put her in double reverse, a bit slack for competition, but showy-like for pupils. Back they went in long graceful glides, back to a smooth stop in front of the pupil.

'See? Now you have a wee whirl yourself, Mr Devine. Dada-dada-Dum – that's right. Once more! Oh, vary nice indeed. Yis, we'll make a dancer out of you in no time.'

The pupil stopped. His face was worried. 'Do you think I'll learn enough to make a showing by next week?'

'Why nat? Why nat? It's all a matter of practice.'

'Yes, I'm going to have more lessons this afternoon. I'll work at it all day, if need be. But I must learn in a hurry.'

This shocked even Mr McDade. 'You mean you want private lessons all day today? You'll not be up to it!'

'No, no. I can do it. But what do you think? Will I be able to dance after them?'

'You'll know the basics,' Mr McDade said. 'Variations, of course, that's another matter. Dancing is a lifetime sport, always new heights to scale, so to speak. Some people take to it easy. Others nat.'

'But I just want to learn the steps. Just so that I won't make a fool of myself.'

Mr McDade smiled. He thought he knew this fella's problem. 'Some people is shy in dancing,' he said. 'Now we have a way to remedy that. Our Get Acquainted Nights. Just for students of this institute. Men and ladies. Vary nice class of people our students are. And quite a number of gents like yourself have found it a great help to meet ladies under normal ballroom conditions, so to speak. Oh, yes. In fact, I can tell you there's been quite a few weddin's in Belfast as a result of our Get Acquainted Nights. We have one this coming Tuesday. You're welcome to drop in.'

'No, I'm afraid that wouldn't suit me.'

'We have afternoon tea dances too,' Miss Craig said. 'Wednesdays. For members only, three to five.'

'No, I'm sorry, I'm afraid not,' the pupil said.

Mr McDade shifted sail. 'Well now, when all's said and done, private lessons cannot be beat. But keep the other in mind, sir. We teach you to dance, but we hope it will also be our privilege to keep you dancing.'

'But could you tell me . . .' the pupil said . . . 'I mean, you haven't answered my question. How long will it take to learn?'

'You can learn the basics in six lessons,' Mr McDade admitted. 'But practice makes perfect, as the saying goes. Now, off you go, the pair of you. I'll start the music.'

He looked critically at the faraway clutch the pupil used. He turned the machine up. He pushed the pupil against Craig's tummy. 'A close stance is the key to body control,' he said sternly. 'Get a good hold on your partner.'

Dada-dada-Dum-da-da-da-DI-da! He smiled at them as they moved off. I must caution Craig about wearin' that jumper, he decided. Makes the place look like a shillin' pally de dung. Not that it matters with this pupil. He wouldn't notice if she had bare knockers pushin' up against him. Ah, well, you meet all kinds.

Young Billy Parton went into the back room where Mr Parton was sitting among the dummies, sewing the firm's labels on a dozen shirts.

'Dada, can you come out a minute?'

'What for?'

'There's a customer trying on sports jackets. Wants pants too.'

Mr Parton bit his thread off. Outside in the shop, a tall chap with glasses was trying to see his back in the mirror. He had on one of the new shipment of Aberdowndies. Mr Parton looked at the man's shoes and trousers. Perhaps this chap doesn't know the price of Aberdowndies, he thought.

'Do you like it, sir?' he asked. 'That's a very nice one.'

'Is this what you call a hacking jacket?'

'Yes, sir. Best of material too. That tweed lasts for years.'

'And how much is this one?'

'Sixteen guineas. We have them made up specially.'

The customer fingered the material. The jacket was a brown herringbone and looked odd on him.

'It fits you fairly well,' Mr Parton said. 'The sleeves need shortening. And, of course, it would look better with the proper trousers.'

He produced dark grey worsteds and held them against the man's leg. The man said, 'Yes'. They took his measurements.

'You'd want the trousers shorter than those you have on,' Mr Parton said.

'I suppose so,' the customer agreed, looking doubtfully at the dirty old suit pants he was wearing.

'The shoulder of this would need a small alteration,' Mr Parton said, touching the Aberdowndie. 'Your right shoulder slopes.'

'Oh? Would that take long?'

Mr Parton looked sadly at the oil portrait of his grandfather on the wall. In a hurry, as usual. The old class of customer had gone forever. 'Tuesday afternoon,' he said. 'That would be the soonest we could manage.'

'Oh? Well, I suppose that will do.'

'Have you thought of a Tattersall with this? Check waistcoat is very much the thing, this year. Show him some Tattersalls, Billy.'

105

'Wouldn't that be a bit, ha, bright?' the customer asked.

'Not at all, sir. Now, look at this one, see? Looks lovely on you. It takes ten years off him, doesn't it, Billy?'

'Very smart, sir,' Billy said. 'Of course, you'd be wearing a more informal shirt and tie. That makes all the difference.'

'The Clonaskilla weave would go well,' Mr Parton said. 'Show the gentleman one to give him the idea, Billy. Lovely, isn't it?'

'I'll take two,' the customer said in a nervous shout.

'You'll be a different man in this outfit,' Mr Parton said. 'There's a lovely tie I saw the other day, would go well with it. Just came in from London. Show him that brown tweed tie with the gold fleck in it, Billy.'

They sold him the tie too. It was a nice order. Indeed, when Mr Parton picked up the customer's old suit jacket to help him into it, he was surprised the man bought so easily. For his old suit was a cheap thing. The sleeves too short, the shoulder padding poor. The man didn't look the type to make a nice order. Won a football pool, or some such.

Mr Parton smiled. He wrote the bill.

'And what was the name, sir?'

'Devine.'

'It will be ready on Tuesday, sir. Without fail.'

Eamon (Tusker) Heron crouched in the entry behind his parents' house, trying to open the back-yard door without waking anyone up. It was after midnight and he should have been home an hour ago. There were no lights in the house, so his Daddy and Mummy must be asleep.

He wrapped his dirty handkerchief around the bolt and pressed against the door so that the hinge would not squeak. He had sneaked out to the Floral Hall with another fellow, trying to pick up two dolls. They had stood all night without getting many dances and it had been a waste of six bob, so it had. Tusker moved the bolt gently and it slid back. The door was open. But just then he heard a noise in the entry behind him. A man and a girl, it was, talking. They must have just come into the entry a minute ago. Sinful thoughts made Tusker tremble. With infinite precaution, he turned to look. They were at the mouth of the entry, not twenty yards away. The street lamps shone right on their faces.

It was his cousin Una! And Dev! What was Dev doing with his cousin? Holy smoke, the fellows in class would never believe this. 'Do-less Dev' with the cousin from Dublin! Tusker's excitement was tempered by lustful regret. Dev would not do anything dirty. No fear.

He was sixteen and he got 'Tusker' from the fellows because he had buck teeth. He was small for his age, but fellows never 'did' him, because his old man was a master. That was Tusker's biggest cross, his old man being a master. Cuffo Heron, the fellows called his old man, because his old man had a trick of punching them on the back of the neck in class. And flippering – how could you expect fellows to like you if your da had just flippered them? Tusker thought all masters were ould cods, even his own old man. But the other fellows did not trust Tusker, and Tusker knew it. He would do any disloyal thing to his old man to show the fellows he was just like them. *He had to*.

Well, this was something he could tell the fellows. Dev was in the entry with Una, his protestant cousin. His Daddy was ashamed of Una, there was something funny about her. His Daddy had said not to mention to anyone that Una was a Protestant. But who cared what his Daddy said? His Daddy could go to blazes, so he could. Tusker would tell the fellows that she was a Protestant and hot stuff. Oh boy, if Dev would only *do* something! But Dev was an old stick-in-the-mud, the fellows would never believe that Dev was up an entry with a girl at night. They'll say I made it up, Tusker thought sadly. But it's true.

So Tusker watched and hoped. He heard Dev say: 'Now, stop worrying, Una, you were perfect.'

And Una said: 'I can't help worrying, Dev. It's going to be much harder with all those people judging me. I'm nervous.'

'But you're much better now. They'll be delighted with you.'

'Oh, I hope so, Dev. Anyway, you've done your best, you've been a darling, really spending so much time on me.'

It's some exam and Dev is giving her a grind in English, Tusker decided. But did you hear that lovey-dovey? *You've been a darleen.*

'No,' Dev said. 'On the contrary, it's been great for me. Being with you these last few weeks has made a new man of me.'

Tusker heard her laugh. No wonder. Then she said: 'Well, I notice you've made a lot of changes in your appearance. New clothes, and shaving off your moustache. You look quite different these days.'

'You think it's an improvement?'

'Of course. But listen, Dev, I must go in now. It's awfully late.'

'Please, there's one thing I want to ask you, Una?'

Tusker strained, holding his breath. Nobody took a girl up an entry without having something dirty in mind. At least feeling her, he hoped. He was afraid even to blink, for fear of missing something. He held his breath, his mind full of lust and fright. If Dev caught him spying, he'd murder him.

But Dev just said: 'Tomorrow night, after the try-out, I wonder if you'd like to celebrate with me? Perhaps we could go to a dance?'

'Oh, that would be lovely. Good idea. But look, Dev, let's talk about it tomorrow. I've got to get in now, before Uncle Tim starts raising the roof.'

'All right, then.'

'Thanks for everything, Dev. Good night.'

For crying out loud, he hadn't even kissed her! Tusker's frustration caused him to shift uneasily. The back door, yawning open, squealed in its rusty hinges. Tusker saw Dev turn and look right down the entry, right at him!

But it was all right. It was too dark. Old Dev did not see. His face was smiling and it was true, what Una said, he was all dolled up the way he never was in school. As Tusker watched, Dev turned away and went out of the entry.

Ah, Jesuz, the fellows will never believe me tomorrow, they'll think I made it up. I wouldn't believe it myself, Tusker thought sadly. But boysaboys, wait till I tell them!

Chapter Nine

From where he stood, halfway up the darkened aisle, Mr Devine could see his judges: Kathleen Boland, Kevin Cooke and Dan Cavanaugh whispered among themselves in the front row of seats. Above those conspiring heads, pale and unreal in the stage lights, Moloney, Mrs Hanlon and Una cried out into the darkness. He listened, trying not to notice the inattention of those whisperers.

He was not afraid. He had done wonders with her. She was every bit as good as Peg Shea had been in the part and they would all be satisfied with her, he was sure. Afterwards, he would take her to a dance, it would be an occasion for celebration. And that evening, somehow, he would ask her, he would tell her his feelings, he would ask her.

There was every chance she would turn him down, of course. That Dublin fellow was still far from finished. But if she did not, well, he had weighed all the pros and cons, he had even estimated the risk he'd be taking. Ardath, for instance. If he married her, he would lose all chances of advancement. They might even ask him to resign. But there were other jobs, weren't there? In England, for instance. During the war, many fellows he knew had gone off to England, some in the English forces and some as civilians. A lot of them were killed, but wasn't it strange that the others had not come back, they had settled there, or gone to Canada or Australia. Just went to show that England and the Dominions might not be bad places to live in, no matter what people said.

Of course, it was premature, even to think about that. She could still be in love with that bloody accountant. And even if she agreed to marry him, they would have to visit her mother in Dublin to get parental consent. There would have to be an engagement. But still . . .

They were coming to the end of the act now. He looked at the front-row judges. They were still whispering. But Una was doing nicely. Nicely. And she looked lovely, didn't she? He remembered a remark of old Professor O'Neill's about a pretty girl's being worth an extra ten per cent in any oral. The two men would find her pretty, even if Kathleen did not.

It was Una's big speech now. He listened. Not bad at all. She moved on the stage as if she were a professional. He smiled in the darkened aisle. I taught her that. He was still smiling when he saw Kathleen Boland coming up the aisle.

'Dev, can I have a word with you outside?'

So they had decided already, then. Fair enough. He followed Kathleen to the back of the hall. Smiling, he held the door open and they went out into the drafty vestibule. She offered him a cigarette from her packet. The red ceiling light cast a bloody pallor over their faces.

'Well . . .' he said. 'It was a hard fortnight, but it was worth it.'

'Do you think so?'

It was as though she had struck him. 'Don't you?' he asked.

Kathleen Boland put out her tongue and picked a tiny shred of tobacco from its tip. She was wearing a green turban and in the red ceiling light she reminded Mr Devine of a pantomime devil he had seen as a boy. She held up the shred of tobacco between her index finger and thumb, looking at it as if it were a pearl.

'Now, don't be upset, Dev,' she said. 'We'll manage all right. But not with your friend Miss Clarke.'

'Why not? Don't you think she's good?'

She still did not look at him. She let the tiny tobacco shred drop to the floor. 'Not particularly,' she said. 'Her accent is still wrong. And anyone can see she has no stage

111

presence. Oh, I know you've done your best, Dev, but it's not good enough.'

'Does Kevin think so too?'

'Yes. We all do. But nobody likes telling people unpleasant truths. So I was elected to do the dirty.'

'I see,' he said dully.

'Mind you, no one's blaming *you*, Dev. But you can't make a silk purse out of a sow's ear.'

'Now, wait a minute. Wait a minute! There's no need to insult Miss Clarke, is there?'

'I'm sorry, Dev. I apologize. But she isn't very good. Honestly she isn't.'

'Oh?' He could be wrong, he supposed; if they all thought Una was poor, perhaps his judgment was influenced by . . . *Love is blind*; that was an old saying.

'And besides,' Kathleen said, 'we can get Peg Shea, after all.'

'But she's having a baby.'

'She's had it already. It was premature. She lost it, poor thing. As a matter of fact, I met her the other day in Royal Avenue and she said she'd love to be back in the group. It would be good for her, too. Take her mind off the other.'

'So that's it,' Mr Devine said sourly. 'You'd all prefer Peg Shea.'

'It's not a matter of preferring her, Dev. She's miles better. But I haven't even mentioned it to her yet. That just shows how much we hoped this Clarke girl would be all right.'

'I see.' Dammit, what could he say? Peg Shea had played in a dozen productions, she could not be passed over for a newcomer. But on the other hand, it was rotten of them to push poor Una aside after she'd worked so hard. Oh, it was all connived at, he was sure. Once they heard Peg was available, they were determined to have her. It was all a clique, this city was made up of cliques, drama cliques, religious cliques, school cliques, and God knows what else.

There was no use in a fellow's trying to fight them: it was a pure waste of time. You might as well hold your tongue and save your breath.

'Well,' he said. 'If that's the way everyone feels, there's no sense keeping Miss Clarke here. It's not fair to waste her time.'

'Would you like me to break it to her, Dev? It might be easier.'

'No, no, I'll do it. I'll take her home now. I won't be back.'

'Suit yourself. You're not walking out on us, I hope?'

He did not answer.

'That would be a dirty trick,' Kathleen Boland warned. 'Holding a grudge because your protégée didn't get the part.'

He looked at her angrily but held his tongue.

'I wouldn't have expected that of you, Dev. Be reasonable.' She put her hand on his arm, as if to soothe him. But he turned away, took off his spectacles and wiped them with his thumb. He was taking it very hard, Kathleen decided. She tried another tack. 'Do you really insist we take the girl?' she asked. 'We'll do it, rather than lose you. But it'll be against our better judgment.'

'No, no, of course not. I'm not trying to force anybody.'

'Well, be a good sport then. Don't be trying to beat us with a big stick. Will we shake hands now? Are we still friends?'

He couldn't very well refuse when she had her hand out. So he shook it.

'You can take Miss Clarke on home,' Kathleen said. 'And I'll cue them for the second act. Next rehearsal is on Wednesday. Right?'

'All right.'

In silence they returned to the hall. Mr Devine signalled to Una Clarke to come down from the wings. Moloney was on stage, acting, but none of the others watched him any more. They saw Dev and the girl go to the back of the hall and waited while Dev helped her on with her coat. When the hall door closed behind them, Kathleen Boland advanced to the edge of the footlights and held up her hand for Moloney to stop.

'How did he take it?' Kevin Cooke asked.

'He got a bit annoyed at first. But he calmed down.'

'What's all this?' Moloney asked, coming to the footlights.

'Peg Shea is going to do the girl's part,' Kathleen told him.

'Since when?'

'Since yesterday. She's back in circulation now. And that girl is hopeless, Tony, if you don't mind my saying so.'

'No skin off my nose,' Moloney said. 'She's no particular friend of mine. Snippety wee thing, if you ask me.'

'I thought she was all right,' Mrs Hanlon said. 'Didn't you, Kevin?'

Kevin Cooke looked at his fingernails. 'Peg Shea would be better,' he said.

'I can't help feeling sorry for the pair of them,' Dan Cavanaugh commented. 'She's only a kid. Poor Dev, he nearly killed himself coaching her.'

'A kid?' Moloney squatted on his hunkers by the footlights, giving them all the gather-round sign. 'I'll tell you a yarn about that kid,' he said.

'Let's get on with the rehearsal,' Kathleen cut in.

'Ah, hold your horses. Did you know she was mixed up with a married man in Dublin?'

'Now, that's enough, Tony,' Kathleen Boland said firmly. 'You should be ashamed of yourself, slandering people and them hardly out of the door.'

But Dan Cavanaugh looked at Kathleen as she spoke and then turned a puzzled glance on Kevin Cooke. Married man, he thought. Well, that makes things a bit plainer. So that's why Kathleen's been dead set against the girl, this last

114

few days. Aye, Kathleen's husband was a first cousin of Heron's wife. Wheels within wheels. And hadn't he overheard Kathleen telling Kevin Cooke that Heron didn't want his niece in the play? Kevin had said then that they mustn't offend Devine and upset the apple cart. Aye, it all made sense now. Kevin didn't care what happened as long as Kathleen was happy. Kevin needed Kathleen as his star for the festival entry. So that's it, Dan Cavanaugh decided. It's all Kathleen's doing. And poor old Dev is the goat, as usual.

Mr Devine had no idea how to tell her. In plays and in the pictures, when you told a female bad news, you sat her down first. He had never seen a woman faint, but then, he said to himself, he was no expert. So, in the vestibule, he pretended that they were having a break and suggested that they go down the street for a cup of tea.

She did not say anything. They began to walk towards the Rosemary Tea Shop. He thought it odd that she didn't ask how she'd done. But, as they neared the teashop, he began to suspect that she knew already. There was something abstracted about her, something distant and cold.

They sat in the alcove, as usual. The usual disgruntled waitress took their order. Now was the time to tell her. Get it over with.

'I, ah, I'm afraid I have some unpleasant news, Una.'

'About the play?'

'Yes. Apparently the girl who played your part last year is available, after all. And – over my objections, mind you – the others want her back.'

She did not seem surprised. 'Oh, well,' she said.

'You see, this girl has a prior claim, so to speak.'

'It doesn't matter, Dev. I was no good tonight.'

'I thought you were splendid,' Mr Devine said quickly. 'Splendid. I was out voted, that's all.'

She opened her small handbag, fumbling. Surely she wasn't going to weep? But she took out, not a handkerchief, but a packet of ten cigarettes. 'I deserve this,' she said. 'Your friends tonight saw through me. They were right, my heart wasn't in it.'

She paused and leaned across the table to touch the tips of her fingers on the back of his hand. 'Ah, poor Dev,' she said. 'Cheer up, you'd think it was you they turned down. It's not your fault.'

There was no need for her to be patronizing, dammit. After all, she was the one who wanted the part, wasn't she? No sense pretending now that she didn't care, no sense treating him as if he were a child.

'Well, I, ah, I thought you wanted the part.'

'Oh to blazes with the part! What do I care about your silly part? What do I care?'

'I'm sorry,' he said, feeling a poker in his back.

'I've no luck, that's all. No luck. Everything I do turns out wrong, nothing ever happens the way it should. Oh, I heard something today, I can't tell you now, but if you knew, you'd see why I'm not worrying about a silly play.'

'Not bad news, I hope?'

'Bad news?' She opened her mouth as if she would laugh, but the laugh became a sob. Mr Devine watched, helpless, as the tears began to run down her cheeks. Although he was ashamed of himself for doing it, he could not help looking at the curtains, hoping nobody would notice. The curtains were open and he got up to close them. Then he walked around behind her chair and put his hands out, as though to touch her shaking shoulders, pulling back in sudden fright as she straightened up, still weeping.

'Now, now, Una, dear. Get a hold of yourself.'

'Give me a handkerchief,' she said.

He had a clean one in his pocket. He unfolded it and saw her hide her face in its white linen. 'I'm sorry,' she whispered.

'Perfectly all right. Don't worry.' He looked again at the curtains, hoping no one would come.

'It's not the play, Dev. It's just the last straw in my bad luck. Oh, Dev, I'm so miserable, so miserable.'

He sat down again. He felt weepy himself now. But he hoped she would not cry any more – if she would only stop crying! He began to talk, hurriedly, one eye on the curtains because the waitress would be coming soon with their teas. 'Now, Una, maybe I can arrange something about the play. I'm sure Peg Shea would give up the part if she knew how much it means to you. I'm sure she would.'

'It's *not* the play, Dev, it's something worse. Something I'd be ashamed to tell you. And maybe it isn't even true, this thing.'

She began to cry again, worse than before. She put her head between her arms and gave way to it completely. At that moment, to his shame, the curtains opened and the ugly waitress entered with two cups of tea. She laid the cups on the table and looked accusingly at Mr Devine. Then she put her rough, boiled hand on Una's shoulder.

'What's the matter, Miss?'

'Never mind,' Mr Devine said. 'It's all right.'

'I wasn't speakin' to you, sir, I was speakin' to the young lady. Now, what's wrong, dear? Can I get you somethin'?'

Una, not raising her head, made a gesture of denial.

The waitress hesitated, looked once more at Mr Devine and withdrew, taking care to jerk the curtains wide open so that she would not miss the goings on, from her place near the serving hatch. Mr Devine hastily got to his feet and dragged the curtains shut.

'Una, please? What's the matter?'

'Nothing. I'm sorry.'

'But look here, is there anything I can do?'

She raised her head and groped blurrily for his handkerchief. 'It's nothing to do with you, Dev. It's something I heard this afternoon. If it's true, I'm the biggest fool in the world. I'm hoping it's not true.'

'What's not true?'

'I can't tell you now. I'll tell you tomorrow. I'll know for sure then.'

'It's not the play, then?'

'No, no!'

'And it's not anything I've done?'

'Of course not.' She looked at him, her hand crumpling the handkerchief, her breathing harsh and shallow as though she had no more tears but could not control the act of sobbing. 'If it hadn't been for you, I don't know what I'd have done these past weeks. It's not you at all.'

'Then what is it, for heaven's sake?'

'I have to make a phone call tomorrow. I'll know the truth then and I'll tell you.'

Know what? Under the table, Mr Devine's hands sought each other, his fingers turning and turning the signet ring as suspicion became sick certainty. The fellow in Dublin – yes, it could be true. And the simple thing she said now confirmed it, as any simple thing would.

'I think I'll go home, Dev. I'm afraid I don't feel up to going dancing tonight.'

'Of course, of course. I understand.'

'No,' she said. 'You don't. But you're trying to be nice to me, as usual.' And she began to cry once more, sitting straight up in her chair, not hiding it. He listened, uncomfortably aware that behind the curtain the waitresses must be listening too.

They were. The ugly waitress (rot her soul!) came in again.

'Would the young lady like a taxi?' she asked in the tone of a woman rescuing a fallen girl.

'Would you like a taxi?' he asked.

'Yes.'

'There's a Silver Taxi just stopped across the street,' the waitress said. 'That's why I ast. I'll catch a hold of the driver.'

She left and Una got up, awkwardly putting on her coat.

He fumbled, trying to help her, wondering why, if this were true, she ever came to the rehearsal tonight in the first place? But what else could she have done? he thought. I'd have come myself. If you're in terrible trouble, the best thing to do is carry on as though nothing had happened.

'I'll ring you tomorrow,' she said. 'Except that's it's Sunday – you'll be at Mass.'

'I'll go early,' he said. 'I'll be back in my digs at nine, waiting for your phone call.'

'All right.'

'I'll see you home now.'

'No. I want to go home alone.'

In the teashop, waitress and proprietress stared at Una as he paid at the cash. The taxi driver was waiting, the back door of the taxi open. In the dark street, Una turned. 'I'm sorry to have made all this fuss.'

'No, no, it's all right.'

He face was close to his, a pale, unreal blur in the darkness. 'Don't hate me for it,' she said.

He stood, unable to speak. He looked uneasily at the waiting taximan. How could he say, in front of this fellow, that he didn't hate her at all, that he loved her, yes, loved her as he had never loved anyone in his life. You could not say that in front of a taxi driver. But still, he must say –

Too late. She turned and got into the taxi. The man shut the door. Mr Devine moved forward to knock on the window, to ask her to roll it down, he had something he must say, something he –

But the taxi moved away. Her face, behind the glass, blurred and was gone. Too late.

He stood there, until he saw the waitress peering at him from behind the teashop window. Then he walked back to the bus stop, his mind confusedly turning, not on the lost opportunity, but on the silly details of the evening, on his long and costly preparation in Miss Craig's arms, his hurrying of the tailor to get new clothes. All useless now.

For she would not dance for many a month. Tomorrow, she would phone the doctor and the doctor would tell her what the tests said. There must be tests for that sort of thing. If positive, she was carrying that Dublin fellow's bastard. No wonder she didn't care about the play. No wonder.

A bus came and he got on. It was crowded with men coming home from the dogs. Loud voices told how Ballina Champion had trapped wide and been beat out at the turn. The books were in money, they were having a good season, the books. Down Agnes Street the bus dragged, dropping disconsolate punters at each stop. So long, Jack, so long, boy . . . Going home, the wages lost, the wife waiting. A barney about money, because Ballina Champion trapped wide behind a ten-to-one shot and some ould dog that came to Celtic Park in a tramcar walked off with the race. The pubs would be empty tonight.

At the corner of Manor Street, Mr Devine stepped down. He stood for a moment looking at his reflection in a shop window, seeing his unfamiliar shaved lip, his expensive new clothes. All dressed up and nowhere to go. He moved away, the image of his face drifting insubstantially over an unimaginative display of Ovaltine tins behind the window glass. A smiling milkmaid offered him a tin, but his ghostly face, declining, slid off the glass window as he turned the corner into Cliftonville Road.

He thought of his rooms, dark and quiet and empty. He turned away from the avenue where he lived, walking slowly past a home for the blind. A sound of music came from behind closed curtains. Sightless faces smiled at unseen music. Mr Devine, the music senseless in his head, saw the moon slide over the turrets of Royal Academy. He paused by a red letterbox, staring up at the moving moon, and his face grew suddenly excited as though he had received an inspiration too startling to control. He began to walk, more quickly now, as though his body must respond to this new and powerful mental stimulus.

Supposing the worst were true? Well then, the Dublin fellow could not marry twice, could he? A husband would have to be found, a husband who would take the child and breed legitimate brothers and sisters to keep it company. She would not refuse him. She could not.

At the bottom of Cliftonville Road he came to a public house. He had never been inside this pub although he had lived for years in the area. He crossed the road now and looked at the place. *Public. Family Department.* He passed by the public, hit by the stink of porter from its half-opened doors. Down the lane a sign said *Lounge*, urging him up a well-lit staircase. In a first corridor, he opened a door and was surprised. There was a big room, a fire in the grate, and a small serving bar. Quiet place. But as he entered, he started back at the sight of a huge grizzly bear who lurked behind the door, paws upraised to hug the stranger.

But the bear had a hat on one stuffed paw and a sign advertising Guinness around its neck. This was a sporting pub. Sad stags' heads stared down from the walls, their antlers worn and shabby as the wooden furniture beneath them.

Mr Devine sat down by the fire and the barman asked his fancy. He was a pleasant young fellow and he put up a bottle of Jameson for Mr Devine to see. He poised a water jug, waiting Mr Devine's small motion of sufficiency. A cheerful, pleasant fellow, and, looking at him, Mr Devine felt a foolish desire to say: 'I'm getting married soon. Will you join me in a quick one?'

But, of course, he said nothing. He drank his whisky in a long, excited swallow, feeling the fumes tickle the hairs in his nostrils. There were only two other customers in the place, a middle-aged man and his wife. Mr Devine looked at the barman and raised his glass in signal. The waiter nodded and brought the bottle.

'Same again, sir?'

'Make it a double this time.'

She would telephone him tomorrow, as soon as she knew

for sure. She probably hoped he would be kind. After all, why else had she asked him that odd question: if he hated her. He stared at the double whisky in his glass, sad now as he remembered. What sort of rotter was he, to be glad at a girl's misfortune, to celebrate the fact? But he was not celebrating. No, no, he was just having a drink and thinking things over. Of course.

His self-assurances were interrupted by two new customers who entered the lounge in a rush of talk. The boy was tall and thin and wore a tan duffel coat. A small green cap lay like a lid on top of his head. The girl ran to the fire, holding out her arms as if to embrace it. Mr Devine stared sombrely at her tight tweed skirt, her breasts lifting the sweater as she stretched her arms to the heat.

But the boy destroyed this silent survey, crying out that it was cold as the hobs of hell, and that they would have Pimm's Number One to warm them. He dropped his little cap on the bar and he and his girl clambered on high stools. The waiter went smiling to serve them. Glasses were set up under the bar lights. The girl laughed, smothering her mouth with her hand as though the boy had whispered a delightful indecency.

Mr Devine watched it all as he slowly sipped whisky. The girl, wiggling her tight bottom on the bar-stool leaned over to link arms with her boy in a *Brüderschaft toast*. Arm-linked, they kissed. Mr Devine looked away, his eyes on the fire flames. The whisky made his eyes water. He had missed all that when he was that boy's age. And since? How many couples had he watched over the years – how many times, when he was a young fellow in his teens, had he told himself he would be lucky like that someday? But when he himself was as old as the boys he saw kissing, he was afraid. Afterwards, as a schoolmaster, well, there was no question of a display like that in public. And so he had never done that: no *Brüderschaft*, no public cuddle.

Sad flames leaped and died. By the window, out of

earshot, the married couple talked in incessant dumbshow. The waiter made a joke and poured again for the boy and girl, leaning his elbows on the bar, including himself in their company. Mr Devine sighed. Alone of them all here, he was alone. He looked back at the fire. Alone.

He signalled for another double. Another double was served. But drink was no substitute, was it? He was like a flower that had never opened. He felt foolish when he thought of that, but it was true. Like a flower that had never opened. He had been afraid to open, afraid. He was ashamed to think how few girls he had gone out with more than once. He would not have confessed it to anyone, not even a priest, but he could count only four. And none of those girls would even remember him today. Not one of them. No girl had ever found him interesting. And he had his pride, dammit, he was not going to plead and beg with them. He could get along rightly, so he could, without any silly girls. Or so I thought then, he thought now. But it's no more true today than ever it was. I was always lonely for a girl to find me interesting, to know one girl half as well as I knew my only sister.

He drank the double neat. Behind him, at the bar, he could hear the young girl laughing wickedly. There was nothing worse in the world than a young girl's mocking laugh. Women were mockers, character-assassins, every single one of them. Fancy putting yourself in a position where a woman could laugh at you. An intimate moment, a ridiculous posture – a declaration of love, for instance. Or, on your wedding night, to hear a girl laugh at you, like that girl behind me now. And it could happen in my case. It could happen.

The flames were dying in the blackened grate. How many men stayed solitary through fear? How many sinned alone because someone once had laughed at them? Male virgin sins, why were they funny, why did people snicker at them?

'This will be the last call, sir.'

'Give me another, then.'

A girl who was in the family way would be an experienced girl, he remembered. She would compare her wedding night with that other night or nights. There was always that danger.

The girl at the bar laughed again. The waiter brought the last drink and he settled up.

He drank it slowly, hearing good nights as the other customers went out. The waiter turned the lights down and put a guard over the dying fireplace. Mr Devine stood up, feeling the effects of it. Carefully, he walked to the door. The waiter unlocked it and wished him good night.

'And mind the stairs, sir.'

At the head of the stairs, he stopped, buttoning his raincoat. Put his hand on the rail and looked down. Drew back guiltily. It would be awkward to pass them. He looked again. Yes, that was what he had missed up to now. On the landing.

Below, at the turn of the stairs, the boy in the duffel coat pressed his girl against the wall. They swayed, kissing. The boy's hands slowly caressed her back.

Mr Devine gave a loud warning cough. His face was congested as he descended, eyes on the steps, hearing them draw apart as he passed, sensing their impatience. Head averted, he opened the door below and went out into the cold wet wind of the street.

They would kiss when he was gone. They would kiss again. He blinked and turned his face to the night wind. He had a right to live too. Una would not laugh at him, a girl in her position. She would not laugh.

Chapter Ten

Mrs Dempsey wanted to know what time it was, she'd be late for Sunday Mass. She hurried into the kitchen, her hair wrapped tight in curlers, little white bandages sticking out like cut fingers all over her head.

'It's half-past eleven, Mama,' Annie said.

'Gracious God! Help me with these pins, I'll miss twelve!'

Annie dried her hands on the dish towel and began to unravel her mother's white bandages, revealing, under each, a sausage roll of grey hair.

'I suppose Mr Devine is gone?' Mrs Dempsey said.

'No, Mama, he's not.'

Mrs Dempsey jerked her head free. 'But he'll be late for Mass,' she said. 'Did you not wake him up?'

'No.'

'Well, call him, this minute.'

Annie went to the connecting door and shouted down to the basement. 'Mr Devine! Mr Devine!'

'Yes.'

'It's after half-eleven.'

They could hear him coming up. He must be sick; he never misses Sunday Mass, Mrs Dempsey decided. Late herself, she called for Bridie to bring her coat. She was putting on her hat when Mr Devine appeared at the head of the basement stairs. He was still in his dressing gown. His eyes were bloodshot and his hair tousled.

'I didn't wake,' he mumbled and they could smell the stink of booze off him. 'Has anybody phoned me this morning?'

'No,' they said.

'Well, I'm going to shave now. If anyone rings, be sure and call me.'

125

Mrs Dempsey could not help asking what the matter was. It must be something serious if he was missing Mass for a telephone call.

'Not bad news, I hope, Mr Devine?'

'No, it's a young lady I'm expecting. A Miss Clarke. If she calls or telephones, be sure and get me at once.'

Saying this, he passed through the kitchen. They heard him go upstairs and lock the bathroom door.

'Fancy missing Mass for a telephone call!'

'You'll miss it yourself, if you don't hurry, Mama.'

'So I will, where's my hat? Get my hat, Bridie.'

'You have it on, Mama!'

He was sitting in the dining room, a cup of tea in his hand, the *Observer* propped up against the teapot, when Mrs Dempsey came back from Mass. It was one o'clock and his bacon and egg lay uneaten on his plate. She hurried on down the corridor to the kitchen, removed her hat and coat and put her apron on over her good dress. After one, and him not finished his breakfast! Well, she would have to move him soon. Her sister was coming for Sunday dinner.

Annie came in, carrying sweeper and broom.

'Did anyone telephone him?' Mrs Dempsey whispered.

'No. But he's on eggs, waiting.'

'Are you chewing gum?' Mrs Dempsey asked sharply.

Annie shrugged her shoulders, her wall-eye asking the ceiling to bear witness how she was put upon.

'Spit it out,' Mrs Dempsey ordered, putting her large floury hand under Annie's chin.

Annie spat it out.

'How often do I have to tell you not to indulge in that filthy habit?'

'Och, there's no harm in it, Ma.'

'Is that the phone?'

They listened. It was the phone, all right, and that was young Bridie coming downstairs two at a time in her hurry to get to it first. *Curiosity killed the cat*! Mrs Dempsey, moving with unbelievable expedition, thundered into the hall and grabbed the receiver.

'Hello?'

'Is Mr Devine there?' a girl's voice asked.

'Who's calling, please?'

'Miss Clarke.'

'Just a minute, please.' Mrs Dempsey put the receiver down. She made angry motions at her listening daughters. 'Go away, you girls!'

He was standing at the dining room door, the Sunday paper trailing in his hand. 'For me?'

'Yes, Mr Devine. A Miss Clarke.'

'Thank you.'

He picked up the receiver but did not speak until Mrs Dempsey had retired to the kitchen.

'Hello, Una?'

'Yes, Dev. I promised to phone you, remember?'

'I've been waiting for your call,' he said, glancing over his shoulder. The kitchen door was shut. Mrs Dempsey and her daughters were nowhere in sight.

'I'm sorry I was such a nuisance last night,' she said. 'But tonight I can make it up to you.'

'Tonight?'

'Are you busy, Dev?'

'No, no, I, ha, I hoped we could see each other sooner. Perhaps this afternoon.'

'It's Sunday, Dev; where can we go on Sunday in Belfast?'

He had not thought of that.

'But I know a place we can go dancing tonight,' she said. 'That is, if your invitation still stands? It's a place called the Ambassadors.'

He was ashamed of his disappointment. If she wanted to go dancing, it meant the doctor had told her it was all right. She was not pregnant.

'Don't you want to go?' she asked.

'Well, of course, I'd love to.'

'Could you meet me about eight, then?' she asked. 'Say in the lobby of the Grand Central?'

'Yes. Yes. But Una, couldn't we . . . I mean, couldn't we meet this afternoon? There's something I want to ask you. Something important.'

'It's raining outside,' she said.

'Yes, I suppose so.'

'Can't it wait until tonight, Dev? Perhaps we can have a drink or something before we go to the dance.'

'It's, ah, Sunday.'

'So it is. Well, see you tonight, then.'

'Una? That telephone call you said you'd make today, that bad news you spoke about. Did you, ah, did anything transpire?'

'Oh yes, I phoned,' she said. 'I'll tell you about it later.'

'I see.' She probably didn't want to speak about it over the telephone, he reasoned . . . but he remembered that he'd have to wait until eight o'clock, not knowing. 'Not bad news, I hope?' he said cautiously.

'Not *good* news, Dev. Anyway, I'll tell you later. Goodbye for now.'

'Good-bye.'

He put the receiver down. Still trailing the Sunday paper, he walked slowly to the kitchen and knocked.

'Come in.'

'They were all three peeling potatoes for their dinner. He nodded vaguely and went through the half-opened basement door, down the flight of stairs to his own place.

'Close that door, Annie,' Mrs Dempsey whispered.

Annie closed the basement door.

'He's doing a line with a girl,' Annie said.

'Och, he is not,' Mrs Dempsey complained. 'You have lines on the brain, my girl.'

'He is too, Mama,' Bridie said. 'He was making a date with her.'

Mrs Dempsey took the eye out of an Arran Banner and rinsed it under the tap. She stared reproachfully at the potato before tossing it in the basin. He was a young man, why wouldn't he be thinking of getting married? It was just that he had been with her so long and never had a girl. She had got used to him, he was no trouble, his rent came in very handy. Mrs Dempsey considered a novena. Maybe he won't marry this one, whoever she is.

'Clarke, her name is,' Annie told Bridie. 'I wonder if she's nice-looking?'

'She must have something to make *him* notice her,' Bridie said. 'He never noticed us.'

'Bridie! A child of your age! God knows, I don't know what they're teaching young girls these days!'

'Oh, go on, Mama.'

'He sounds just like a man in love,' Annie said sadly, her wall-eye turned plaintively on her mother.

'He does not! Oh, gracious God! What'll I do if I lose my boarder?'

The Ambassador's Club was at the mouth of a small lane, less than three minutes' walk from the city's centre. Yet it was hard to find. In daylight, the entrance was clogged by heavy vans loading paper supplies from a warehouse which occupied one side of the lane. Opposite, in a warren of cluttered storerooms, small garment jobbers sought and gave orders on the telephone. At night, when the warehouse was locked and the jobbers' phones were silent, a neon light blazed at street level; beneath it, a heavy old commissionaire took up his sentry go. Mr Devine did not know the place existed. He had never been in that lane in his life.

But now, unbelievably, he and Una Clarke stood in the entrance hall, receiving metal cloakroom tags from an attendant. A man in a shiny dinner jacket sat by a card table. There was a little matter of membership, he said. It could be settled for ten-and-six. Mr Devine signed the ledger and was given a gilt-edged card which he must show at the head of the stairs. There, a lady in black silk and silver-buckled shoes welcomed him and asked for ten shillings' admission. In return, she gave him two tickets to dance. All being in order, they were permitted to enter the ballroom.

It was a long narrow room, with small tables on either side of the dance floor. At the far end, on a small platform Denis Donegan and His Debonaires merrily juggled maracas and waved flouncy Gaucho sleeves. Denis's sister, Eileen, did the vocal, smiling from time to time at the dancers below, as Con Smythe supplied a breather by a little diddle on the keys.

'*Mam-bo, Mam-bo*!
'*Mam-bo, Mam-bo*!'

In the centre, high above the dancers' heads, a large reflecting globe spun slowly, struck by a spotlight from the balcony. Waves of yellow, green and purple washed over the walls. There were a great many people and the only free tables were those directly under the orchestra. A waiter led them over and, because it was Sunday, the drinks were soft.

Shielding his eyes against the glare, Mr Devine tried to smile at Una. Yellow lit her hair as she smiled at him. Yellow changed to purple as the spotlight spun. It was half-past nine and he still didn't know.

He tried to close out the microphone voice above him, tried once more to make order of his guesses. Was she or wasn't she? It was hard to say. She had met him at the Grand Central; she was waiting in the lobby and there had been futile talk of trying to get a drink. He had the impression that she'd already had a drink. There was something hectic about her tonight – a wild, angry amusement in her talk. He wished they would turn that damn light off, it was right in his eyes. How could a person talk in a place like this?

'*Mam-bo, Mam-bo*!
'*Ai-Ai-Yi*!

'*Ba-rha-rum! Boom! Boom!*'

The drummer hit the drums a final skelp. Eileen Donegan bowed before the microphone and the Donegan Gauchos put the maracas between their feet and picked up the more conventional instruments. The dancers broke the pattern, dissolving to their seats as the spotlight died in a final, green after-image. Normal ill-lighting livened the room. The crowd here was a young crowd, Mr Devine noticed. And tough. Lots of little gougers and their girls. At the door of the Men's, four boys stood, no older than the boys he taught in senior year. But what a difference there was in those miniature men with their sharp lustful eyes, their knowing appraisal.

Well, now was the time to clear the air. He leaned across the table and said: 'By the way, Una, how did you – '

But the microphone spoke above him, drowning all normal sound.

'*Next dance will be a medley. Gent's Excuse-me.*'

The pianist took a drag on his Player's Weight and poised it on the edge of the upright's lid. His foot hit the floorboard with metronomic precision. Lead off, and off they went; they were dancers here, they came for that: holding girls' hands, they edged past the tables to the dance floor. Slow fox. Remembering his lessons, Mr Devine asked her if she would like to. She would. If she was willing to dance, then she might not be . . . He thought of that as he led her onto the floor.

Erect, holding his partner in the close stance that is key to body control, he guided her to the centre of the floor, one hand on the small of her back, the other holding her fingers up and out. Snakelike boys glided past and she moved close: he felt her hair touch his face as she put her face against his shoulder. A warm, weak feeling filled him at the thought of this slight surrender. But it was only the way people danced. He thought, wryly, perhaps that's why Irish people like dancing so much. It lets the sexes be intimate, but pretends it's all good sport. Carefully, remembering Miss Craig's instructions, he reversed his partner.

'You're a good dancer,' she said. 'I wouldn't have thought it.'

'Oh? I've, ah, taken some lessons in my day . . . Una, there's something I want to ask you.'

'You mustn't,' she said. 'You want to know what's wrong, don't you?'

'No, no, I just – '

'Well, promise not to ask me, Dev. I'll tell you later, perhaps. I just don't want to talk about it now.'

'Of course. But as a matter of fact, it wasn't that. I wanted to ask you something else.'

'*Ba-Rah-Rum!*'

The drum signalled the change. Without any pause, the Donegan Debonaires switched to waltz time. For a moment, he lost what he was going to say in the effort of remembering Miss Craig's waltz instructions. Una's hair tickled his nose as he whirled her around. But he did not move his head away. It was worth any discomfort to be so close to her. Now, he must ask her. Propose. Explain.

'Una, I, ah, as a matter of fact, I've been thinking about you a great deal recently. I should have mentioned it to you sooner. It concerns myself . . .'

. . . And around in one desperate sweep, he waltzed her, around and around again. She had not interrupted. He must say it now.

'Well, as a matter of fact, Una, I wondered if you would ever consider me. You see, I'm very fond of you. Very fond.'

He had forgotten to keep dancing. Around them other dancers circled, waltz-timing, bumping slightly as they passed. The spotlight, turning, blinked its basilisk eye. Her hand pressed his, her arm nudged his shoulder, guiding him to movement. They began to dance. She had not spoken.

He must remember the steps. He must not talk, he must

let her think it over. Unwilling to discover what her face might show, he raised his eyes to the spinning globe above, blinking at the myriad lustres of its surface, each tiny jewelled facet striking off a coloured pinpoint of light as the spot light struck, sending a snow flurry of coloured pinpoints around the room.

'Excuse me.'

Someone was tapping him on the shoulder. He stopped dancing. A young gouger stared at him, impatient.

'Okay?' the gouger asked Una, taking her hand as if to draw her away from Mr Devine. But she pulled her hand free.

'No thanks,' she said.

'It's a Gent's Excuse-me,' the gouger cried, outraged. 'I'm cuttin' in.'

'I'm sorry,' she said coldly.

'It's the rule.' The gouger's eyes showed horror at this anarchy. 'It's my turn, Gent's Excuse-me. Be a good sport now, c'mon.'

She looked at Mr Devine as if asking his help. Mr Devine said apologetically: 'I'm sorry. The lady doesn't want to.'

'Chesus Krys!' the gouger cried. 'What's she so stuck-up for?'

Mr Devine's face lost its apologetic look. Stepping forward he gave the gouger a quick push, sending him stumbling back. 'That's enough,' he said. 'Go away.'

'You lukkin' for trouble?' the gouger muttered, offering his clenched fist like a salesman showing a sample.

Mr Devine, about to dance with Una, stopped and removed his spectacles. Holding them in his hand, he advanced towards the gouger. He did not speak. He stared.

The gouger lowered his fist. Something warned him of his danger. He considered an obscenity as a face-saver, but looking again at Mr Devine's strangely naked eyes, decided not to risk it. Mr Devine put his glasses on once more and rejoined his partner.

They danced, holding each other close as lovers. She had not wanted to dance with anyone but him; was that not an answer, some kind of answer? But still, she had not spoken.

She had not spoken. When the medley finished and they sat down, he saw her take the straw from her orange crush and slowly begin to shred it. A new guess surprised him: perhaps she was afraid to speak. How could she answer without revealing her troubles? He watched the straw become shreds under her fingernails. He looked away unable to witness the embarrassment his declaration must have caused her. After a moment, she stopped. She picked the straws up, rolled them in a ball, and said:

'I'd better explain something, Dev. It's about me and Michael, the man I told you about in Dublin.'

He waited: she would tell him now. He hoped she would use some euphemism. It was too painful to hear; a thing like this.

'Yes, I remember,' he said. 'The chap you had a crush on.'

'Well, it's all over now,' she said. 'After today.'

'Today?'

'I found out the truth about him today,' she said. 'He's weak and selfish and rotten.'

'What did I tell you?' Mr Devine said gloomily.

'I've been a fool, I admit. Today, when I phoned Dublin, he confessed it to me. His wife is pregnant.'

Mr Devine was almost certain she said that. But he must have heard her wrongly. Or maybe she and this chap were married? No, no, not that. Maybe it was a roundabout way of saying that she was pregnant herself, that she was his 'wife' in that sense? It must be.

'A girl I know wrote me a letter,' she said. 'I got it yesterday. That's why I was in such rotten form last night. I could hardly think straight when I was on that stage, trying to say my lines. So I decided to find out. I phoned him this morning when I knew he'd be alone. His wife always spends Sundays with her mother, you see.'

'I see,' Mr Devine said stupidly. See *what*, in the name of God?

'It was true all right,' she said. 'And the worst part is he made her pregnant while he was still going around with me. That's what I can't forgive him.'

Why not? But if he said that, he would appear stupid. She obviously thought he understood. So he said: 'That's terrible.'

'You see what I mean? Oh, what dirty pigs men are! I could kill him, so I could.'

The band above them burst out with terrifying *brio*, jamming all conversation. She stood up impatiently and he heard the odd word – 'away' – 'dance'? He led her out on the dance floor, foxtrotting hastily towards the other end of the room.

'Yes,' she said. 'After what he promised. To think that all that time he was secretly *sleeping* with her.'

So it was the fellow's *wife* who was pregnant, after all. Una was not pregnant. Then what was she upset about, for heaven's sake?

'If I were to go back to him now,' she said, 'he'd go down on his hands and knees to me. But there's a fat chance of that. I told him today. I'm finished with weak-kneed whiners.'

'I should think so,' Mr Devine said, confused but emphatic. 'You're far too good for him, a lovely girl like you.'

'Lovely? I'm not lovely, Dev, and you know it.'

'You are. You're the loveliest girl I ever met. To think of you wasting your time with the likes of that fellow.'

'Let's not talk about it,' she said. 'I don't even want to think about it. Let's just dance.'

So they danced, not speaking, and she touched her cheek to his. The warm, lost sensation came back, hopeless, delicious. If this only settled it, he thought, if we could just go on dancing with nothing more said, with everything solved, unspoken.

But the dance ended. The dancers clapped. Denis Donegan made an announcement about Tuesday night. When he had finished, the music started. The dancers had not moved from the floor. They danced again, Una and he among them.

'*This dance will be a Ladies' Excuse-me.*'

'Now, somebody will try to take *you* away from me,' she said.

'Ha, ha, don't be ridiculous.'

'What's ridiculous about it, Dev? You're quite a nice-looking fellow. And so prosperous in your new togs.'

'Oh, nonsense, I'm just a schoolmaster, dull sort, eh?'

'You're fishing for compliments, Dev.'

'No, no.'

'Well, then, you don't have a high enough opinion of yourself. I've often noticed how humble you are with people. As if you thought they were better than you. I think Catholics are prone to that sort of humility, don't you?'

'Priest-ridden?' Mr Devine said quietly. 'Is that what you mean?'

'Of course not!'

'Well, we've never discussed this, Una, but, ah, do you object to Catholics?'

'No, Dev. Not at all. Don't get huffy, now. I must say, they don't seem free to me. They have to believe certain things or suffer the consequences.'

'Well, doesn't everybody nowadays?' he asked.

'I suppose so. But you know what I mean?'

'No, I do not know,' he said angrily. 'I'm pretty free, dammit all, I'm quite a heretic in many ways. You'd be surprised how many Catholics are.'

'How much of a heretic? Would you want your children brought up as Catholics, for instance?'

He saw what she was driving at. Well, dammit, she wasn't going to trap him. 'If you were to marry me, for instance,' he said. 'I'd give up everything for you.'

'Oh, Dev.'

136

'Anything!' His voice had risen to its nervous half-shout. 'I'd even give up my religion if I had to.'

He was so upset, he fumbled the dance step and dragged her to a stop. 'Let's dance,' she said hurriedly. 'Please!'

'I want you to believe me,' he insisted, his eyes dilated behind the lenses of his glasses. 'I mean, it's important to me that you believe me.'

'Yes, yes, of course I do. Let's dance for a minute. Let's not talk any more.'

They danced. At the end of each dance, she did not let him go. They stood in the dancer's circle, waiting for the music to begin again. They did not speak at all. After a while, she put her head back on his shoulder; he could feel her hair against his cheek. He did not say anything. He must not spoil things again. He must be content with this.

As they danced a slow waltz, she said: 'I'm very fond of you, too. I might even be in love with you. I don't know.'

He blinked his eyes behind his spectacles, trying to keep that damnable self-pity back; behaving like a woman, he was. He must hold his tongue, he had plagued her enough. Now, she was just trying to be nice to him.

'I've thought about you a lot, today, Dev, and how good you've been to me, ever since we met. That's why I wanted to go out with you tonight, even though I didn't feel like going out. You were looking forward to it so much last night, and I spoiled it for you.'

He felt his body go stiff. Dammit, was she trying to say she felt sorry for him?

'You made me feel important,' she said. 'You made me feel that I mattered. Do you know what I mean?'

He nodded.

'I haven't gone out with many boys,' she said. 'And none of them were ever as thoughtful as you. I suppose every girl likes to get her bit of devotion. I'm no exception.'

'*Next dance will be a medley.*'

'Do me a favour,' she said. 'If anybody taps you on the

shoulder ignore them. I want to dance every dance from now until the end.'

'Yes,' he said.

'I just want to forget everything. All right?'

'All right.' What else could he say? Nothing had been settled, it was still all up in the air. But at least she had not turned him down, had she? So they danced. They danced all the way to the good-night waltz. They joined in a circle and sang *Auld Lang Syne*. Con Smythe hit the keys: *God Save the Queen*.

The waiters, already in their overcoats, swept butts from under the tables. At the cloakroom, they were last in line and the man in the shiny dinner jacket was holding the front door open for them. The commissionaire had gone home. It was all over, and unless he could think of something, some way to hold her, some way to prolong the evening, she would go home and nothing would be settled.

In the dark lane she turned, undecided. 'Isn't there anywhere we can go? Is every place closed?'

'I'm afraid so.'

'Nowhere we could have a drink?'

'I, ha, I don't think so.'

'What about your place?'

'My place?'

'Yes, your digs,' she said. 'Don't you have a drink about the house?'

Mr Devine joined his hands, touching his signet ring, turning it. 'Yes, of course,' he said. 'As a matter of fact, I have some gin, I believe. Of course, there may not be much left.'

'Look here, do you want me, or don't you, Dev? You won't hurt my feelings by telling me the truth.'

'But of course. I, ah, I'd hate to break up now. Come to my place, by all means.'

'All right. How do we get there?'

She had decided for them: he thought of Mrs Dempsey

and flittered away from that thought. He had never had a girl in his place, especially at this time of night. Mrs Dempsey was very strict. But it was too late to think about that now. He found himself saying something about a bus and before he had time to say much more, they were on a bus and going.

At this time of night.

At least, he hoped, nobody would see them going in.

Maybe, if they were very quiet?

Maybe, it would be all right.

The basement flat was dark and quiet as the house above it. He put the hall light on and hurried ahead of her, wondering if the place was tidy. What a fool he had been to bring her; the flat was shabby, disgraceful, it gave the lie to his new clothes, to the wine he had ordered with dinner, to all his efforts to be gay and smart. Once he put the lights on in his den, he would lose her respect. It was like an old pensioner's place: a disgrace. He was too ashamed even to make an excuse for it. He took her coat and hung it on the hall stand. He heard her go into his den. Where the hell were the glasses? And how much gin was left in that bottle he bought last Christmas? He found the bottle and two small glasses and hurried in after her. She was standing by the dying fire, looking at his photograph collection.

'Is that you?' she asked, pointing to a dark young man with a tennis racket.

'No, Mick Hanratty his name is. That's me over there.'

'Oh, with the glasses. Yes.'

There was one decent chair and, God knows, it was not decent either. He swept it clear of magazines and newspapers before offering it. The place was filthy, filthy, he realized. But she did not seem to notice. She refused the armchair and sat on the rug by the fire. As she settled, her skirt lifted with a soft puff, rising above her knees. Mr Devine looked away. He had some orange crush somewhere, sticky, unused and warm. He put some gin in the glasses and made two gin and orange drinks.

'Here you are. Not very good, I'm afraid.'

'It's grand. Sit down on your chair and be comfortable. Do you live here all alone, Dev?'

'Yes. I get my meals from the people upstairs.'

'I envy you, living on your own.'

He looked beyond the brightness of the reading lamp, at the dusty bookshelves, at the old suitcase under the window sill filled with undarned and dirty socks, He said: 'It can be lonely, living by oneself.'

'But you can have friends in.'

'I, ah . . . Schoolmasters don't seem to make many friends,' he said. 'I've often noticed that we don't seem to have much outside life. Other masters say the same thing.'

'But you have relatives. Family and so forth.'

'Both my parents are dead. I have a sister, but she doesn't live in Belfast.'

'No girls?'

'No.'

'Oh, I can't believe it,' she said.

Mr Devine looked down at his hands. Unaware, he had been turning his ring. 'Yes,' he said. 'As a matter of fact, you're the first girl I've ever had here, apart from my sister.'

'But you're so understanding,' she said. 'I mean, that thing I told you tonight about Michael, you understood what I felt at once. I thought you must have known a lot of women, to be so . . . well, it must be intuition.'

On the mantelpiece, the man with the long moustaches looked at him, the lady in white silk brocade smiled her stiff, unnatural smile. Did you ever have a woman tell you a story like this, Dada? Would you have understood this riddle? A man makes his wife pregnant and a girl says it betrays her. Where was your intuition, Dada? But his father, smiling for that long-ago photographer, would not have understood: he had married Mary Ellen McGrath and had two children by her. There had been no other girls in his father's life. He would not have considered the question relevant.

140

'You knew,' she said. 'Most men would have missed the point. I told you he'd promised to divorce her, didn't I?'

'Yes.'

'He said if I went to Belfast and waited for a year, he would manage to go to London and give her grounds. I said I didn't care, I'd be correspondent, even.'

Mr Devine looked at the fire. He could not bear to look at his father while this talk went on.

'Does that shock you, Dev? You see, I was in love with him, I was ready to do anything he wanted. I never guessed that he wasn't in love with me too. He couldn't have been, could he? I mean, if he was sleeping with her all the time. Oh, it's disgusting, disgusting!'

She bent her head suddenly and he could see the white nape of her neck. 'Well, I mustn't talk about it any more,' she said. 'I could kill him, though, when I think of it.'

'Don't think about it,' Mr Devine said hoarsely. 'He's not worth thinking about.'

'No, you're right.' She raised her head and looked right into his eyes. 'Dev, was it true what you said tonight? Is it true that you love me?'

He nodded, his hands fumbling with his ring. He nodded again.

'Say it, Dev. Say it again, just to please me.'

Mr Devine looked at her, his eyes blinking behind his glasses. 'I love you,' he said hoarsely.

Kneeling on the rug, she closed her eyes, her face tilted upwards. Mr Devine took a deep breath and said: 'I love you, I love you, Una.'

'Kiss me.'

He bent to kiss her and at the last moment remembered his glasses. He dragged them off and held them at arm's length while he bent to kiss her. He kissed her mouth completely.

'Again,' she said. She put her arm around his neck, pulling his head down. It was a damned awkward position, he realized, trying to bend over and kiss someone kneeling at your feet. But the moment his lips touched hers, he forgot his awkwardness. Her mouth was warm, her warm cheek touched his. A hot trembling sensation came on him. He slid out of the armchair like a man in drink. On his knees, facing her, he put his arms around her. 'I love you,' he said hoarsely. 'Oh, God, I love you.'

He felt her push away. He must be hurting her. Contrite, he released her at once. But she smiled and lay down, full length on the rug. He saw that his dirty slippers were in their cardboard box, a few inches from her head. He leaned over, as if to kiss her, and shoved them behind the fender.

'This is better,' she said. Her eyes were closed and she was waiting. He kissed her again. Her mouth seemed very large and warm. To his disquiet, her tongue immediately began to probe. He had heard fellows talk about French kissing, it was something dirty, they said. Damn her soul, who taught her that! *That married man.*

'What's the matter, Dev?'

'Nothing. Ah, nothing at all.'

'What's wrong, don't you want to kiss me?'

'Of course.'

'Do you want me to go?' she said, sitting up.

'No, no.'

He looked at her knees as he said it. Her skirt was disarranged. She was daring him. It crossed his mind that maybe she was used to lying on fellows' rugs in the middle of the night. Maybe she was. Likely she was.

'Well, then,' she said, lying down again.

For answer, he made a pilgrimage towards her, on his knees, shuffling awkwardly, his hands outstetched to touch her. He sensed that this was the moment of sin: that once he had gone this far, he would have to follow wherever she led. But he was afraid to stop now. He did not know how he could. Anything he might say would offend her.

'Put the light out,' she whispered. 'There's enough light from the fire.'

That meant he had to stand up again. When he switched the reading lamp off, he saw that she was right; the fire threw a soft, reddish haze on the rug, the worn armchair, the glasses on the table beyond. Looking down, he looked into her eyes: they did not look like her any more. They gleamed strangely, reminding him of the eyes of his sister's cat before the darkened turf hearth in the kitchen in Dungannon. Afraid, he knelt once more, as though in genuflection before the altar of her body. Here, on this rug beneath his parents' wedding picture, the solitary day-dreams of his youth had improbably been made flesh. She dwells among me, he thought. She dwells among me.

'Now I'll tell *you*,' she said. 'I love you, Dev. I love you.'

Gratefulness filled him. He put his hands on her neck and kissed her on the lips. But her mouth opened, her tongue probed. The reverence was profaned. He knelt back swiftly on his heels, hearing the short shocked gasp of his own breath.

'Say you love me,' her voice commanded.

'I love you.'

'And I love you too.'

He knew, at last, the meaning of this. She wanted it said over and over, as though, like prayer, repetition would buy grace for the thought. He bent once more, his lips touching her neck. But he overbalanced and half fell on her.

'Oh, I'm sorry, Una. Terribly sorry.'

'That's all right.' She sat up and looked at the fire. She said, in an embarrassed voice: 'I suppose you take precautions. I suppose you have something.'

'What?'

'Oh, never mind.' She stood up and put her hands on the mantelpiece, still looking down at the fire. 'I'm not used to this,' she said nervously. 'So go into your room until I get ready. I'll be with you in a minute.'

Surely to God he couldn't have heard her right? He got up slowly, afraid to look at her.

'Don't put any light on in there,' she said. 'I'd rather it was dark.'

She was still looking at the fire, waiting for him to go. He went to the doorway. In the familiar hallway gloom he moved by instinct, finding the cold brass doorknob of his bedroom. There was moonlight in his room, a weak light which vaguely showed his heavy, solid bed, the dresser and a chair on which a pair of trousers lay like broken legs. He realized that he was carrying his glasses in his jacket pocket. He put them on and looked in the dresser mirror. The face which looked back was weak with fright.

He listened: there was no noise in the sitting room. What was she doing, what did she mean, would she take her things off? And he, what must he do now?

How did I ever land in this situation, he wondered, his fingers seeking, touching, turning the signet ring. How? In this, his own solitary bed where he had sinned a thousand times in sinful imaginings, repented nightly in mumbled acts of contrition, in this bed this very night, real sin would be consummated. There was no getting out of it. She would be here in a moment.

And he, what should he do? Undress? Be in bed and waiting? Or just sit here? With shame, he thought of his naked body. He would look awful, his turned-in knees, his narrow chest, and, *merciful God!* long white underwear. A comedian in long drawers, someone to be laughed at. Or would he frighten her, would she scream? Mrs Dempsey in her bed above would hear it all. She would send for the police.

Never, oh God, in thought, word or deed, will I sin again, if tonight, in Your Infinite Mercy, You will spare me this. I will honour You all my life if only this will not come to pass.

But why should Our Lord grant a miracle in a sordid

affair like this? And only a miracle could help him now. *Was that her, already?* Get out of these long combs, for God's sake!

Fumbling, as though he were drunk, he pulled off his tie and collar. Shirt over his head. Socks off. It was cold in the moonlit room and as the cold chill of the linoleum touched his toes, another coldness came upon him. He would fail. He did not feel able. He would fail. Desire was a fantasy, a sinful, secret lusting that ran wild with unfulfillment. Desire was a mental lusting, a making of improbable dreams. But this was no dream: reality was getting ready in the next room. Naked, waiting to be sinned with; waiting to be touched, to be dominated, to be lain on. Oh, let her not come. At least, until he could get these things off. Now! Shove them under the bed.

But now, in the dresser mirror, his long pale body was shamefully exposed. His legs seemed knock-kneed, and his hair was tousled like an idiot's. He backed into the shadows behind the bed. Was that her? Yes, he could hear her coming up the hall. Would she laugh like the girl in the pub last night? Would she?

'Where are you, Dev?'

She was at the door. She had not seen him yet. And, *oh God* she was not naked like him. She was in her slip! He should not have taken everything off, she would laugh now, she would laugh at him. He looked wildly around the room and then hid in the only place that offered concealment, squatting down behind the far side of the bed, hiding himself. He was finished, she would burst out laughing when she saw him. Finished. He closed his eyes, crouched like an animal. He would say he was sick. He would say he was taken sick.

'Dev? Where are you?'

Her voice was very loud. He would not have time to put something on. If she called again, Mrs Dempsey would hear her. That greater fear made him start up from his crouch, his pale face appearing to her over the edge of the bed-spread.

'I, ah, I was just . . . I mean I was putting something away. Just a moment.'

Half standing, half crouching, he backed towards the wall, dragging the wardrobe door open to screen himself from her eyes. There was a smoking jacket inside, a fancy silk thing Kevin Cooke had sent him as a Christmas present. He pulled it on, aware that it barely reached his thighs. Uneasily, he emerged, tying the strings, his long white legs cringing nakedly in this strange attire.

Una Clarke was sitting on the edge of the bed. The moonlight shone on her face. She was wearing a white slip and her feet were bare. She smiled nervously.

'Hello, there.'

He tried to phrase it – he had been taken ill, something he had eaten, no doubt. But he could not say it. For at that moment, she lay down on the bed, as carefully as if she were about to undergo an operation. She closed her eyes and waited, her arms hugging her breasts. There was a little mole on her shoulder. Her lips moved in a barely audible whisper. 'Are you coming, Dev?'

He walked towards the bed like a man, condemned. In sinful dreams he had seen himself as master, male, menacing. But now, he was sick as a boy who had not prepared: the role had been reversed, he was victim, he would be punished for his failure. He would fail. He sat down on the bed beside her, seeing the slight shudder of anticipation his presence caused her. She was so unlike the sinful imaginings: a young girl in a white slip, her eyes closed, her bare feet side by side. She was waiting.

In fumbling, awkward haste he leaned over and kissed her on the lips. Her arms reached up, gripping his shoulders, pulling him down on her. Her hands, he realized, were cold as his own. Clumsily, he slid away from the touch of her breasts and lay down, fellow victim, beside her. They did not speak and in the silence of those long seconds, the ticking of his alarm clock on the bedside table was loud as a metronome in the room. She was waiting: morning was a lifetime away. He must act.

He opened his eyes, turning his head to look at her. Her face was inches from his, her eyes were open and watching. Panic turned his bowels in sickness. He sat up in bed.

'What's wrong, Dev?'

'Nothing.'

'Well, lie down then. Lie on top of me. I'm cold.'

'I, ah . . . I . . .'

He could not finish. He jumped off the bed and ran to the door of the room. But where could he go, half naked, at this time of night? He stopped by the door, as though some invisible policeman, appearing from his old sinful dreams, had put a hand on his shoulder, declaring an arrest. He stopped, but he did not dare look back at the bed.

'Dev? Dev, what's wrong with me? Tell me, you'll have to show me what to do. This is my first time.'

His white, sick face reflected the window moonlight as he turned to stare. She was sitting on the edge of the bed and her face was frightened too. *Her first time.* Oh God, why didn't she say that sooner? But now it was too late. He could not confess that he too . . . she would not believe him. He said, in a hoarse whisper:

'It's not your fault. Not your fault.'

'Oh, God, this is awful. Awful!'

'I'm sorry,' he said, hanging his head.

For a long instant there was no sound from the bed. Then, frightened, he heard the sound of crying. He raised his eyes and saw her tearful, angry face.

'Don't look at me,' she screamed. 'Oh, Christ, don't look at me like that!'

'Please, Una, let me explain, I ah . . .'

'Oh, Christ!'

When she ran at him, he could not help cringing back,

thinking she would strike him. But she only wanted to escape; she brushed past him in the doorway, white in the moonlight, crying as she ran. He heard the door of his den slam as she shut herself in. He walked slowly to the bed and sat down. She would go home now. She would dress and go. It was all over: he would not be forgiven.

For a long time he sat unmoving, his bare feet touching the cold linoleum on the floor. Somewhere in the city a clock struck and he turned to his bedside alarm. In the green circle of numerals, the long phosphorescent minute, the short fat hour, pointed confirmation. Three o'clock. He fingered his ring, turning, turning, as though to wind up his courage. She had not left yet. He had heard no sound. Cold and stiff, he rose and went into the hall. A strip of electric light showed under the closed door of his den. He could hear her weep. He knocked gently on the door.

'Go away.'

'Una, please?'

'Go away.'

He rubbed his shanks together uncertainly and trailed back to his bedroom. He sat down on the bed once more, his face towards the clock. When the thin minute, the fat green hour pointed to four, he got up and went out into the hall again. The light was still on. He did not knock, but turned the door handle. He went in.

She was fully dressed and was lying face down on the rug. She did not move or speak when he entered. A lock of hair, stirred by her breathing, hid the confusion of her face. Exhausted by weeping, she was asleep.

Very quietly, he sat down in his armchair. She did not wake. For a long time he stared at her face, wondering whether he should risk picking her up and putting her to rest on his bed. But she might misunderstand. Better leave her. He went on tiptoe into the hall and found his grey overcoat. Carefully, he came back and stood holding it like a cape before him. He stood above her, preparing to spread it over her body and legs, and in that instant, looking down on her defenceless sleep, the desire he could not summon came quick and troubling. He felt his hands shake: the overcoat shook. Now he could: he could fling himself upon her like some beast, tearing away her clothes, letting loose his passions. He closed his eyes. Was that not his sinful imagination once more, the imagination which atrophied reality? No, he could not, he would feel only shame and terror if those eyes opened, if she accepted, if she waited for him to make love. Gently he lowered the coat, covering her legs. He sat down in his armchair, chin touching his breastbone, his eyes reflecting the ruin of the fire.

Chapter Eleven

A back-yard pallor struck through the narrow garden, lighting the barred basement window. Four iron shadows lengthened across the room, falling on a high-heeled shoe, a glass with lipsticked rim. Like felon's stripes, the shadows covered Una Clarke's sleeping body. From far off, a factory siren cried. Mr Devine opened his eyes and stared, uncomprehending, at the ashy grate, the high-heeled shoe beside the fender. It was morning.

There was no sound in the house, no sound in the street. It must be very early. She should leave before anyone was up to see her. She must go back to the Herons before the Herons woke up. He saw Tim Heron's angry face: but he did not wake her. For when he woke her, they would have to speak, he and she. That was the worst of all.

At half-past six, a horse and cart came up the avenue and he heard the horse stop outside. As the milkman came up the path, he began to whistle. Would it wake her? The milkman's bottles rattled, the whistling continued. Mr Devine looked at her. Her eyes were open, watching him.

'What time is it?' she asked.

'After six.'

'Why didn't you wake me?' she said, throwing the coat aside, jumping up, smoothing down her skirt. 'I've got to get home at once. I didn't expect to be here all night.'

'I'm sorry. I didn't like to disturb you.'

She looked around for her handbag, found it and propped a tiny mirror against the framed photograph of Mr Devine's parents. She began to comb her hair quickly. For a few moments, neither of them spoke. Still combing, she said: 'I suppose I should thank you, At least, I'm the same as I was before I came here.'

'Una, I'm, ah, I'm awfully sorry about what happened.'

'It's my fault,' she said, in a falsely cheerful tone. 'I wanted to get my own back on Michael, you know. I deserved to be let down a peg.'

'I, ah, I never should have allowed you . . . It was my fault, Una.'

'Well, let's not talk about it,' she said, with a laugh which sounded more like a small scream. 'Gosh, I'll have to run. Aunt Maeve wakes up at seven. If I'm not in before seven, there'll be ructions.'

Mr Devine had a sudden picture of Maeve Heron, a sodality stalwart, always mixed up in pilgrimages, bazaars, homes for Fallen Girls. The worst person in the world to find out about a thing like this. He must get her home at once!

She put the mirror in her handbag, fitted her shoe on her foot and hopped, half-stumbling, into the hall. He tried to help her put her coat on but she was into it before he could touch her. 'Have I got everything?' she asked, not looking back.

'I, ah, I think so. Will you be able to get home all right? The buses must be running now.'

'I hope so.' She was at the door, waiting as though he were some salesman she wanted to be rid of. He hesitated, his hand on the lock. It could not end like this, she could not possibly run off like this, without a word.

'Is the door locked?' she asked.

'No, no.' He opened it, careful not to let it squeak. He looked at her hopefully as she passed him in the doorway. She seemed as embarrassed as he was himself. She said, not looking at him, 'I'll give you a ring later on today, if you like?'

'Yes, yes. Please.'

'All right. Good-bye.'

'Good-bye. And be careful of the gate, Una. It's noisy.'

She hurried on down the garden path and, despite his warning, she opened the gate with a jerk. It made a noise like an untuned fiddle. She did not try to close it, but ran off down the avenue as though she were a girl late for work. Perhaps it was all for the best, her hurrying like that. Less painful for both of us. And no one's seen her, thank God. He shut the door.

And heard a door shut. It could not have been an echo, could it? He stood, his heart jumping, his eyes on the ceiling. Above him, in the narrow hall, footsteps went back into the kitchen. They were Annie's footsteps, he was sure. She saw. She must have.

Like a judgment, far off, a factory whistle cried. What time is it, in the name of God? He pulled out his watch. Seven o'clock.

Una would be late.

At 9 A.M., after half an hour of religious instruction, the first classes of the day assembled. Mr Devine, arriving punctually, went to Junior V, where a group of first-year boys waited him. They were boys who had barely passed their entrance examinations; they would always have trouble passing examinations. The approved thing was to make them memorize as much as possible. Seating himself at his desk, Mr Devine ordered a dunce from Newton-wards to come to the front of the class.

'Begin,' he ordered, and did not listen as the boy began to recite. How could he think of teaching on a morning like this; he was too sick. Should he report sick, should he go to the Dean's study and leave a message that he was ill? If he could only go back to his digs, he might be able to phone Una and find out if she got in all right. But what if Maeve Heron answered the telephone, what if they had caught Una coming in this morning? Oh, no! They couldn't have, they couldn't. But if they did, Tim Heron is right next door to me. Teaching Senior II this very minute.

> 'Higher still an' higher,
>   From the earth thou spring-est
> Like a clouda fire;
>   The blue deep thou wing-est – '

'Next boy,' Mr Devine interrupted. 'O'Brien, you carry on.'

Over O'Brien's faltered beginning, a droning murmur could be heard. It was an *entr'acte* sound: it meant the class next door was unattended. Mr Devine rose up at once from his desk and went out into the corridor. As soon as his back was turned, Junior V hastily consulted texts for a look at the verses to come. But they had no luck. Dev came in again and closed the classroom door.

'Continue,' he said.

Heron's class was unattended. Heron had not come to work. The reason Mr Devine had not noticed it sooner was because Young Connolly had left the door open between his class and Heron's, to keep an eye on the boys. This was often done by one master to cover up for another who might be late. It was twenty minutes past nine now, and Tim Heron was usually very punctual. There was always the chance that Heron was sick.

> 'All the earth an' air
>   With thy voice is loud,
> As, when night is bare,
>   From one lonely cloud – '

'All right,' Mr Devine said. 'Halloran, you carry on.'

> From one lonely cloud,
> The moon rains out her beams . . .'

Halloran paused, stuck for the next line. Normally, Mr Devine would have caned him on the spot. But this morning, he merely said: '*And heaven is overflowed*. Go on from there.'

> 'Wat thou art we know nat;
>   Wat is most like thee?
> From rainbow clouds there flow nat
>   Drops . . . Drops . . . ah . . .'

'*Drops so bright to see*,' Mr Devine prompted. 'Sit down, Halloran. Kelly will continue.'

Kelly stood up. He knew his verse. He declaimed, in a sudden gabble:

> 'Lika high-born maiden
>   Inna palace tar,
> Soothin' her love-laden
>   Soul in secret ar . . .'

'Conlon next,' Mr Devine said.

But as Conlon rose to his feet, some back-seat boy called out: 'Sir, there's somebody at the door.'

'What?'

There was someone at the door. The door opened slightly and Tim Heron put his head in. He beckoned to Mr Devine and withdrew his head. Mr Devine rose from his desk, his bowels queasy. He said to the class: 'Get your books out and study the text. Anyone who talks will be punished.'

He left the classroom door ajar, as a warning that he would be listening for any noise. In the corridor, Tim Heron waited, his whitish lips pulled into a tight pursestring of anger, his fierce, electric-blue eyes glancing furtively up and down the row of classroom doors as though he feared the President would spring out like an angry jack-in-the-box from one of them. He was, Mr Devine noticed apprehensively, still wearing his overcoat, still carrying the worn briefcase he used to travel to and from the school. He had the air of a man about to leave again – a hurried, angry visitor.

'Young Connolly kept dick for you,' Mr Devine began. 'The President hasn't been around yet. Nobody's noticed you were late.'

But Tim Heron shook his head as though he had been given an incorrect answer. He thrust his face close, his right eye blinking rapidly in nervous rage. His voice was hoarse: 'Look here, Dev, were you out with Una last night?'

'Yes, Tim, I was.'

'What time did you see her home?'

Mr Devine hesitated. What was he to say? What had Una said? He must be careful not to put his foot in it.

'Well?' Tim Heron raised his voice. 'Answer me, what time did you see her home?'

'Ah, why, Tim? Is anything the matter?'

'*Did-you-see-her-home?*'

'No, ah, as a matter of fact, I didn't. She went back by herself.'

'What time was that?'

'Whisht!' Mr Devine murmured, with a warning look at the half-opened classroom door. 'As a matter of fact, it was rather late.'

'Seven in the morning,' Heron said harshly. 'Aye, I would call that late.'

His body trembled as though he only held it in check by a great effort of will. Mr Devine started back, despite himself. So the jig is up, he thought. They caught her coming home this morning and she said she was out with me.

'Seven,' Tim Heron repeated. 'Maeve caught her climbing in the back window at seven in the morning. And telling lies too!'

'Lies?'

'Aye. She said she spent the night with a girl she knows. All right, said I, give me the girl's name. So she gave me a name and address I never heard of. And when I went to that address this morning, nobody there ever heard of this girl. The whole thing was made up.'

Mr Devine tried to look shocked.

'Aye. And then I remembered that she said she went out with you, earlier. So I came on over here to find out if that much was true, at least.'

'Yes, ah, we went to a dance together, Tim. She may have met a girl friend while we were at the dance, I'm not sure.'

'And then what?'

'Well, ah, she went home. It wasn't very late, ah, about midnight, I believe.'

'All right then,' Tim Heron said, his bony face thrust close, his paper-thin hair sticking up like antennae: 'Where the hell was she from midnight to seven, will you tell me?'

'I, ah, I don't know, Tim. But I'm sure there's nothing to worry about, old man.'

'Are you now? Do you think so? My niece is out all night and telling lies about it and you think that's all right, do you? My God, you have some notions of worries, so you have.'

Mr Devine shrank back from that hostile face. He fidgeted, pulling his gown straight on his shoulders. 'Well, Tim, there's no reason to bite my head off, is there?'

'I want an honest answer, Devine! Were you out with her all night, or weren't you?'

Devine. His own name, laid across his back like a whip. In all the years he had known Tim Heron, Tim had never spoken to him in this tone of voice. *Devine.* As though I were a stranger, a liar who had tried to trick him. But I *am* a liar, Mr Devine remembered guiltily. No, not a liar, I'm just trying to calm him down. No sense upsetting him, is there? A little white lie never hurt anyone.

'No, Tim,' he said. 'I was not.'

For a long moment Tim Heron did not speak. His fierce blue eyes narrowed, as though he could not see clearly. Finally, he said: 'Is that true, Dev? Word of honour?'

'Yes, Tim.'

Mr Devine watched the jerking stone of Tim's Adam's

apple move, convulsive in the scrawny throat, as Tim digested this bitter medicine.

'I'm sorry then,' Tim said. 'Sorry I lost my temper, Dev. You see, I thought you were the one she was with.'

'That's, ah, that's all right, Tim.'

'God knows who wouldn't be upset, I ask you?' The fierce blue eyes widened, asking. 'God knows *where* she was.'

'I'm sure it's just some prank, some misunderstanding,' Mr Devine said. 'Una is a nice wee girl; a good girl, I'm sure.'

'Is she? Ah, you don't know her like I do. I've good reason to be worried, I tell you.'

'Yes. But Tim, don't you think we should be getting back to class? I mean, the President will be making his morning rounds.'

'I'm not working today,' Tim Heron said, thick anger coating his voice once more. 'I'm responsible to that girl's mother in Dublin, so I am. Do you think I could teach classes all day and me worrying myself sick like this? No fear!' He shook his head, emphasizing it. 'I'm going home to make a few inquiries,' he said.

'But, the President . . .'

'Ah, to hell with the President!'

'But, Tim . . . ?'

'So long now, Dev. Keep this to yourself, now will you?'

'Right, Tim.'

Heron thrust his briefcase under his arm and went back down the corridor, his steel-cleated shoes making small angry sounds on the terrazzo flooring. Mr Devine pulled his gown about his shoulders, watching that bent back disappear. God help Una! he thought. But what could I do? I didn't know what story to tell him. I had to say something.

He turned towards his classroom. They were very quiet, weren't they? Not a whisper. Some extra sense, born of ten years' training, warned him as he crossed the threshold. Not

157

one boy looked up. All were quiet, pretending study. He sat down at his desk and put his chin in his hands. Door ajar. And Heron's voice was loud. He stared at the rows of bent heads, the dirty collars, the stringy ties. No boy dared look him in the eye.

'Conlon,' he said. 'Continue.'

'Where, sir?'

'Where we left off.'

> 'Wat objeks are the fountains
>   Of thy happy strain?
> Wat fields or waves or mountains . . .'

If one of them would catch his eye, he would know. He had not taught them for ten years without being able to sense these things. He would know, the moment their eyes met his. But they avoided his stare.

'Next boy. Denny.'

As Denny began to recite, Mr Devine suddenly rapped on his desk for attention. Make them look up. They looked up, startled. Eyes met his eyes, then slid away, avoiding him.

'No talking,' Mr Devine said. 'No talking in back there!'

Denny started his verse again and the class was quiet. *They knew.* They were waiting now, twenty-eight little wireless transmitters, primed with scandal, ready to broadcast it all over the school, all over the city. Oh God, is this my guilty conscience, or did they hear us? Could they have understood what we were saying? What did we say, exactly? But he could not remember.

'Yet if we could scorn
    Hate, and pride, and fear;
If we were things born
    Not to shed a tear . . .'

When the bell sounded, ending the first period, Young Connolly waited outside the classroom door, with the pleased look of a man who has heard of an enemy's downfall.

'Did you see Heron this morning?' he asked Mr Devine.

'Yes, ah, yes I did.'

'That bloody man is in for trouble,' Young Connolly said. 'I was keeping dick for him this morning and he never even had the grace to thank me.He came in and left again, without a word.'

Young Connolly was still smarting over his rejection by Heron's girl, Mr Devine knew. He was not a reliable witness.

'But do you know the best of it?' Young Connolly said. 'Heron never told the President he was going home! He came here and took off again, without a word to anyone. I tell you, Dr Keogh is fit to be tied.'

'Is that so?' Mr Devine said, in a faint, faraway voice.

It was nine-forty. Four more classes before lunch. And with one master already off work, there was no chance that the President would excuse another one. No, I will have to stick it, Mr Devine told himself. I will have to stick it until lunch time. Maybe then I could phone Una and find out what's going on. Oh God!

Sweating green walls, snuffling radiators, window sills which blew cold draughts into the back of the neck awaited him in the small room where he met his second class of the day. Twenty boys – the class of Senior II – sat at their desks, hastily cramming their set piece for his interrogation.He looked at them as he entered and one or two looked up, with an uneasy good morning. That was normal. He was reassured. The gossip had not spread yet: there had not been enough time. He sat down at his desk and laid his cane along the pencil trough.

Senior boys were the ones to worry about, though, if the gossip *did* start.Some of them were candidates for the priesthood, full of conscience, prone to confessing all doubts to their study circles. But would a senior report a

159

story like this? Which of them would dare tell a priest such a tale? Would they know the meaning of it? Most of these boys were, he knew, wholly or partially uninformed about the facts of life. They might not know what Tim Heron was driving at. They might report it simply because they did not realize how serious it was. But woe betide us, if they do.

His pupils would show no respect: of that he was sure. Master were tyrants and, like tyrants everywhere, their coin of fear was repaid in secret mockery. Every one of us, lay or clerical, is watched for weakness, Mr Devine told himself. We are not loved, we have three hundred mouths to mock us; three hundred little calumniators that could finish me and Heron in a morning.

It was a frightening prospect. But he was still master: the cane lay in front of him, he could flog them, every blessed one of them. That was how the Dean would act: double the dose, hand out the medicine. What was the use of medicine though? It was the Dean's medicine, the school medicine, which made this kind of boy. When he himself had been a pupil at Ardath he had not loved his masters. That was the rule of teaching: boys respected the cane, the cane was what got results in his day, and still did. But if a master showed a weakness, he was paid back. If they *did* hear us, he thought, they will make the most of it.

He rapped his knuckles on the desk, calling them to attention. Habit made him glance at the blackboard. As usual, it was covered with Father Kelleher's Greek squiggles.

'Daly,' he said. 'Clean that board.'

The class began.

Midday. Mr Devine passed among the rows of eating boarders, his head like a marching soldier's, carefully fixed on a neutral point ahead. He avoided any eye, walking with nervous purpose to the lay staff table, choosing a seat far away from the others. He fitted his napkin under the fold of his jacket, held his breath as though he were about to dive, and then, at last, looked at his fellow men.

Moloney was putting chunks of white bread in his soup. Comiskey and Turley were talking about the budget. Young Connolly asked for the salt. Nothing unusual, nothing to indicate that any of them had heard a rumour. The clerical table was likewise busy. The President was talking and the other priests listened, nodding agreement from time to time.

He picked up his soup spoon. Maybe he had imagined the whole thing. Certainly, despite his fear, despite his sick stomach, the morning had passed like any other. There was no sign that Junior V had overheard Heron's talk, no sign that any rumour had been passed on. So maybe there was nothing to worry about. Only his behaviour reproached him now; still what else could he have told Heron? He did not know what story she expected him to tell. Ah, well. Somehow he must get through the day.

'Good afternoon,' a voice said. No one looked up. Mr Geohegan sat down, hitching his chair closer to Mr Devine. He glanced down the table for a friendly smile, but, as usual, none of the others looked at him. Unabashed, he turned to Mr Devine, uttering his usual prefatory cough. For once, Mr Devine was deaf: he did not nod and smile. Today he had not the heart to listen to the games master's saga of domestic struggle. Today, he had enough worries of his own. Geohegan could go to hell.

He spooned the soup placed in front of him and sipped it ritually, but the first taste almost made him retch. He was sure he could not eat a bite today: his stomach sat in uneasy threat on his every movement. So he pushed the soup away, raised his napkin to wipe his mouth and was suddenly seized with irritation as the games master reached over and tugged his sleeve. By God, he felt like telling Geohegan to leave him alone, telling him to stop pulling at a fellow like some beggar. But he thought better of it. He said nothing.

'Will you be long at your dinner?' Geohegan asked.

Well, that was too much, that was the bloody limit. He turned in his chair and stared at the games master. Would you look at the cut of this fellow, with his mouth hanging open and four fountain pens sticking out of his pocket as if to advertise the fact that he can read and write?

Mr Devine took a deep breath. When he spoke, his voice was sarcastic, his inflection one he normally reserved for particularly stupid pupils.

'If you were at all observant, Geohegan,' he said, 'surely you would notice that I am in the process of *beginning*, not *finishing*, my *dinner*, as you call it.'

'Beg pardon,' Geohegan said, humbly. His fingernails, Mr Devine noticed, were in need of cleaning; his flannel trousers were stained with bicycle grease and he had a pimple on his chin. No wonder the other fellows wouldn't sit near him. An impossible bloody man, with his ginger hair and his letterbox forehead. Why was I ever civil to him, Mr Devine asked the ceiling, why? And here's my thanks; he plagues me – today of all days.

'I didn't want to interrupt you, Mr Devine. But I thought I should mention something, do you see? Something that concerns you, in a manner of speaking.'

'What the hell are you talking about?' Mr Devine asked coldly.

Geohegan looked down the table at the other diners. He put his hand over his mouth, in a pseudo-genteel effort to stifle a cough. Then he bent his ginger head to whisper: 'Something in the boys' jakes, Mr Devine. I seen it a wee while ago. And, no offence, but if it was me, I'd do something about it, if I was you. I hope you won't be offended at me mentioning it. But you and me have always been friendly, so I thought I'd pass the word along.'

Dog-like, having placed his dead rat at Mr Devine's feet,

he waited for a sign of understanding. And when Mr Devine looked queasily at the other diners to see if they had overheard, Geohegan nodded to reassure him that this was secret, a private thing between the two of them. Mr Devine folded his napkin and stood up. Geohegan did likewise. Together they left the refectory.

In the main corridor, after reassuring himself that no one was about, Mr Devine took hold of Geohegan's arm. 'Is it something on the walls?' he asked. 'Something they wrote on the walls?'

'Yes. I hope you weren't offended at my mentioning it.'

'No, no, on the contrary.'

'You know, Dr Keogh often pops in there at lunchtime to look for boys smoking. I thought it'd be a good idea to get it off before he sees it.'

'Yes, yes. Quite right. Where is it?'

'This way. Wee bastards they are. Wee hoors' gets.'

Mr Devine remembered that Geohegan had been a sergeant major in the Free State Army. Still, it was a shock to hear someone use language like that in the school corridor. However, he reminded himself that this vulgar streak was the reason Geohegan had mentioned the walls. No other master would have.

'What, ah, what did they write, Geohegan, old man?'

'They done it in ink,' Geohegan said. 'Read it yourself. I'd have rubbed it out, but it needs washing with carbolic soap and water to shift it. It needs two to do it. One to keep an eye out for the priests. I mean, it's not a master's place washing walls, is it?'

'I suppose not.'

'So I thought if you'd give me a hand, I could get soap and hot water from the kitchens. You can keep an eye out in case anyone comes.'

'Yes, good idea,' Mr Devine said warmly. Dammit, he felt like a fool; he felt like blubbering. To think he had just been rude to poor Geohegan. It was poetic justice, wasn't it?

163

No other master would have been so worried about the menial aspect of washing lavatory walls. That was what Geohegan was worried about. But no other master would have helped. Oh, God bless little Geohegan, he was one of nature's gentlemen.

'When, ah, when did you notice it, old man?'

'I caught them at it. Three boarders. They ran away when I came in.'

'But when was that?'

'Just before dinner, pardon me, *lunch*.'

Well, half an hour ago, that was not very long, not many boys could have seen it and probably none of the staff except Geohegan. If we can get it off now, there probably won't be much harm done. But what did they write? *Merciful God, what did they write?*

He and Geohegan walked briskly across the yard, avoiding the puddles in its broken macadam surface. The old jakes were an eyesore beside the school's new brick gymnasium. Built seventy years ago, they showed two scarred doors in a flat surface of dirty whitewash, the whole capped by a slate roof with a third of its tiles missing. The masters did not use this jakes, but Mr Devine realized that Geohegan must pop in there often, it was so handy to the gym.

The entrance to the jakes was blocked by a small boy, buttoning. The boy, seeing that the two master were really coming inside, fled before them. Three seniors hastily dropped their cigarette butts in the urinal and sauntered out by the other door. A stench of urine, stale nicotine and strong disinfectant filled Mr Devine's nostrils. Sickened, he stared along the row of half doors. No one was using them. *Now where was this thing?*

The silence died in a sudden flow of rising waters as the urinals overflowed and purged themselves. The walls of the place resembled an old blackboard, covered with meaningless scribbles, gouged initials, and the rusty stain of dripping water pipes.

'It's behind you,' Geohegan whispered.

It was. How could he have missed it? It was done on a fairly clean space right beside the entrance. There were three figures drawn in ink. Two wore mortarboards and carried canes. The third figure had a triangular base to show it was female. Underneath it was lettered: UNA.

How did they know her name?

There was scribbled doggerel too. He stepped up to look more closely.

> Now boys a dear
> and did you hear
> the news that's going round
> Dev and Cuff have had a fight
> cause Cuff's wee niece stayed out all night
> and they say Dev put out the light
> and pulled her drawers down.
> So Cuff's away
> and they say
> Dev cannot face his job today.
>
> PS HER NAME IS UNA CLARKE.

Another hand had written the postscript in large printing. Mr Devine lifted the sleeve of his gown, spat on the wall and tried to rub the last two words out. The ink ran but the words would not obliterate.

'No use doing that,' Geohegan said. 'Wait here and I'll get soap and water. I'll be back in a tick.'

'Don't be long, old man.'

But Geohegan was gone. The urinals discharged once more. Water filled their smelly gutters. He went over, soaked the hem of his gown in the gutter and returned to his anguished task. Get her name off, at least. But it was no use. It would not come off.

Someone was coming. He could hear boys' voices outside.

He ran along the row of toilets. He heard the boys coming in the other side. Cautiously, he opened a door, hoping it

165

would not squeal. Once inside, he realized that his feet showed. If they looked, they would see it was a master. He climbed on top of the stinking toilet bowl and squatted on his hunkers. He could hear boys whistling and talking, not ten feet away. If only Geohegan would hurry up.

The boys left. The urinals roared again. He was just getting down from the seat when he heard new voices.

'Is that it?'

'Oh, holy smoke!'

'Boy, if Father Mac sees *that*, we're for it!'

'Hurry up, you guys. Phil, you keep dick.'

'Hurry up, Jimmy.'

'It won't come off, for crying out loud. It's a ballpoint pen.'

'Och, you're not trying. Rub harder, for flip's sake.'

'Away back to the door, Phil.'

'Go on, Phil!'

With infinite precaution, Mr Devine raised himself from his squatting position until he stood upright on the toilet bowl. Leaning forward, he grasped the edge of the door with his fingertips and was able to see over the top of it. Two junior boys stood by the wall. They had a bucket of water and were soaking clods of earth in it. As he watched, they began to scrub the graffiti on the walls with the wet clods, slowly obliterating his and Heron's matchstick legs. That was a good idea, earth and water, Mr Devine reflected, he should have thought of that himself. He sighed, feeling a painful strain of his outstretched arms. The effort of supporting his weight on his fingertips, the effort of leaning forward like a man about to dive, was beginning to make him perspire and tremble.

'Anybody coming?' one of the boys asked.

There was a third boy posted as a look-out at the door. 'No,' he said.

All teachers had favourites: no matter what one thought of the little brutes, some were less obnoxious than others.

Better-off boys were usually better behaved, for instance. But these three boys were – let me see, he said – Coogan, Devlin and Glover. Three young lumps of boarders, nothing out of the ordinary, at all. Why are they doing this for me? Or are they doing it for Heron? That was not likely. Tim Heron was hated: always had been. So it must be for me they're doing it. Good to think there's some loyalty left in this world, three boys using their lunch hour to do this, it was moving, so it was, it moved him; he was not ashamed of the weepy feeling it gave him. Arms outstretched, trembling on tiptoe, he closed his eyes, letting his head hang in relief. It was good to think there was a little loyalty in them after all. A little human consideration, a small way of showing their appreciation.

But a second thought came to mind. Maybe these boys were the ones who drew that filth.

'If Father Mac had seen this, we'd have been hammered,' one of the boys said.

'Me,' said the one called Coogan. 'I'm the one he'd have blamed.'

The doggerel was almost indecipherable by now, covered over by black smears. What did Father McSwiney have to do with this? Why would he blame Coogan? Was Coogan known for this sort of thing?

His mind made up, he jumped down from the toilet to the floor; he slammed the door open, letting it bang against the wall. He rushed out, his gown awry. Corny Coogan and Jimmy Devlin dropped their earth clods. Phil Glover bolted.

'Did you do that?' Mr Devine shouted, pointing at the wall.

'No, sir.'

'You did, you did!'

'No, sir, we were taking it off, sir. Please, sir.'

'Why were you cleaning it off?' Mr Devine shouted. 'Answer me, why?'

Corny looked at Jimmy. Saw his terror's twin in Jimmy's eyes.

'Answer me!' Mr Devine shouted. 'Why were you taking it off?'

They could not answer.

'Who did it? Speak up!'

'It was some seniors, sir.'

'What's this got to do with Father McSwiney then?'

'Nothing, sir, please, sir. But he'd blame us, sir.'

There was no sense in what they said but by now he was as confused as they. The urinals roared again. He became aware that some other boys were peeping in the door, watching them.

'Go away,' he shouted. The faces disappeared.

'Now,' he said to the two in front of him. 'Do you want the cane, or do you want to tell the truth?'

He unhooked his cane from its usual place under the armpit of his gown. But as he did, Geohegan entered, holding soap, a scrubbing brush and a bucket of steamy water.

'Get out,' Mr Devine told the boys. 'Get out of here!'

He raised his cane like a man herding cattle: the boys fled. The scarred wooden door banged as they escaped across the school yard.

'Okay,' Geohegan said, putting the bucket down. 'You keep dick, and I'll get cracking.'

He removed his shabby sports coat and handed it to Mr Devine. He rolled up his shirt sleeves, exposing muscles like bunches of scout knots. His right arm, Mr Devine noticed, was tattooed: a faded shamrock enclosed a harp, the whole ringed by black, animal hairs.

'Better get moving,' Geohegan said, picking up the scrubbing brush. Mr Devine nodded. He put his cane away and went out into the school yard. A shower was just starting and the yard was deserted. He backed towards the doorway of the jakes once more, and as he did, he heard

168

something drop at his feet. It was one of Geohegan's cheap fountain pens, fallen from the breast pocket of the jacket Mr Devine carried. He picked it up, clipping it carefully back in place, remembering that less than an hour ago he had sneered at its owner's education. Sergeant Geohegan, common little Geohegan. And now he was being saved by that same little man.

'Did you put this muck on it? Geohegan called out.

'No.'

'Makes it harder to clean off.'

Raindrops spattered the puddles of the deserted yard. Behind his back, the urinals flushed once more. He peered inside, seeing Geohegan erase the last of the scrawled doggerel beneath the graffiti. No priest would know, no master would whisper that rhyme to another in the quiet of the common room. But even so – it was known. As he stared back across the rain-washed yard, he seemed to hear three hundred boyish voices chanting in eerie unison: . . . *drawers down, drawers down.*

Una must never know of this. *Never.* He must swear Geohegan to secrecy at once. But they knew her name. Had Heron mentioned her by name this morning? He could not remember: but he remembered that Heron had a son in senior year. Sick vomit rose in his mouth and was repelled. He could not look in front of Geohegan. Would he never finish, back there, what was keeping him?

'How are you getting along, Geohegan, old man?'

'Nearly done.'

The bell, immediate, deafening, shook the main building, its electric shriek filling the yard. Mr Devine dodged back out of sight as though he had been shot at. The wall was mercifully clean. Geohegan had almost finished.

'I mustn't keep you late for your classes, Geohegan, old man.'

'All right. All ship-shape now.' Geohegan dropped the brush into the steamy pail. 'I'll just cart this stuff back to the kitchens,' he said. 'My kids are always late anyway. You'd better duck on back to work.'

'Yes, yes. And . . . I say, I mean, I don't know how to thank you, old man. I mean, I . . .'

'No bother,' Geohegan said. He was drying his forearms on a blue pocket handkerchief. Humbly, Mr Devine held out the shabby sports jacket, waiting for Geohegan to slip it on.

'I'll never forget this,' he said, his voice quavering. 'It's damned decent of you, Geohegan.'

'I'll have a gander at the jakes in the new building,' Geohegan said. 'Might as well, now I have the bucket.'

'Oh, would you?' Mr Devine's voice broke. 'I don't know how to . . . It's damned decent, damned decent of you. Thanks very much. Thanks very much indeed.'

Geohegan looked at him with an odd embarrassed stare. He bent to pick up the bucket. 'Go on,' he said. 'You'll be late for class.'

Chapter Twelve

Whenever a master at Ardath wanted an easy time, he would begin his class by writing several questions on the blackboard. Sheets of ruled paper were then handed out to the boys, who devoted the ensuing forty minutes to writing detailed answers for each question. This was known as an examination test. The boys wrote steadily, stopping from time to time to simulate thought; and a few moments before the bell, their papers were collected by the master and carried to the masters' common room, where they were placed in the box which supplied kindling for fires. That afternoon, in each of his classes, Mr Devine passed out ruled paper.

His sick feeling had been replaced by a heavy apprehension, reminiscent of childhood when something has been broken and someone will tell. The day's events recalled themselves in a series of ugly pictures: Mrs Dempsey's Annie closed a door: Tim Heron hurried down a corridor, deflected in his search for truth: a hairy arm, tattooed with a shamrock, scrubbed a stinking wall. And perhaps, at this moment, another picture was being formed: a priest, come to search the jakes for signs of minor vice, stood silent before new evidence of major iniquity.

Meanwhile, he must survive this last class of the day. Hands clasped under the ragged tail of his gown, he paced the aisle of desks. It might be his last class, ever. It was hard to imagine, after ten years, but it was possible. It was possible. He remembered Paley, the drawing master who liked his beer. One day, Dr Keogh walked in on a class and saw two big bottles of India ale in a bucket under Paley's desk. One of the bottles was half finished. No one saw Paley after that day. The story handed down, embellished by class after class of boys, was that Paley was drunk and dancing a jig in class with a whisky bottle in either hand. Drunk man in class. Now, that was tame, compared with a master who spent a night with another master's niece. Oh, they could make a story of that all right. *The evil that men do lives after them*. Old Shakespeare had their measure, sure enough.

He paused and looked over the rows of bent heads at the rain-misted window beyond. Evil, that was the ironic part. Practised voluptuaries could have hidden all traces of last night, they would have sinned undetected. But she and I, innocents the pair of us, are found out the first go off. And who'd believe us, if we told the truth? I spent the night with her, Tim, but nothing happened. How could I expect anyone to believe me? How?

Instinct told him it was time to finish. He looked at his watch.

'All right. Two minutes to go. Pass the papers along to the end of each row. Quietly now.'

He went up the line at a pallbearer's pace, collecting the sheets. He piled them on the desk, shuffling them neatly into a box stack. Then the bell rang, the last bell of the day. He left the room before the ringing ceased.

A few minutes' walk from Ardath, in a winding suburban wilderness of crescents, drives and avenues, Mr Devine waited in a telephone booth, his fingers on Button B.

'Hello?' a woman's voice said.

It was not Una. It might be Maeve Heron. He pressed the button. 'Is Miss Clarke there, please?'

'Who's speaking?'

'This is, ah, Diarmuid Devine here.'

'She's not in,' Maeve Heron said in a different, colder tone.

'Well, ah, do you know when she'll be back?'

She did not reply. A child's cry, dismal and exasperating, sounded somewhere in the background.

'Hello?' he said. 'Do you know when she'll be back?'

'No! I don't see what you want her for, anyway. My husband spoke to you this morning, didn't he?'

'Yes, he did. But – '

'And you said you didn't know where Una was last night?'

'Well, yes, as a matter of fact – '

'My husband may believe you, but I'm not sure *I* do,' the angry voice said. 'My husband's often too trusting for his own good. It seems to me, Diarmuid Devine, that you have something to answer for. A man in your profession! And Tim always was friendly with you. He helped you many a time, so he did.'

'What, ah – now look here, Maeve, I don't quite understand?'

'He's sick today, poor Tim, do you know that? Sick with worry, so he is. He's just gone out to see the doctor.'

'Oh, I see – I'm sorry to hear that. When, ah, when do you expect him back?'

'Not till six or after. He has a long way to go. Across town. Oh, I think you should be ashamed of yourself, Diarmuid Devine!'

'But, please, I – '

'None so blind as those who will not see,' Mrs Heron said. 'Anyway, I'm not putting you in touch with Una. I may as well be frank, I think you've done enough harm already. That girl is only twenty. You are older, you should know better!'

'Now look here, just a minute – '

But he heard the jarring signal which meant he was disconnected. She had cut him off. Maeve Heron, a woman he had always tended to ignore, a big motherly creature, all politeness and platitudes. He could not link his memories of her with that voice shouting at him as if he were a dog she was ordering out of her flowerbeds. Why was she so angry, all of a sudden? What did she know?

As he stepped out of the phone booth, the door, springing shut, nudged him rudely into the anonymous avenue.

It was frightening to think that people he did not know, in places he had not thought of, might be sitting this very moment, discussing and condemning his every action. And all over the city, now, the day boys were on their way home – little talking newspapers, primed with scandal. Aye, our teachers had a row today. What teachers? Och, the child is daft. Not daft, maybe – what was that again? Two of our teachers had a row about a girl.

He decided to go back to his digs. He remembered Una's promise to phone him that afternoon: that was before all this trouble started. He was not looking forward to the questions she might ask. How could he explain to her that he hadn't *meant* to let her down, that he hadn't known what to say? No, it would not be a very happy conversation.

But when he reached his own avenue, he began to run, prompted by a sudden belief that she would be waiting for him at his digs. Two housewives, pram pushing, stopped to stare as he ran past. What was so peculiar, he felt like asking them, in the sight of a man running? He had a stitch in his side by the time he stopped at his own basement door to fumble for his key. There were two letters on the hall stand but, dammit, they were not from her. Without waiting to take his coat off, he hurried down the hall to the foot of the stairs and called up to the kitchen.

'Mrs Dempsey! Mrs Dempsey!'

The kitchen door opened at once, as though Mrs Dempsey had been standing behind it, waiting for his summons. She stood, enormous in the doorway, staring down at him with the serenity of the apex figure in a monument to motherhood.

'Has there been any message for me, Mrs Dempsey? Did anyone phone?'

Without speaking, Mrs Dempsey held up a letter. Impatience made him start up the stairs, but she was already descending, majestic, slow, solemn. He backed down the stairs and nodded his thanks as Mrs Dempsey proffered the envelope. She raised a large floury arm to pat her grey hair bun into place, saying:

'A young woman delivered it.'

He tore the envelope open. Inside was a sheet of copybook paper with a pencilled note:

Dear Dev:

I don't know what story you told Uncle Tim but things are in an awful mess here. They caught me coming home this morning and now the roof has fallen in. You didn't help it seems, if what Uncle Tim tells me is true. I hate to drag you into this, but I'm in an awful mess as Uncle Tim threatens to tell my mother and have her come and get me. Mummy and I have had enough rows already and this would really break her heart.

So I need your help, Dev. We've got to tell the Herons something that sounds true, for a change. And you must back me up. My suggestion is we say I got tight and fell asleep at your place and you were afraid to take me home in that condition. I think they might possibly believe that, if you to tell it to them. You're a friend of theirs, after all. I hate to ask you to do it, but believe me, Dev, I am forced to. Could you come to the house this afternoon when you get this note? I will be at the window, looking out for you.   Una

'What time did she deliver it?' he asked.

'This morning. After eleven it was.'

He read the letter again. He had completely forgotten Mrs Dempsey. When he looked up and saw her still standing there, he felt a quick irritation. Dammit, he had no time to talk to her, why didn't she go away? He looked at the letter again.

'I'd like a word with you, Mr Devine, if you don't mind?'

'Yes, Mrs Dempsey, what it it?'

She was, he noticed, not wearing her apron. Without it, in her best black velveteen, she had the undressed air of a soldier in mufti. He was further disconcerted when she moved the thick turret of her body in the direction of his den, saying: 'Could we go in here, if you please? My daughter is in the kitchen, you see.'

What did she mean – what must her daughter not hear? But the moment these questions posed themselves, the answer became plain. Mrs Dempsey's face made it all too clear. A mottled flush spread from her floury cheeks right down the descending staircase of her chins. Uneasily, Mr Devine put the letter in his jacket pocket and followed his landlady into the warm, stuffy silence of his den.

'Ah, do sit down, won't you, Mrs Dempsey?'

'Thank you, Mr Devine, I'll only be a moment.'

But she sat down. Backing slightly, she let her great velveteen rump meet the edge of the armchair, like an airliner's undercarriage swinging slowly into position. She looked up, her several chins diminishing in the process. She made a small throat-clearing sound. Then, fixing her large-lidded eyes on a point some inches past Mr Devine's left shoulder, she said:

'I'm afraid I'll be needing this wee flat soon. I'm afraid I'll be obliged to ask you to make other arrangements, Mr Devine.'

Mr Devine joined his hands over his stomach, his fingers seeking reassurance in the touch of his father's ring.

'Well, ah, that's bad news,' he said. 'I mean, I've been so long here. Still, I suppose all good things must come to an end.'

'Yes,' Mrs Dempsey said.

'Well, ah, when would you be needing the place?'

'To the end of the week is as long as I can give you, I'm sorry to say.'

'I see.'

For several seconds the only sound in the room was the puff and falling noise of the slacked fire. Mrs Dempsey's face now had a well-slapped look, two red weals discolouring her cheeks. Mindful of her impeccable sodality attendance, he thought how embarrassing this talk must be for her. It was, he felt, the least he could do to give in gracefully.

'Well, I'll be very sorry to move, I'm sure. But you need the space, and that's that. Very well, then.'

Mrs Dempsey's large eyes blinked rapidly, remaining fixed on the neutral point behind his shoulder. 'Yes, I'll be sorry too, Mr Devine. Very sorry. But you understand, I must think . . .'

She gasped for breath and continued in a frighteningly higher register:

' . . . I must think about my girls. I have young girls in this house, my own flesh and blood, well, even though you have been here so long and even though I will miss the money, I have their morals to consider after all.'

She gasped again, and Mr Devine said quickly: 'Yes, yes, of course. I'll try to move at once. I could send for my things later, if you've no objections?'

It was dreadful, dreadful, but he knew without looking that she was beginning to cry. Her great bosom rose and fell; her face began to quiver from nose to last tiny chin. With mysterious legerdemain, a tiny lace handkerchief materialized in the palm of her hand, and was pressed against her mutinous muth. She rose, sobbing, and swayed past him, disappearing into the darkness of the hall. Should he say something? Go after her and pat her huge, heaving back? But she was going up the flight of stairs now. He could hear a Panurgean sniff as she paused at the threshold of the kitchen, composing herself to face the curious, divergent stare of her eldest offspring.

Mr Devine sat down in his armchair. He felt no sense of being wronged. He was very fond of Mrs Dempsey, he realized; she'd been a good landlady all these years, and it was rotten to have put her in this position. About moving . . . Well . . . He looked around the room, every book where he knew it was, every object fitted carefully where it would be easy to get at. Since the war, good digs were at a premium. But he had no time to worry about digs now. There was the letter in his pocket. He opened it and read it once more. She was waiting for him at Heron's house. She wanted him to tell . . . My God, he could see himself telling Old Tim the likes of that! . . . It was nearly as bad as the truth. And Tim had a terrible temper, he was capable of anything, he might even take the whole story to the . . . No, no . . . But if the students gossiped, Tim would hear about it sooner or later and then he might go to the . . . Aye. He'd take it to the President. *Oh Merciful God, how did I get mixed up in a thing like this?*

But he must get a hold on himself; he mustn't panic. There must be a way out, he told himself. Tim Heron wouldn't be home until six; he was visiting the doctor. And meantime, Una was waiting. If he went at once, perhaps he could get her to change her mind and tell some other story. There must be some other story they could tell. He'd have to hurry, though. Her letter said she'd be waiting at the window.

But the bay window wore a net curtain: it was impossible to see if there was anyone behind it. Mr Devine walked up and down in front of the Heron house. The net curtain did not move. She gave no signal. He would have to ring the doorbell and hope for the best. Reluctantly, he opened the gate, walked up the short, flagged pathway and dragged on the old-fashioned bellpull. It was a quarter to five. Surely Tim Heron would not be home yet.

The door opened slowly. Clinging to the handle like a hooked fish was wee Frank, the Herons' youngest boy.

'Is Miss Clarke in?'

'Who?'

'Una, is she in?'

'Yis.'

'Well, will you tell her someone is here to see her?'

178

Wee Frank swung to and fro on the doorknob. He gave no sign that he understood.

'Will you tell her there's somebody to see her?' Mr Devine said in a low, urgent voice. 'Go on, like a good boy.'

Wee Frank let go of the doorknob. He turned towards the back hall, yelling: 'Dad-eee! Dad-ee! There's a man at the door.'

'No, no, not your father. I want Una Clarke. Una!'

'Mam-eee, mam-ee, there's a man – '

Somewhere in the interior darkness, a door opened and a female voice said: 'Who is it?' Mr Devine did not know that voice. He reached forward and shut the door so that the person would not see him. Having done this, there was nothing left to do but to make himself scarce. At first, he backed down the steps, hoping that if the door opened he could still pretend he was waiting. But when he reached the gate and no one had appeared, he turned and walked very quickly down the avenue, beginning to run as he reached the corner of the Cavehill Road. Once round the corner, he paused. Maybe Maeve Heron had paid no attention to the wee boy. He hoped so. He crossed the road and paused again, feeling ridiculous. Supposing someone had been watching from a window, supposing one of the Herons had seen him backing away? He leaned his forehead again the coolness of the iron railings of a small public playground. It was better to have dodged away, wasn't it, than to have faced Maeve Heron in her present temper?

But at that moment he heard someone running across the road. Towards him. He did not dare look. It must be the wee boy, running after him. It was not.

'Dev!'

She put her hand on his shoulder and when he turned to face her, she said: 'Are you sick? What's the matter? You look awful.'

He tried to smile, but his mouth refused. 'Hello, Una.'

'Come on,' she said, taking his arm, walking him along

179

the row of iron railings. 'What on earth did you go away for? I was just coming to the door.'

'I, ah, I thought it was someone else. The child began yelling, you see.'

'Uncle Tim is out,' she said. 'There was nothing to worry about. Aunt Maeve was upstairs.'

'Oh.'

'Look, let's go in here,' she said, stopping at the playground gates. 'Let's sit down. We've got to discuss this.'

The playground was empty, but as Mr Devine and Una went in, four children entered with them. The eldest, a boy grown too big for his short trousers, jumped on the merry-go-round and set it whirling. His three little sisters, traces of their tea still ringing their mouths, rushed past Mr Devine and clambered onto the spinning platform. The boy jumped off, disgusted at their imitation, and ran across the tarmac, leaping high to grip a set of iron exercise rings. He somersaulted, and as the adults passed by, he dropped to the ground, leaving the iron rings to jangle uselessly, their chains entwining.

'The swings,' he cried. 'Peggy! Eily! All of yiz on the swings.'

Mr Devine and Una halted to let the three little girls rush past in obedience to their leader's order. The playground shelter was locked, so he led Una to a nearby bench, scarred with initials, its back to the iron railings and the cold wind from the waterworks pond. From where they sat, they faced a municipal tennis court, unused in this season, nets down, gates locked. Una huddled herself closer to him, producing her usual battered package of ten cigarettes. She bent to light one, crouched to screen the match from the cold autumn wind.

'What a mess we're in,' she said. 'How stupid people are.'

He was grateful. Not one word about last night, not one reproach for his conduct. She had tact, at least. 'Your uncle sounds upset,' he said. 'Very upset.'

'It's not only last night he's upset about,' she said. 'It's knowing about me and Michael in Dublin. You see, he's afraid something similar will happen here. That's why he wants to tell my mother.'

'But that's nonsense. I mean, nothing happened.'

'But who'd believe us? Who'd believe me? You see, in Mummy's eyes, I've blotted my copybook already. If she hears about this, I'll be dragged back to Dublin in chains.'

And who could blame her mother? Mr Devine thought. But he remembered what Una had said last night. She was a good girl, despite appearances. He wished there were some way he could let her mother know that. But as she said, who would believe him?

'That's why this story about me being tight might be the answer, Dev. I've been tight a few times before – at dances. And Mummy knows that. If we could make Uncle Tim believe I passed out in your digs, he mightn't even tell Mummy. After all, you couldn't take me home if I'd passed out completely. You'd have had to let me stay the night.'

Couldn't very well send her home in that condition, Tim . . . And how did she get in that condition? Tim would ask. And Maeve Heron, who thinks the worst of me already, how would she interpret a story like that? Oh, no. No!

'Well now, I couldn't say a thing like that, Una.'

'Why not? What *are* you going to say then? That you slept with me?'

Mr Devine felt for his ring, turning it, turning it. 'But dammit, it looks awful, a thing like that,' he said. 'It looks, well, it looks almost as bad, don't you see?'

'It's not as bad. He thinks I slept with some man he doesn't know. He's afraid I'm pregnant.'

Mr Devine stared at the gravelled tarmac, at her shoes beside his, at her ankles, at the match she had tossed dead on the ground. What on earth could he say? He could not look her in the face.

'I told him to send me to a doctor, if he was so

suspicious,' she continued. 'Oh, it's an awful mess, awful! He and Aunt Maeve are behaving like a couple of raving lunatics.'

'Oh, now, you're exaggerating, surely.'

'I'm not exaggerating one bit. I'm in a terrible mess, Dev, don't you realize that? If Mummy finds out, I'm sunk. Sunk!'

His eyes sought the shelter wall beside him as though searching for a sign. *J. L. loves M. B.*, he read, his eyes wandering among the wall's obscure scratches, the chalked endearments, the forgotten trysts. Sick, he remembered that other wall, the filthy doggerel wiped clean by a hairy, tattooed arm. *And they say Dev put out the light . . .* 'They say' – they *are* saying it, all over the city, at this very moment . . . *and pulled her drawers down.* Ah, if she had seen that filthy stuff, what would she be saying to me now? Worse, worse.

'Don't you see, Dev,' she said, putting her hand on his sleeve, 'the reason they'll believe it is because it's shocking? It's what they expect. And if *you* tell them, they'll never doubt you.'

He looked at her with the furtive, sidelong glance he sometimes used on women who sat next to him at the cinema. As though she were a stranger and would be offended if she saw him do it. For a young girl, she was unpleasantly shrewd, he decided. Tim Heron *might* believe a story like that, if I told it to him. If she's so knowledgeable about other people, then what has she decided about me? Cold distrust filled him. He did not know her at all: he was with a stranger.

'You see,' she was saying, 'it would be no use, coming from me. Ever since I told Uncle Tim that fib this morning, he won't believe a word I say.'

'But I don't know if he'd believe *me*,' Mr Devine said, uneasily. 'I'm not very good at telling things like that.'

Exasperated, she tossed her cigarette away. It blew along

the macadam, touched the iron railings and was lifted through them by a puff of wind, to roll and fall into the waterworks bushes beyond. She said – her voice high, hysterical – 'What do you want me to do, Dev? Do I have to get down on my knees to you?'

'No, no, but . . . ah . . .'

'But what? What do I have to do to shame you into helping me?'

And to his . . . *Oh my God, somebody will see her, in public, get up, damn you!* . . . she knelt down on the tarmac beside him, her hands gripping his knees, her pale face staring up at him. 'Is that what you want?' she cried. 'Must I beg?'

'Una, get up, for goodness' sake. Please! Now get up and we'll think of something. Everything will be all right.'

But she did not move: she stared at him, not speaking. He took hold of her elbows and dragged her to her feet. 'Please,' he mumbled. 'I hate this.'

'I hate it as much as you do. But you've got to help me, Dev. You've got to!'

She had gone on her knees to him; she thought he was selfish and cruel. Didn't she know he'd do anything for her, he'd cut off his right arm, if it would please her? But to tell Old Tim a story like that, to stand in front of Old Tim and say you had got his twenty-year-old niece so drunk she passed out – Well, he simply couldn't see himself – it was beyond human power.

She doesn't understand, he decided. She's too young to understand. Tim couldn't ignore a story like that; Tim is one for justice, for his right; he would consider it his duty to see me sacked.

'I might try,' he said. 'But maybe we can make it sound a little less shocking, eh? Maybe we can think of something else?'

For an answer, she got up and walked away. Birds fell

from the dark air, braking on wingtips, skimming the playground railings, soaring to distant rooftops.

'Wait,' he said. She stopped. Her anger stood between them like a dangerous presence. Eager she was, to rush in where angels . . . Yes, he thought, that is the difference between us.

'Are you going to tell him, Dev?'

'Well, couldn't we – '

'There's nothing else to tell him,' she said. 'I've thought it all over. I'll have to tell him myself then.'

'But it'll be the same thing. Una! He'll come to me and want to know why I did it.'

'That's too bad, isn't it?' she said. 'You should have thought of that when you let me down this morning.'

So she knew. Heron must have told her what he'd said. But what did she expect him to say? How was he supposed to know what lie she'd told her uncle?

'I should have,' he began. 'I mean, I wasn't very brave, I'll admit. But you see, I didn't know what to say to him. You see, Una, you're not a Catholic. To us, drunkenness is a mortal sin; a man who'd let a young girl he was out with get stocious drunk is almost as bad as a fornicator.'

'A man,' she said bitterly. 'A *man*. Do you ever think about anybody but yourself, Dev?'

'Una, wait a minute. Una!'

But she did not wait. She walked past the deserted swings, anger hurrying her steps. In a moment she would be at the gates, in a moment she would be back at Heron's, raging mad, ready to tell anything. Panic leaped in him. He began to run after her, and the children stopped playing to watch. The man was running after the woman.

'Una, wait, Una, I want to explain. Una!'

But she walked on, even when he caught up with her. She did not turn her head. 'You're wasting your breath,' she said. 'There's only one thing I want to hear now. Tell me you're coming to see Uncle Tim.'

'Wait, Una, I want to tell you something.'

'Something that'll soothe me down, no doubt. That's your special talent, isn't it, Dev? All things to all men.'

'That's not fair, Una.' But was it? It had the power of truth, he realized: it was the unspoken rebuke he had feared all his life. Did everyone see through him the way she did? But damn her, what right had she to talk? She was not so bloody perfect herself.

'All things to all men, am I? I love you; is that just a joke to you? Oh, it's a joke, I'm sure. Just an ass of a schoolmaster, a Papist too, no good at kissing and loving, just a big joke. No great chartered accountant that runs back to his wife.'

'Stop it! Stop it!'

He dodged his head back, too late. His cheek burned as though her fingers were nettles. His glasses hung crooked over his ear. He put them straight and saw that she was crying.

'Ah, Una, I'm sorry. I don't know what came over me.' He took her arm, pulling her to a stop once more.

'No, I deserved it.'

'You didn't. I'm a coward,' he said. 'You'd be mad to marry a fellow like me.'

'Marry? Who's talking about marriage?'

He held up his hand as if to shield himself from another blow. 'No, I'm sorry. I shouldn't have said that, either. I'm not even the right religion for you. I wouldn't marry a Catholic, if I were you.'

'Are you proposing to me, Dev?'

'No, I'm just . . . I mean to say, I'm just pointing out the advantages and disadvantages. Disadvantages, now – there are plenty. You don't love me – how could you, after last night? I'm a flop; I'm ashamed of myself. Ashamed.'

'Just a minute,' she said. 'What do you mean, *you're* a flop?'

His mournful face searched the street, in terror that

someone might overhear. 'Well, I am,' he murmured. 'I couldn't . . . you know what I mean.'

'But I thought it was me,' she said. 'I thought it was *me*.'

'You? Oh, no, not you. I mean, you were . . . You don't think surely . . .'

'But what else *was* I to think, Dev? You wouldn't even touch me. I saw your face, you looked disgusted. As if I was ugly and awful.'

'No, Una, no! To tell the truth, it was – well, it was the first time for me. I never was with a girl, so you see . . . ?'

'Are you a pansy, or something? They say a lot of people who take up acting are pansies. You can tell me, Dev; I won't be shocked.'

'A pansy?' His voice rose to an indignant high-pitched shout. It was ridiculous, but the moment she accused him of it, he felt he talked and acted like one. 'Of course not,' he continued, deliberately making his voice deeper. 'Dammit, I'm just a, well, a virgin, do you understand? A lot of people are. In fact, a hell of a lot of people are.'

'Oh God,' she said. 'If it wasn't so pitiful, it would be funny. Funny!'

'Well, I'm glad you find it so, ah, amusing. I'm sorry you got the wrong impression. I never realized you thought it was *your* fault.'

'What did you expect me to think, Dev, for heaven's sake?' She began to laugh, but it was a relief, like crying: there was no humour in it. 'What a fool I am,' she said. 'What an utter fool.'

'It was all a mistake,' Mr Devine said anxiously. 'We were both innocent. It means . . . Well, it means . . .'

But he could not put what it meant into words. It had begun to rain and they walked down the Cavehill Road, turning at the street corner as though by common consent, walking back again, heads bent forward, staring at the pavement like conference delegates pondering a question.

'I'm not good enough for you,' he began again. 'You see,

186

I never was in love before, I didn't know what to do. I've lived too much alone for a young man, I realize that now. I never knew much about girls, you see, love and all that was – theoretical, with me. Imaginings.'

'But why didn't you explain this before?' she said. 'Why didn't you tell me you were as innocent as me?'

'Well, I, ah, I've always found it hard to discuss my private feelings with other people. To admit things, do you see? I'm always afraid that somebody will laugh at them. I was afraid you'd laugh at me, if I told you.'

'I wouldn't, you know that.'

'Yes, but that doesn't help when you're afraid of something. You're unreasonable. Being afraid is an unreasonable thing most of the time.'

He had stopped walking now and he turned to her, his eyes magnified behind blurred lenses, his mournful face wet with rain. They had halted beside a bus stop and a bus slowed down, waiting for them to get on. Mr Devine, realizing this, shook his head at the bus conductor. The bus drew away from the pavement and, watching it go, he found himself returning the stare of a stout woman passenger, her face pressed against the rain-blurred glass, as though rebuking him for talking about such things in the open street.

Una walked on and he followed. Her hands were deep in her coat pockets, her hair was wet with rain. He watched as she deliberately stepped into the small pavement puddles, breaking the reflected image of her face as it swam in each tiny pool. At the street corner, she stopped and waited for him to stop too.

'I couldn't marry you, Dev,' she said. 'I'm sorry.'

'Of course, it may be too soon for you to think of marriage,' he said – anxious, as always, to make the other person's refusal seem just.

'It's not that.'

'Well, you may be right, Una. I'm not any great catch, I know.'

'Dev, will you for heaven's sake stop agreeing with me? You're not making it any easier.'

'I'm sorry,' he said humbly.

'I was awfully selfish, Dev. I was flattered when you said you were in love with me, when you seemed really to care about me. After Michael's behaviour, it was reassuring.'

'You wouldn't have to be in love with me, Una,' he said, trying to ward off the finality of her words.

'No, Dev, that's where you're wrong. I *would* have to be in love with you. We're completely different types. I want to fight against what life's doing to me, and you're afraid to. Live and let live is your motto.'

'But you don't understand,' he said desperately. 'I could change. If I had you to fight for, I could be different. Completely different. And damn the consequences.'

She shook her head. 'No . . . It's hopeless, Dev, hopeless. I don't want another weakling. I need someone who's strong, someone who'll help me. Besides, I'm not going to marry anyone just because I feel sorry for them.'

He felt his hands join, his fingers pressing his father's ring as though they would break it. *Sorry for me*. This was what happened when you were foolish enough to invite it. *Sorry for me*, she said. Could she have said anything more cruel if she tried? *Sorry for me*. What right has *she* to be sorry for me?

She could not leave bad enough alone, he noticed. She went on, every word making it worse. 'Oh, you're nice, Dev, and you wouldn't hurt a fly. But you've just proved that you'd betray your own mother to avoid a row. God knows how you think you could live with the likes of me. I'd make you miserable, so I would. And the awful thing is, you'd never dare tell me.'

'Very well,' he said, and heard his voice switch to a high, breaking tone. 'I'm sorry I bothered you then.'

'Don't say that, Dev. I'm sorry too, I shouldn't have lost my temper. Please forget what I just said.'

Forget it. How was he supposed to forget it; who did she think she was? 'I'm not offended,' he said, trying not to shout. 'I'm not in the least offended.'

'I'm sorry, anyway.'

They began to walk once more, and this time she continued on towards the street where she lived. 'Well,' she said, 'I can't tell our drunk story to Uncle Tim, I see. I suppose I'll have to say nothing and let him think the worst. He'll send me back to Dublin, you know.'

He did not answer. He did not even seem to be listening. She tried again, as they reached the small street. 'I'm going in now; I'm not going to tell them anything. Your secret is safe, Dev.'

She was surprised when he entered the side street still at her side. For a moment she began to hope that he was really going back to the Herons' with her. Perhaps, after all, she had shamed him into doing it. Now that she had turned him down, perhaps he felt obliged to show he held no grudge. But at the Herons' gate, he stopped. He raised his hat, formally, the rain wetting his sparse sandy hair.

'I hope we're still friends,' she said. 'I hope you won't hate me for saying what I did.'

'Of course. I'm sorry I made such a fool of myself.'

He waited, still holding his hat over his head, like an absurd snapshot, caught by a street photographer. He seemed to expect something more, some word, some sign. A tenderness weakened her resolution. It was so awful to be the rejected one. She knew: she thought of herself, rejected by Michael. But then she thought of Michael, and Michael's weakness. Dev was weak too. Horribly weak. And still, behind it all, she felt there was something to love in this pathetic figure, holding his hat above his head in farewell. She went over to him and, although she knew her Aunt Maeve might be watching, she put up her face to be kissed.

But he did not kiss her.

'Good-bye then,' she said.

'Good-bye.'

He put his hat back on his head as she reached the Herons' front door. It was not locked and she went in without looking back. He felt his hair wet, under the hat. He waited, as though he expected her to come out again. The rain stopped. It was getting dark. After a while, he went away.

Chapter Thirteen

The Very Reverend Daniel Keogh had a great liking for tea. All day and well into the night college servants brought fresh pots to the presidential study, setting them down under the bright light of a lamp which burned sixteen hours out of twenty-four. The President, sifting endlessly among his clutter of papers, would reach out from time to time to pour a fresh cup. Tea, he lives on tea, the kitchen staff said.

He was old, he had little appetite, he had much to do. So many papers, so many tasks: the sleeves of his soutane shone and pens fitted easily against the thick callous on his forefinger. But these outward signs could do no more than hint at the constant and diverse labours which Dr Keogh had accumulated to screen him from the boredom of his tenancy: there was a history of Catholic diocesan organizations to be revised; there were notes for a book on Cardinal Celina; sermons for special retreats, orations for parish centenaries, memoranda on certain aspects of canon law. Above all, in chaotic and cancerous growth, were notes, drafts and reference periodicals for his *magnum opus*: a record of Irish clerical pilgrimages to the Vatican in the nineteenth century, with an account of the reasons for, and the results thereof. In addition, school business yearly required more correspondence. Yes, there was much work to be done. Too much, according to some people. There were those who hinted that the President expended too much valuable time in exegesis of matters whose relation was marginal to his position as administrator of Ardath. Others murmured that the pressure of forms and regulations in the Welfare Age was more than any man of his years should be expected to cope with: his load should be lightened. However, Dr Keogh did not agree. He had always had a taste for scholarship, for administrative correspondence, for overwork. He hoarded his labours, he clung to his tasks. To him, they were privileges. He would not relinquish them.

In addition to his clerical labours, the President left his desk during the morning hours to tour the classrooms, chat briefly with the staff, teach a class of Greek to senior students and preside over luncheon in the refectory. In the evenings, he had special interviews with boys who might have a vocation. Twice a week he presided over a study circle of senior boys who would shortly begin their training for the priesthood. These study circles were an excellent method of keeping in touch with the student pulse. In the evenings also, he often found time for a chat with Old John Harbinson, the deaf hall porter, who was assigned to bring up his tea. Old John would place the teapot in the empty space from which he had removed its predecessor, waiting respectfully in the shadow of the desk lamp until Dr Keogh found time to look up and say:

'What do you hear today, John?'

This was not a cruel joke. Old John, mooning in corridors, shuffling through common room and study hall in his elastic-sided slippers, was a piece of college furniture, rarely noticed by students or staff. Deaf, feeble-minded, old: it was an act of pure charity to keep him on at all, the Dean said. The President did not agree. He too had been accused of being feeble, old, unnoticing. He and John had a little understanding. John's job was safe.

Now, as the chapel bell sounded three times, Dr Keogh stirred his tea. The fresh pot was cold, because Old John's chat had taken longer than usual and had been more than usually interesting. Shivering a little – a touch of his malaria again – the President raised his large grey head and listened to the noise of boys in the yard below. In a few short minutes the bell would be stilled, the boys would reach the chapel and evening devotions would begin. There would be an hour of blessed quiet, an hour of repose. Dr Keogh shuddered, crouching low over his desk as the old ague gripped him once more. He held the teaspoon up to the light and absently, like a small, old child, licked sugar from its concave surface with the tip of his tongue. He shuddered again: his Roman penance, he called it.

Years of sunshine, of contented work and study in the Irish College, years among men with keen minds and keen scholarship. And, as after the pleasures of sin, the purgatory of banishment to this, his cold homeland, to old age and obscurity among small, intriguing souls.

The President raised his head once more, his eyes closed, his withered face turning towards the warm sunlight of the lamp. His thoughts returned to the story Old John had been telling him, a serial it was, a serial which had taken some curious and disquieting turns over the past week or so. A serial which might involve Monsignor Sullivan (a very able man) and Canon McAuliffe, an important member of the Board. Shut eyes reddened by the lamplight, Dr Keogh thought too of his Dean of Discipline, Father Alphonsus McSwiney, tall, redheaded, his clerical clothes of the best material and cut. Anxious McSwiney, moving on the edge of the circle, a word to the Monsignor, a word to the Canon. A word here, a word there. Yes, according to Old John, the story was widespread, the boys were excited by the scandalous aspect. Yes, only a matter of time now until the parents begin to write letters, until the telephone rings with some boy's father on the end of the line, a discreet question, diffidently phrased. It could be serious. It could.

The President reached into the frayed skirts of his soutane and withdrew two quinine tablets. He cupped them in the palm of his hand, ready to swallow. McSwiney was too apt a choice as Dean of Discipline, he reflected. McSwiney relied too much on force. The cane was all very well, it was a time-honoured method of knocking a few fundamentals into rough boys. But it – and McSwiney – had limitations, he sometimes felt. Moderation was not a part of the Dean's philosophy. McSwiney believed in an iron hand, ungloved.

The President's mouth formed a small rictus of amusement at the thought. Any show of mercy or tolerance would call the Dean to attack, and Dr Keogh thought he knew precisely how the Dean would answer that call: a sacrifice brought bloody to the feet of the Board of Governors, a promise of similar sacrifices in the future . . . if only the Board would see fit to appoint a new broom, the old broom could be tossed out to rot in some country parish. The President shook the tablets gently in his hand. Yes, any weakness on his part now, and Father McSwiney would be knocking on the Monsignor's door, informing, condemning, asking for his due.

On the other hand, the President thought, the Monsignor and the Board members surely know my worth. There is more to administration than new soutanes and theatrical offerings. Aye. His grey face trembled in the warm lamplight, his contempt mixed with the ague that was warmth's legacy.

He swallowed the tablets.

As the boarders entered the study hall after evening devotions, the Dean of Discipline waited by the door, his presence a guarantee of orderly conduct. Father Creely, the invigilator, passed up the far aisle, reading his office. He mounted the rostrum and sat down, turning a breviary page. There was no idling. The boarders had only three hours left to complete the many exercises set for the following day. Slow boys, who could not finish that evening, would have to rise at six and work until breakfast.

The Dean, his elegant shoulder cape thrown back to show the lining sheen, moved up the study hall like a man herding sheep. At the rostrum he paused and leaned against the lectern, watching the boarders take their seats. Father Creely raised his eyes from the breviary, waiting for the Dean to speak. Expectantly, he placed a small picture of Our Lady of Sorrows between the pages to mark his place. But Father McSwiney did not speak. Once more he resumed his walk among the busy boarders. Father Creely, who confessed to a more than ordinary curiosity, couldn't help wondering what was going on. The Dean seemed to be looking for some sign, some betrayal, among those bent, boyish heads, those dutifully studious faces. Closing his breviary, Father Creely stepped down from the rostum. He watched as the Dean moved towards the study hall door. He followed.

In the corridor, Father McSwiney turned, waiting for Father Creely. He had a puzzled look on his large white face. 'There's something up,' he said.

Father Creely glanced through the opened doorway at his charges. All was in order. 'Is that a fact?' he said, politely. 'I didn't notice anything out of the ordinary.'

'I know boys,' the Dean said. 'And I keep my ears open. Do you remember that argument between Heron and Devine last week?'

'Yes, very well, Father. Has there been some new development?'

'Heron's boy, Eamon, had a crowd around him before devotions,' the Dean said. 'I heard one boy asking him about his cousin from Dublin. In a joking manner. Then they saw me, and of course . . .'

'Do you think those three lads told what they heard?'

'I'm not sure, Father. I have a notion there's more than that to it.'

'Maybe Heron and Devine have had another row, do you think?'

'Now you're getting warm,' the Dean said. 'That's a possibility.'

Both clerics stood silent, staring down the moonlit corridor. Father Creely glanced back at the scene in the study hall. All was quiet. Pens marked paper as though the students were reporters recording some inaudible oration.

'Well, keep your ears open, Father,' the Dean said, at length. 'Let me know if you get wind of anything.'

'I will, Father.'

'And send Young Coogan out to me, will you?'

'Very good, Father.'

The Dean folded his arms and walked a few paces away from the study hall doors. If this fuss was about Heron's niece, he had covered himself nicely by mentioning it to the Monsignor the other day. And of course the girl was not in the play any more, so the play would not be affected. All the better, if Heron and Devine were having a row – two lay masters fighting and the President did not even know about it. Disgraceful, the Dean said to himself. Disgraceful. The Board should be informed at once.

If the President handled this affair in his usual way, it would be by doddering along and doing nothing. And that, the Dean said to himself, is simply not good enough. No, it was the Dean's duty to mention it to the Board. To show them a firm hand was needed. A new broom, so to speak.

Through the corridor windows a pale moon cast slanting rectangles of light on the tiled corridor floor. Into one of these a boy stepped, his face whiter than the pale night light. The Dean, hearing the footstep, turned with a swish of skirts.

'Father McSwiney? Did you want me, sir?'

'Yes, Coogan. Come along with me.' The Dean put his large white hand on the boy's shoulder, feeling the muscles flick convulsively as though he had touched some young frightened animal. Gently, he guided the boy away from the study hall into the lonely, moonlit corridor.

'I think you are a truthful boy,' the Dean said, pausing under a moonlit rectangle. 'Yes, I think you are a good boy, Coogan. Now, I want a truthful answer.'

196

'Yes, Father.'

'I know all about it, mind you,' the Dean said. 'I just want to hear your version, Coogan.'

His strong fingers pressed hard on the cheap stuff of Coogan's jacket. 'Well, Coogan?' he said softly.

'What, ah, what about, Father?'

'Now, Coogan, don't start off that way. You know very well what about. We all know what's going on, don't we? I've heard some funny stories today. Now, I want you to tell me what you have to do with this business. Start at the beginning.'

Father McSwiney was confident. Ardath was not an English school, thank God, it was Irish and Catholic. There was therefore no nonsense about putting boys on their honour to own up to their wrongdoings. Boys did wrong. To find out what they had done, you picked a former wrongdoer and threatened him. No boy would be foolish enough to suffer for another's crime. If the boy did not tell, you gave him what for. No boy, in Father McSwiney's experience, was stouter than a good cane.

'I didn't do anything, Father,' Coogan said in a rush of fear. 'It wasn't me. I never even knew about it.'

'That's not the way I heard it, Coogan. You were in the middle of it.'

'Honestly, Father, I only tried to wash it off.'

The Dean's hand tightened on Coogan's shoulder. He glanced up and down the moonlit corridor and then shoved Coogan against the wall. He did not know what Coogan was talking about. He had no patience. He wanted to find out.

'So you washed it off, did you?' he said in a sarcastic voice. His thick fingers closed on the short hair at the back of Coogan's neck. With a grimly cheerful smile he lifted Coogan slightly off his feet, like a man picking up a puppy. It was very painful. Coogan gasped, aware that he must not yell.

'What was it you washed off, you little liar? Answer me now!'

197

Confused, in pain, Coogan vaguely tried to remember what had gone before. His thoughts spun in a wavering circle, trying to find a way to end this agony. Above him, his large white face split in an angry smile, Father McSwiney waited for confession. Coogan felt as if his hair must surely come out in the Dean's hand.

'It was po'try,' he whimpered. 'Some of the seniors did it, Father. Not me, Father.'

'What seniors?'

'Kelly and Magowan, Father.'

'What did they write, Coogan?'

'I, ah, I don't remember, Father.'

'Don't you lie to me,' the Dean said. He tightened his grip. 'Start at the beginning. What was it, why was it, and how did it come about? And be sharp, my lad, or you'll be sorry.'

'It was some fellows in Junior III,' Coogan whimpered. 'They heard Mr Devine and Mr Heron talking this morning. They had a row, at least a kind of a row.'

'That's the good lad,' the Dean said. 'That's more like it. Now, don't worry; I believe you, Coogan, I'm sure you had nothing to do with this. Now, what was it, this row between Mr Devine and Mr Heron, what did they hear?'

Coogan told him.

Chapter Fourteen

The whining fidget of Mrs Dempsey's electric carpet sweeper crossed and recrossed the floor above. He opened his eyes and could see. Glasses on? Why, he never wore them in bed. But he was not in bed, he was in the armchair and his back was sore. He sat up straight and saw the dead fire. The yellow eye of the lamp reproached him in the morning light. He switched it off. What time was it?

His watch had stopped. He put it back in his pocket, unwound. It was a bad omen, its stopping like this. Since his father's funeral he had never forgotten to wind it at suppertime and it had not been stopped except for cleaning. But now it was an omen. Everything had stopped. He had not done the normal things, he had not even gone to bed last night. He took off his glasses to rub his eyes. It was as though he had been delirious and the crisis had passed, leaving him weak, aware, reminded of lost time by the sight of things undone. What time was it! *Late!*

He hurried into the hall to look at the eight-day winder. Relief made his slack. The hands were at a quarter to eight and the pendulum moved. It was strange, was it not, how the body behaved precisely as though it was an ordinary morning? He always woke at a quarter to.

He went into his bedroom, reproached by its order, the blankets neatly tucked in, the sheet turned down to receive him. He had not used it since she lay on it. He had not been able to. Now, he rumpled the pillows and pulled the blankets free. He must undress. Normally, he went upstairs to shave in his dressing gown and slippers, passing through the kitchen where Mrs Dempsey would be preparing his breakfast. He began to take his clothes off, sports jacket, new trousers, shirt. And remembered why he had bought them. He sat down on the bed, his hand still holding his shirt. In the dresser mirror he saw his face.

It was a face which once had worn a moustache, a face which once had smiled and sought to find an answering smile, a face which once evinced a certain uncertainty. But it had changed: it no longer asked or desired. It knew: it was afraid.

He stood up and reached for his pyjamas. If he did not wear his dressing gown and pyjamas when he went up to shave, Mrs Dempsey would think it odd. But what odds if she thought it odd? She had kicked him out, hadn't she? She had told him to leave by the end of the week. What was the use now of keeping in with Mrs Dempsey? She could go to hell.

Still, he knocked as usual before entering the kitchen, and offered his usual 'Good morning'. Mrs Dempsey did not reply. She knew it was not good, the morning. Bent over her sink, her huge back like a shut door on his greeting, she gave his effort at normalcy the rebuke it deserved. He would have been worried about that, a week ago. Now, he did not care. He had other, graver, fears.

Fresh graffiti on stinking lavatory walls, a parent on the telephone asking for goodness' sake if there was any truth in this? Dr Keogh and the Dean in private conference. A college servant, a summons to the President's study . . . Mr Devine, what on earth is this we hear? Dammit, he could refuse to discuss it with them, no business of theirs. Well, in that case, Mr Devine, we must ask you to . . .

Then why go to college at all? Why not wait here for the letter saying that regretfully, in view of recent . . . and on account of various factors known to us, Mr Heron having been consulted, and having given his account of the matter, it would be advisable, as of this date . . . otherwise compelled to terminate . . . wishing you success in your future endeavours, yours very truly, Daniel Keogh, MA, DD.

But still, Una had promised that he would be kept out of it. Very good of her! Saint Una Martyr: sent to Dublin in disgrace. *Of course she was expecting him to own up*; she hoped to shame him into it, didn't she? Well, why should he? *I can't marry a man just because I feel sorry for him*, she said. All right then, he thought. I can't ruin my career for a girl just because I feel sorry for her.

Conscience? But why did he feel this harsh, tight pain? He could remember her in so many places these past few weeks, he carried in his head a score of pictures, each clear, each bringing her face to his mind's eye, each taunting him with what he had missed.

Yellow lit her hair as the spotlight spun: firelight shadows flickered as her eyes gleamed beneath him on the rug: on the bed it was moonlight, and the white body lay close to his, waiting as though for an operation, an operation he could not perform. And the last picture of all, in a darkening sky, her face in the rain uptilted for a kiss. A kiss he did not give.

The harsh, tight pain was the pain of loss. He had sinned in losing her. Sin demanded punishment. Amen. So be it.

In dressing gown, his face shaved, his towel laid like a priestly manciple over his left arm, Mr Devine went down to breakfast.

'Rourke. Clean that board.'

Danny Rourke picked up the felt and wood duster and rubbed chalk in a swirl that clouded the morning light. Junior III waited as Mr Devine sat down, putting his cane before him, in preparation for his first class of the day.

'*Ode to a Skylark*, was it not?'

'Yes, sir,' several voices answered.

This is Junior III. These are the boys who overheard Heron and me yesterday morning. These are the boys I have to thank for that filth in the jakes.

'Very well. Stand up, Halloran. What year was Shelley born?'

'Ah – you didn't, sir – you didn't set that for the exercise.'

'Stand out, Halloran. Next boy. When was Shelley born?'

Silence. He smelled panic. No one had the answer. No one had been told to prepare this information.

'Stand out. Next?'

When seven boys waited punishment, Mr Devine stood up. Two apiece. As hard as he could hit. He sat down once more, but he had only begun. More questions. Stand out! Next boy? Stand out! Next boy? He caned. He caned again. By the time the period was over, Junior III had suffered. Escaping, they passed the word along.

Dev was in a terrible wax.

Coogan had been caught writing in the jakes by Dev, someone said.

Dev was in a wax.

It wasn't Coogan, someone said, it was three seniors wrote the limericks.

Dev was in a terrible wax.

Dev and Sarge washed the limericks off themselves, someone said.

Dev was in a wax.

Tusker Heron said Dev and his cousin Una were up an entry.

Dev was in a terrible wax.

Old Cuff Heron knew all about Dev and his niece, someone said.

Dev was in a wax.

She was from Dublin. She was hot. Old Cuff was raging about it.

Dev was in a terrible wax.

Dev flippered sixteen kids in his first forty this morning.

Dev was in a wax.

Wing collar awry, fierce blue eyes blinking, his thin grey hair water-plastered to his skull, he was waiting outside

Junior III. Waiting for Mr Devine's first class to end. You did not have to look twice to know he was out for blood.

He took Mr Devine's arm, hurrying him through the crowd of boys, out in the morning mist of the annex yard.

'Did you not get my message?' he said.

'What message, Tim?'

'Damn, I rang up three times last night to your digs. I left a message.'

'I'm ah, I'm afraid I didn't get it.'

Tim Heron hunched his shoulders, turning away to peer across the empty yard. His black gown was rent up the back like a ragged tailcoat. He said:

'Do you know what's happened? Do you know the whole school overheard us yesterday?'

'I, ah, I heard a rumour. I wasn't sure.'

'Dirty filthy stuff up in the jakes. About you and my niece!'

'When?'

'It's there now,' Tim Heron said. 'The Dean himself took the trouble to inform me.'

'Oh God!'

'Aye. Now, once and for all, Dev, what happened? Were you telling me a lie yesterday?'

'No, Tim, no.'

'I'm responsible to that girl's mother, Dev. I've got to get to the bottom of this before it ruins all of us.'

'Well, I don't know anything more than I told you, Tim.'

'You were out with her that night. You admitted it yourself. What happened?'

'Nothing, Tim. Honest to God.'

'Devine, I've known you a long time. I helped you get this job, as you may remember. I've always thought of you as a friend.'

'Of course, Tim. You've been very good to me.'

'All right then. I'll tell you the truth, Dev, there's no sense hiding it any longer. That wee niece of mine isn't as innocent as she looks. She had a crush on a married man in Dublin before she came here. Nearly drove her mother distracted. I agreed to take her and get her started in nursing. I promised her mother I'd keep an eye on her. Do you follow me? Now, she refuses to tell me where she spent Sunday night. I warned her that unless she owned up by this morning, I'd have to tell her mother. I don't want to do that, Dev. Her mother has a bad heart, it might kill her, so it might.'

'Well, don't tell her mother, then,' Mr Devine said. 'Why worry her? Maybe you're upsetting yourself for nothing.'

'And what if the girl is pregnant, Dev? What'll I say, if that happens?'

'Oh, now, Tim, surely you're exaggerating. Pregnant!'

'Am I? Am I, Dev? I'm asking *you* that.'

'Oh, now look here, Tim, I told you I had nothing to do with it.'

'Aye,' Tim Heron said. 'Aye. Any young fellow might say the same. It's a hard thing to own up to, especially to a relative of the girl in question. But there's Una's future to consider. If you're responsible for ruining her reputation, you should be shot, so you should.'

'But I'm not!' Mr Devine cried.

'Well, I don't believe you, to tell you the truth. And I'm not sure the priests will, either.'

'Now just a minute, Tim, just a minute! You're not going to the President with that story, are you? Do you mean to say you'd blacken my character on no evidence at all?'

'It's blackened already!' Tim Heron shouted. 'Dirty trash about the pair of you is up where every boy can see it. How long do you think it'll be before the Dean tells the old fellow and up you go on the carpet?'

'Thanks to you, Tim. Shouting out your private affairs where a whole class of boys could hear you.'

'If you hadn't been squiring her to dances, there'd have been nothing to shout about, Devine!'

They were face to face now, their arms listing from their sides, their bodies struck with the ague of rage. In that moment of adrenaline fury, it seemed as though they would strike each other. But the moment could not be sustained: their bodies grew slack and listless. Confusedly, Mr Devine tried to remember the reason for his sudden anger, but found he had forgotten. He was aware only that Heron hated him; that Heron despised him. And with reason: he had lied to Heron to defend his dignity. He could no longer look his old friend in the face.

'So you're forcing me to ring her mother up and break this news to her,' Heron said bitterly. 'Forcing me to take strong measures because you're not man enough to own up.'

'Nobody's forcing you. It's your own dirty mind, Tim Heron.'

Heron's thick flanged eyebrows furrowed as though a student had dared to strike him. By God, it was not like Dev, this talk. Not like Dev — a civil fellow if there ever was one — this shouting match. Guilty bluster, Heron thought. What else could it be? Oh, Maeve was right, she says it must have been Devine, she's right.

His eyes immediately informed Devine of his decision. He turned away, as though the conversation had ended, as though, by the insult, Devine stood self-condemned. Into the annex he hurried, his ragged gown like twin streamers behind him. If Devine would do the like of that to a young girl, then he deserved all he got. And he'll get plenty, Tim Heron decided, his right eye blinking in rage. He'll get plenty.

He heard a door slam as he entered his own classroom. That would be Devine in Senior I. That blaggard!

Twelve large boys sat at their desks when Mr Devine entered Senior I. They were quiet. They'd heard he was in a wax.

'Collins. Clean that board.'

'It's clean, sir.'

'I'll be the judge of that. Clean it again.'

He sat down at his desk, ritually laying his cane on the pencil trough before him. *Betray your own mother*; yes, she was right, I betrayed, not ten minutes ago, I betrayed. And she hasn't told on me yet, she hasn't said a word. But Tim Heron thinks the worst of me, nonetheless. Oh, I wanted to tell him the truth, I honestly did, but I couldn't. I was afraid.

He bent forward, propping his face in his opened palms. The tight pain in his chest was worse than ever. It was, he decided, a feeling as if he wanted to weep. This would be a nice place to weep, wouldn't it, with twelve boys watching him. He said, in a hoarse whisper:

'*Ode to a Skylark*, was it not?'

'No, sir.' The voices were surprised.

'Oh? Oh, yes, it was *The Lady of Shalott*.'

'No, sir. That's in Junior year, sir,' an insolent back-row voice informed him. He looked at the back row. These are the senior boys, of course. What were we doing in this class yesterday? I could always give them a test or something, except that I have no ruled paper with me. Perhaps I could tell them I am not well and ask them to read something and keep quiet? But no; when he saw their faces, he knew that would never do. These boys were almost ready to shave, their faces ugly with the signs of adolescence. At that age, they were dangerous.

'Very well,' he said. 'Enlighten me, gentlemen.'

'*Julius Caesar*, sir.'

'Thank you, Gray. You have a better memory than your master, so it seems. Stand up now, and let us make sure. Cast your mind back to Act One, Scene One. Now, when Flavius proposed that the images be disrobed, Marullus replied: "May we do so? You know it is the Feast of Lupercal." Now, tell me, Gray, why should that make a difference?'

They had done Act One a fortnight ago. Gray waited for a prompt that never came.

'Stand out, Gray. Next boy?'

206

So the whole school knew; the walls of the jakes were covered again.

'Stand out, Donlan. Next boy?'

You wouldn't hurt a fly, she said, but you'd betray your own mother to avoid . . . She did not tell on me.

'Stand out, McKenna. Next boy?'

The next boy, a seventeen-year-old from Larne, rose in weak truculence. 'Wasn't it because they weren't allowed to disrobe the images because of a religious ban?'

'I'm asking you, not telling you,' Mr Devine said, 'What was the Feast of Lupercal?'

Silence.

'Stand out. Next boy?'

Someone knocked on the classroom door. The next boy hesitated. To the great relief of his pupils, Mr Devine stepped down from his desk and opened the door. In the corridor, his hoar face anxious with news, Old John, the hall porter, waited.

'Mr Devine, sir, wanted to the tellyphone.'

'Oh?' The phone was at the other end of the college, across the annex yard and through the main building. It would take a while to get there. Damned inconvenient: 'Who is it, couldn't they ring back?'

But Old John smiled and nodded, unhearing. 'Yes, sir, the tellyphone.'

'All right, John.'

Mr Devine looked back into his classroom. 'I'll be back in a minute or two,' he said. 'If one boy makes a noise I'll cane the class.'

They received this in silence. He shut the door and followed Old John as the hall porter shuffled across the yard, his arms dangling like weights on either side of his ancient body, as though trying to keep it on an even keel. Mr Devine looked at the classroom windows of the main building, praying to God nobody was looking out. It was no use asking this old doorknob who's on the telephone. You would have to shout too loud. And what was the use in asking? It must be her.

In the porter's lodge, Old John pointed to the telephone dangling on its cord, spinning in a slow circle like bait on a line. As he lifted the receiver Mr Devine heard the porter sit at the table.

'Mr Devine here.'

'Dev. It's Una Clarke.'

It was strange to hear her voice again. She spoke in a whisper, as though she too were afraid of being overheard. 'Did you speak to Uncle Tim this morning? He said he was going to talk to you.'

'Yes, I did.'

'What happened?'

He paused, trying to think of a reply which would not shame him. He had a vision of her, waiting in some back hallway, clutching the phone to her pale cheek, her dark hair untidy, her eyes afraid. What could he tell her that would not be painfully true?

'He talked about telling your mother,' he said.

'And you didn't explain. You didn't say anything at all?'

'Well, Una, I didn't, ah, I couldn't very well . . .'

'All right,' she said coldly. 'I just wanted to make sure. Do you think he's been in touch with my mother yet?'

'No, I'm pretty sure he hasn't,' Mr Devine said feebly. 'He said he was going to, though.'

'When?'

'Well, he's taking classes now. Not before lunchtime at the earliest, I would say.'

'All right. Good-bye, Dev.'

'Wait. Hold on, just – '

But the phone gave back a senseless buzzing sound. He hung up. Old John nodded pleasantly as Mr Devine hurried out of the lodge. He watched the master running down the corridor. He smiled.

Mr Devine, hoping he would not be seen, did not allow

himself to think of what had been said on the telephone. He worried instead about getting back to his class before his absence was noticed. When he arrived, Senior I was still quiet. Twelve boys watched him. Four of them stood out, waiting to be caned. What for? He could not remember. He waved them back to their seats and looked down at the books on his desk. The books were unopened. Where were we?

'Where were we?' he asked.

He saw their astonishment. What did they know, why were they staring? Had they been gossiping while he was at the telephone? One by one, he challenged them, magistral, grave, the stare that said *submit*. But there was something unusual in their eyes. Was it contempt? He looked at one of the oldest boys: the boy stared back. That boy despises me. No, no, it's imagination, look again, look at the others.

His eyes, no longer master, searched each face in turn. Did they know, did they believe the rumours? The cane was no help now. The class was quiet: the quiet of tension.

'We were doing *Caesar*, sir,' one of the boys said.

'Ah, yes. The Lupercalia.' He opened his book and began to read:

'The Feast of Lupercal was a feast of expiation celebrated on the fifteenth of February in honour of Lupercus, the god of fertility. It was remarkable for the number of ancient rituals which were observed. The chief of these was the course of the Luperci, or priests of Lupercus, who, after making their offering, ran from the shrine of the god on the Palatine through the streets of Rome, their only clothing being an apron cut from the skin of the slaughtered animal. They struck all they met with thongs, also cut from the same bloodstained skin. Barren women . . .'

Someone had giggled. Some boy, among the twelve, had stifled a short, obscene chuckle. Which one? He stared at each in turn. All waited, their faces carefully grave. Hoarse, he resumed:

'Barren women placed themselves in the path of the flogging priests, believing that by means of the strokes, the reproach of barrenness would be taken away from them. As a day of atonement . . .'

There it was again. He raised his eyes, but the boys' faces were like twelve putty masks.

'. . . as a day of atonement, this day was named *Dies Februatus.*'

He looked up from his book. 'That question is sometimes asked by the examiners,' he said in a hoarse voice.

But they were not listening. His private life was a dirty joke. They were not listening.

He was no longer master.

By noon, the rain had stopped and a mist drifted off Belfast Lough. Over Ardath College the sky was lurid, as though the day had already exhausted its strength. In the shadows of the handball alley day boys met in furtive groupings to copy exercises that should have been done the night before. Dinner in the refectory was bread and Irish stew for the boarders. The staff ate chicken *rissoles* and Brussels sprouts. At the far end of Big Field, a master walked alone on the touchline, slowly approaching the Gaelic football goal posts where two bullies played at goal with a smaller boy's lunch as catch. They tossed the lunch package, running and throwing, ignoring the small boy's frantic circlings, his treble appeals for *pax*. As the master drew nearer, the bullies fled, dropping the parcel in a puddle. The small boy, near tears, retrieved his lunch but discovered it ruined. The master paid no attention. He walked by, his eyes on the fading whitewash of the touchline.

He did not notice. He had come out here because on a wet day nobody in their senses would walk in Big Field: nobody would soak shoes in the muddy grass. He did not want to see or be seen: dirty rhymes were up again, dirty gossip went the rounds. A master who had human failings was a master to be mocked. Even now, the President and Tim Heron were probably in conclave. But what could they do, as long as Una kept quiet? Nothing. And if he stuck to his story, there was no evidence to disprove it. Dr Keogh always took the easy way out. He could not sack a master on a rumour, an unfounded rumour. No, it will all blow over, he told himself. It will all blow over. At Christmas break he would go on a walking trip in Wicklow, he would walk it out of his system. And in the meantime, he would keep busy, helping Kevin Cooke with the festival entry.

At the edge of the boundary line, he stopped and looked over at the grey stone façade of Priests' House. At this moment, in the President's study, his case might be under discussion. Heron will tell them the girl is going back to Dublin.

Do I have to get down on my knees to you? she had asked.

He no longer cared. The painful grief had left him. Instead, he felt lucid and weak, as though he had drunk too much and had purged himself by vomiting. He walked back the way he had come, raising his pale face to stare at the sky. Far away, a grey laurel of cloud drifted into the bald brow of Cave Hill. He felt detatched from his fate: it was happening to someone else, to a young and foolish man he once knew. He remembered that man as a boy, a boy who often took Sunday walks over Cave Hill and stared down at Belfast from the sheer drop of McArt's Fort. A boy who dreamed of marrying Madeleine Carroll, the film actress, and taking her to the Riviera where they would commit unknown flesh sins the priests warned against in sermons. Was it any wonder that boy, now a man of thirty-seven, was in trouble today? He had not lived a real life: he had been dreaming.

The grey cloud thickened and Cave Hill was cut in two. Every dreamer must one day wake. Until a few days ago, he had thought well of himself. Of course, there had been moments, moments that must come to everyone, when heaven and hell are only words without meaning, matched against the fact of the breathing stopped, the heart stilled. He had avoided those moments, he had put dreams to work when they came to frighten him. One of those dreams was that he had not yet been tried, but that, if tried, he would not be found wanting in the needs of this world. Love and loyalty. A week ago, he would have said he was capable of both. They were only words, last week. But now he had failed in both. Why did I even fail to sin? he asked himself. To fail to sin, perhaps that is my sin.

But that was also an illusion, a way out. That was avoiding reality once again. Keeping quiet, being afraid to own up, that was the real sin. If he kept quiet, no one would know, no one but Una. One day she might marry and tell her husband, some Protestant like herself. Protestants had an easy attitude to things like that. If I had been a Protestant, this would never have happened, he thought. I would have had my fill of girls by now, I would never have had to worry about going to confession. Confession is no help to people like me, people who hate to tell their sins to anyone, even to a priest in the dark. We are the ones who fear that sacrament, who get no comfort from its absolution. And yet, I suppose I will have to tell all this, some day. Bless me, Father, for I have sinned. And he will say: 'Promise me that you will not commit that sin again, my son.' Father, I may never be able to. And it is true. How can I try again with another girl, how can I try without remembering Una and worrying that I will fail a second time? So do not worry about that sin, Father. Tried it once and didn't like it.

He paused and turned to stare at the grey stone face of Priests' House, at the shaded trees of Priests' Walk, running in a double row all the way to the main building at the other end of the playing fields. The rotten echo of the bad joke lingered. Was this the meaning of failure: were all failed lovers false cynics? He had often heard that pig-talk in bars, man-to-man jokes about women the boasters had slept with.

Were all those boasters cowards like himself, were all the dirty jokes frightened window-dressing to hide the limp truth? Was he one of many, one of a secret army, one of thousands of secret flops?

A man was hurrying along Priests' Walk, his body moving jerkily behind the imperfect screen offered by the row of tres, his torn gown, like broken black wings, trailing his footsteps. Tim Heron! He must be going to Priests' House. He must be on his way to see the President.

Involuntarily, Mr Devine began to run across the wet football field, swerving like a centre-forward in an effort to cut across Tim's path.

'Tim!' he shouted. 'Tim!'

In the path between the trees, Tim Heron pulled up short like a horse that meets an unexpected ditch. He peered between the tree trunks , watching the runner in Big Field. And the runner, coming closer, was alarmed. The familiar, angry conspiratorial manner was gone, the fierce blue eyes were clouded and tired. Standing there, waiting patiently underneath the dripping branches, Tim Heron seemed done, defeated, lost.

'Is it you?' he asked.

Mr Devine stopped on the path, his hand pressed against the painful stitch in his side. 'Tim, I want a word with you.'

'Yes.'

'Are you going to see the President? Did he send for you?'

'He did. I just got the message.'

'You've been home then. Did you see Una?'

Tim Heron looked at him with dislike. 'What business is it of yours?'

'Did you tell her you were sending for her mother?'

'Not yet.'

'Look Tim, I want to talk to you. I want to explain something.'

Tim Heron drew back, his mouth set in a sneer as though

Mr Devine were an offensive beggar. 'What is it?' he said. 'I'm in a hurry.'

But Mr Devine ignored the snub. He put his hand on Heron's shoulder and walked him in the opposite direction from the Priests' House, glancing from side to side as though he expected an enemy to spring out from the trees which flanked the path. When he spoke, his voice was a confessional whisper.

'I, ah, won't keep you long, Tim. But I have to tell you, ah, a very difficult thing. Now, promise me, you'll not interrupt until I finish. Then you can say or do what you wish. Will you promise that?'

'All right.' The whisper, the solitude, the secrecy: all of it appealed to the conspirator in Heron. He too looked around to make sure they were alone, and then, satisfied, he walked on, his eyes on the ground. He could sense Devine's nervousness. It was better not to look at him. Let him tell his story his own way.

'Tim, I didn't tell you the truth before. I – ah – I'm very fond of Una, she's a marvellous girl, Tim. You see, I'm in love with her, I'm not ashamed to say it.'

'Are you now?' Tim Heron used his classroom tone. 'You were ashamed an hour ago, it seems to me.'

'Wait, Tim, you promised to hear me out.'

'Get to the point then, Devine. The President is expecting me.'

'Yes, Tim, I'm sorry. But Tim, you see – ' Suddenly, Mr Devine pulled at the older man's arm, twisting him around. His mournful face was pale and anxious, his eyes were dilated behind his spectacles. 'You see, Una *was* at my place the other night.'

'Ahh!' Tim Heron grunted the word out, as though he had been punched in the stomach.

'Now wait, Tim. Wait! It was my fault she stayed. *My fault.* I persuaded her to come in for a minute. And then I gave her drinks, Tim. I made her squiffy.'

He paused, watching the rage take possession of Heron's face, watching the sudden blinking of Heron's eye, the trembling of his hands. 'Do you follow me, Tim?' he said. 'I had no good in my mind. But nothing happened, Tim, as God's my witness. Nothing happened!'

'Hah!' Tim Heron grunted.

'You don't believe me, Tim, I know. But there are two reasons nothing happened – two reasons. When you hear them, you'll believe me, Tim.'

'They'd better be bloody wonderful!'

'Listen, Tim. The first one is that Una is a virgin. Do you hear me, Tim? A virgin. She told me so herself.'

But Heron gave a laugh like a cockcrow. 'A virgin!' His thin lips pursed in contempt. 'What virgin did you ever hear of would let herself get drunk in a man's digs at that time of night?'

'Now wait, I'm going to explain that. You see, I wouldn't let her go. I detained her against her will. I made advances. And do you know, she wept, Tim. She! She told me she had never, on her word of honour.'

'Keep your voice down, man,' Heron muttered. 'No need to shout.'

'I'm sorry, Tim. Now listen. Listen!' Mr Devine stopped speaking, his face contorted as though he were fighting a desire to sneeze. But it was not a sneeze. Behind his glasses, his eyes blurred. 'Do you believe me?' he asked in a high, nervous shout.

'Who'd be daft enough to believe you?' Heron said. 'You admit you got her stocious drunk. How do I know what you did after that? A liar like you makes his story fit the occasion.'

'But – ' The tears were quite visible now although Mr Devine did not seem to notice them. 'Here's why you can believe me,' he cried. 'Because I'm a virgin myself! So help me God it was the first time I ever tried.'

'That's the best yet. Who do you think you're codding, Devine?'

'I'm not codding! And do you know the reason why? Because when I did want to do it, I couldn't. I couldn't! I hadn't got the feeling in me!'

'How far did you get?' Tim Heron asked coarsely.

'I, ah, I had no feeling. I couldn't do it, don't you understand?'

'How far did you get?'

'I just kissed her and then she said she had never done it in her life. But even before then, I knew I couldn't do it. I am not normal, Tim, I had no feelings, I didn't want to do it.'

'But you did try, then? You don't make sense, man.'

'I wanted to know, don't you see? I wanted to know if I could!'

'So you picked my niece to try it on. By Christ, you have a nerve, telling me the like of this.'

'But that's why I'm telling you! Because you've got to believe me. She's a good girl, Una. A good girl.'

'Good girl, my flaming foot! Why did she stay the night then?'

'I wouldn't let her out of the house, Tim. I begged her to stay. And she was afraid of me, I talked and talked, and finally she fell asleep in my den. I let her sleep.'

'So she slept in your den, did she? And what were you doing while she slept?'

'Worrying,' Mr Devine said. 'Worrying about myself and about the fact that I'm not normal.'

Despite his anger, this last honesty seemed to embarrass Tim Heron. He looked away at the line of trees. 'Why didn't Una tell me, then?' he asked.

'For my sake. She was ashamed for my sake. I suppose she was sorry for me.'

'Sorry for you!' Heron's face reddened as though he had trouble breathing. 'I'll sorry ye, you useless snivelling liar, you – '

'Wait, Tim, wait. I wanted her to marry me, do you see? She turned me down. But I meant it honourably, Tim!'

'Good Christ!'

'I'm telling you now because, Tim, you mustn't tell her mother. You mustn't send Una home; you can let her stay here and do her nursing. I won't see her again. You mustn't worry her mother, do you see?'

'Too late,' Heron said, harshly. 'I rang my sister an hour ago.'

'Oh, no, you must ring her up and tell her it was a mistake. A mistake. I only told you this to stop you doing that.'

'Bloody useless coward that you are!' Heron shouted. 'You're too late, Devine, too late! The damage is done! Peg'll not leave her with us now, after the worry we've caused her. Oh, somebody should shoot the likes of you, rotten filth that you are!'

He was choking in the effort of speech, his eyes blinking in uncontrollable fury. As though by instinct, he fumbled in the armhole of his ragged gown and drew out his long cane. He advanced, mouth working soundlessly, swinging the cane in a wide arc. It slashed across Devine's cheek and his glasses fell in tiny fragments on the path. Blinded, he knelt to grope for them, presenting to Heron's frenzy his long back in abject posture. Again Heron raised the cane striking the kneeling figure in his path. Forehead to the ground, hands covering his bruised face, the victim uttered no cry. The only sound in that quiet walk was the whistling of the cane, the dull drumbeat of repeated blows, the harsh tearing breath of the punisher. Again and again, Heron struck, cutting on neck, shoulders, thighs.

A priest ran up the path, the skirts of his soutane clutched up to free his black trouser-legs. His heavy boots sent gravel flying as he ran.

'Stop! Stop!'

But Heron could not stop. He scythed again and again, hitting with thick persistence.

The priest was on them now. His arm shot out and

217

dragged the older man's wrist in an arc, twisting the cane from his grasp. Confused, his face dulled with the lust of punishment, Heron staggered to the edge of the path and sat down drunkenly on the grass. The cane lay abandoned on the gravel.

Father Creely bent down and dragged Mr Devine to his feet.

'Get up! Get up!' he said in a shocked whisper. 'What if the boys see?'

He circled slowly, scanning the walk, the playing fields beyond. There was no one in sight. He ran in among the trees and emerged again, satisfied.

'It's a wonder,' he said. 'A wonder! The whole college might have been watching. We saw you from the windows up there.'

He pointed at Priests' House. Heron, sitting on the grass, stared dully upwards. At a window, far above, two white faces were flat against the pane. One was the President. Blinded and in pain, Mr Devine did not see. His cheek was swollen by a large red and white weal, his ear was cut and bleeding. He fumbled for a handkerchief and wiped his face.

'Come on, now,' Father Creely said. 'The President wants both of you, at once.'

He took Devine's arm and turned him around in the path. His other arm hooked into Heron's. Like a policeman making a double arrest, he led them down the path and up the steps of Priests' House. He hurried them up the main staircase. In the corridor above, the President was waiting, small, untidy, alarmed.

'I will see Mr Heron first,' he said. 'Father, will you take Mr Devine to your room and wash his face? I'll send for him shortly.'

The green baize door was open. Dejected, his thin grey hair falling over his face, his rent gown awry on his shoulders, Mr Heron allowed the President to lead him inside. The green door shut on him with a soft thud.

'This way,' Father Creely said. 'And hurry, please.'

At the corridor stairs they paused while Father Creely made sure the coast was clear. Then Father Creely led him up the stairs and into a large room. He was told to sit on a black iron bedstead covered with a white counterpane. A moment later he heard water running from a basin tap.

'Here. Put that on your cheek, it may reduce the swelling.'

A cold damp cloth stung the cut cheek. A pulse in his swollen ear beat steady as a metronome.

'Do you have another pair of glasses?' Father Creely's voice asked.

'Only at home.'

'Would your landlady know where to find them?'

'Yes, I think so.'

'I'll send one of the day boys on a bicycle. Wait a minute.'

The door shut and he was alone. He stood up and walked uncertainly towards the washbasin. By peering closely in the mirror, he brought his face in dim focus. The weal over his cheek ran from ear to nose. The white ridge, surrounded by red inflamed skin, was familiar. It was like many a cane blow he had given his pupils. He swabbed at his bleeding ear. The water made it bleed still more. His collar was flecked with blood.

He groped his way to a chair which stood by a kitchen table on which Father Creely's exercise corrections lay. There were pictures on the wall of an old man and woman. Parents of the priest? An oleograph of the Sistine Madonna smiled from over the bed. He closed his eyes, bending forward, rocking himself with the pain. The soft flesh at his ribs was swollen and raw. Caned. No one saw except us, Father Creely said. And Heron is with the President now. Explaining himself. Excusing himself. Telling the whole story.

He peered at the Blessed Virgin on the wall. He had never been in a priest's quarters before. Our Blessed Mother

219

watched the bed on which Father Creeely slept. He thought of another mother who had been told bad news that morning, a mother who was coming to take her daughter back. I told for nothing: the harm was done.

There was a noise at the door. Father Creely's soutane swam into focus. Tiny buttons glazed and worn, black male boots beneath the black skirt.

'Feeling better now? I sent a boy. He should be back with your glasses in half an hour.'

'Thanks.'

The skirt moved away. He focused on the floor, with its worn patterned carpet. He heard the priest sit down on the bed.

'What on earth happened, Devine? Did you both take leave of your senses?'

'It was my fault,' Mr Devine said.

'Well, if he had justification . . . In any case, you both jeopardized your position here. Imagine if you had been seen!'

Mr Devine pressed the wet handkerchief against his cut cheek. The blood had congealed on his ear. He touched the earlobe with a finger. It pained. He heard the priest cough.

'You'll pardon my asking, but had this to do with Heron's niece?'

'Yes.'

'I thought so. There's a shocking story circulating among the boys. Shocking!

Mr Devine closed his eyes. Sour vomit rose and was repelled. They knew, they all knew, the priests, the boys, everybody. Tim Heron was discussing it with Dr Keogh now. It was all over the school. He could never hope to stay here after this. Never.

Father Creely was speaking: ' . . . heard it myself some days ago, didn't believe any of it, of course, but now, in view of this, I see no alternative. Does irreparable harm.'

'Yes. I know.'

The priest coughed again. His disapproval made the silence ominous. Clearly, he expected the very worst from all this.

After a while, someone knocked on the door. Father Creely went into the corridor. The newcomer sounded like Father McSwiney. He and Father Creely were very thick, Mr Devine remembered. He listened as the Dean's footsteps retreated. Father Creely returned and sat on the bed. 'Dr Keogh is taking a long time,' he said. 'We'll all be late for class.'

You will, Mr Devine thought. No more class for me. He nursed his pains as the footsteps returned. The Dean entered the room. He looked at Mr Devine and then said to Father Creely:

'He'll see him now. Wants me too.'

'To arrange the redivision of labour, no doubt,' Father Creely said. 'Class schedules will need juggling.'

'Aye. Take Devine's class down to the study hall, will you, Father? Give them something to keep them busy. I'll let you know what transpires as soon as we're finished.'

'Right you are, Father.'

The Dean put his hand on Mr Devine's shoulder.

'Come on,' he said. 'Dr Keogh is ready for you.'

Chapter Fifteen

The strong lamp above the President's desk dropped its yellow circle in the centre of the room, leaving the rest in an outer darkness of weak daylight. From the doorway, Mr Devine could distinguish the top of a grey stubbed skull moving behind a barricade of papers and books. Then as he advanced into the lamplight, one of the paper piles was removed and, through the aperture this afforded, Dr Keogh peered out with the anxious air of a small man on the fringes of a crowd.

'*Harmp*! Sit down, won't you? Here.'

An empty chair faced the presidential desk and as he spoke the President's index finger jabbed downward, willing Mr Devine into it. It was placed on the edge of the lamplight circle and, when he sat, Mr Devine was blinded by the glare. He blinked and looked at the carpet. Two long black legs grew from a nearby armchair as Father McSwiney settled himself. Tim Heron, also studying the carpet, sat on the President's left.

'*Harmp*! *Harmp*!' the President said, false-clearing his throat, calling the court to order. 'I have asked Father McSwiney to be present, gentlemen. I hope there are no objections.'

No one said anything, but Mr Devine, his face paining, his ear throbbing, had the impression all three men were staring at him. He joined his hands in his lap and tried to focus on the initials of his father's signet ring.

'*Harmp*! I have already listened to Mr Heron's account of this unfortunate affair. What occurred today is deplorable. Deplorable! It's a wonder the pair of you were not seen by the entire school.'

'Disgraceful,' the Dean said.

'Unfortunately, it is not just a private dispute between two masters,' the President said. 'It concerns us all.'

'Indeed,' the Dean said.

The President leaned back in his chair. He placed his fingertips together as though he were about to pray. He raised his praying hands and used their jointed index fingers to push his steel spectacles up the incline of his beaked nose. The significance of this gesture was not wasted on his audience, for it was his favourite pulpit preparation. The President was about to announce his text.

'Woe to the scandal giver,' he said. '*Harmp!*'

He tilted his head upward, his beaked nose sniffing the warm lamplight. 'The purity of young souls has been endangered,' he said. 'Scandal – woe to the scandal giver! Better that a millstone be tied around . . . and so forth. *Harmp!*'

Mr Devine, his eyes narrowed in an effort to focus on the President's face, drew back as though the angry blows had recommenced. It was not in Dr Keogh's nature to discuss any misdemeanour without blood-and-thundering his way up to it. First the sermon; then the punishment. But as he bent his head, paining and ashamed, Mr Devine heard the Dean's feet shuffle uneasily, close by. Father McSwiney was no man for sermons. He believed in results.

'Quite so, Doctor,' he said. 'Something must be done about it.'

'*Harmp!*' The President's large head turned in the Dean's direction. 'Very well, Father. Let us return to the beginnings of this disgraceful affair. To a day last week when a junior boy overheard a conversation between these two gentlemen.'

Mr Devine, his eyes shut against the bright lamplight, sensed the startled glances of both the Dean and Tim Heron. *What conversation was the President referring to?*

'Apparently, Mr Heron did not wish to have his niece

223

take part in a theatrical performance, arranged, I believe, on your behalf, Father McSwiney.'

The Dean said: 'Yes, I remember. At the time, I did not bring it to your attention, Dr Keogh. It was a minor matter.'

'*Harmp*! Troubles of this kind are like venial sins, Father. If not corrected, they lead to graver sins.'

The Dean's voice was hostile. 'I hardly thought that the play was a school affair.'

'You punished this boy and two others for gossiping about the matter, did you not?'

'Yes.'

'Then it was "a school affair", as you call it. Have you heard the rumours which have been circulating in the past few days, Father McSwiney?'

'Yes, I heard something about them.'

'I see. No doubt you did not feel it worth mentioning? A minor matter.'

Mr Devine, his head bent, his eyes shut, heard the Dean's cold voice: 'Excuse me, Dr Keogh, but I did not consider it a minor matter. I was investigating these rumours. I did not want to accuse anyone unjustly.'

'Very sound, Father, very sound. However, I do not think Mr Devine has been unjustly accused of an interest in Mr Heron's niece. You were fond of the young lady in question, were you not, Devine?'

The dropped 'Mr' was ominous. The inquisition had begun. Mr Devine raised his bruised face to the glaring light. By narrowing his eyes, he was able to outline the steel and stubble blur of Dr Keogh's face. Why didn't they sack him and be done with it? Why should he be lectured like a first-year boarder?

'Well, Devine. Were you fond of this young lady?'

'Yes.'

'And two nights ago you went – *harmp*! – dancing with her. Is that correct?'

'Yes.'

'She did not return to Mr Heron's house until seven o'clock in the morning. She was unable to account for her movements the night before. Mr Heron, her guardian for the period of her stay in this city, was naturally upset. When he asked you for an explanation, you denied any knowledge of her whereabouts.'

Mr Devine blinked rapidly. When he opened his mouth to speak, he was astonished at the angry shouted tone of his reply. 'What's the use of asking me, Doctor, since you know already?'

'Will you please answer my question, Devine?'

'Yes.'

'And later – today, in fact – you confessed to Mr Heron that you had not been telling the truth. That you had spent the night in question in the company of his niece.'

'Yes.'

The President's spectacles flashed as he swivelled in the Dean's direction. 'Singular confession, wouldn't you agree, Father McSwiney? Under the circumstances, Mr Heron is scarcely to be blamed for reacting with some display of wrath.'

'I wouldn't blame Tim at all,' the Dean said. 'Only he should have thought of the effect he'd create if he was seen whacking Devine in public. It would make anyone believe the worst of these rumours. And they do seem true, I'm sorry to say.'

'Quite so, Father. Now, our concern with all this is the possible damage it may do to the college and to the morals of the student body. That damage has already started. This morning, I received two telephone calls from offended parents. There will be more. Do you know what one mother said to me?'

'So the parents have got wind of it already?' the Dean asked in a shocked undertone.

'Indeed. This parent went so far as to refer to Devine as a "whited sepulchre".'

'Apt,' the Dean said. 'Too apt.'

Without premeditation, Mr Devine found himself standing. From the empty chamber of his skull he heard his voice echo out.

'I don't have to stand for that, Dr Keogh. Give me the sack, if you want, but dammit, I'm not standing – '

'Sit down then, Devine,' the President said. 'I have not finished yet.'

'You're not hearing my confession,' Mr Devine cried. 'I'm not on trial here.'

'Sit down!' the Dean shouted. 'Sit down when you're told!'

'I won't sit down,' Mr Devine said. He turned, his eyes unsteadily focusing their hatred on the white blur that was the Dean's face. He could feel their shock; his enemies sat silent, staring at him.

At that moment, an explosion (quarrying? target practice?) rumbled over the slopes of Cave Hill, shook Priests' House and echoed across the playing fields to boom hollowly in the city below. It was as though heaven had thundered at his impudence. In one moment of defiance he had negated the years of obedience and respect. But the cuts were painful on his face; the echo of angry clerical voices still sounded in his ears; he remembered who he was, where he was, and why he was here.

He repeated, in a nervous half-shout: 'Dammit, I will not sit down, Dr Keogh. I'm a grown man, I will not be treated like a schoolboy. This is my private life you are discussing.'

'Precisely,' the President said. 'You are not on trial. Therefore, I would be obliged if you would accord me a minimum of politeness.'

'I won't answer any more questions.'

'You seem to feel that I have offended you, Devine. If that is so, I apologize.'

The Dean and Tim Heron stared at the President.

Apologize to Devine? After the shocking disrespect he showed for a priest? Was the old fellow really going gaga?

'I apologize,' the President repeated. 'I merely wanted to point out the danger to all of us in these rumours. Now, if you please answer one more question, Devine?'

'No, Dr Keogh. This is my private life. My *private* life, do you hear?'

The President leaned forward, ignoring the Dean's triumphant look. He stared at Mr Devine, and when he spoke his voice was gentle. 'For Miss Clarke's sake,' he said, 'I would like you to assure me that the story you told Mr Heron earlier is true.'

'Yes, it's true. Do you think I'd tell him that – do you think I *liked* telling him that?'

'One moment, Mr Devine! Nothing immoral occurred the other night, then?'

'Nothing.'

'I believe you,' the President said. 'And for the girl's sake, as well as yours, I am very glad to hear it.'

'Now, just a moment, Dr Keogh – ' the Dean's flat, angry voice broke in. 'You don't mean to tell us you're going to accept *Devine's* version of this affair?'

'Mr Heron's version, Father. You must remember we are discussing Mr Heron's niece.'

'Who's no better than she should be, if what we hear is true,' the Dean said. 'Not even a Catholic.'

'Charity, Father, charity. I think you should apologize to Mr Heron for that last remark.'

'He told me so himself,' the Dean snapped.

'Oh, come, come, Father, I'm sure Mr Heron has nothing but the highest regard for his niece. Is that not so, Mr Heron?'

Heron, who had not said a word all this time, raised his head and answered in a quavering voice. 'She's a good girl. Yes, I was unjust, very unjust.'

'Since when has everybody changed their minds?' the Dean asked angrily. 'What's going on here?'

'Sit down, Father McSwiney, please. May I remind you that this is not a debating society?'

'Well, I just want to see some regard for the truth. I mean – ' The Dean fumbled his sentence, stopping, his large white face a study in frustration.

'Sit down, Father. And Mr Devine, won't you sit down too? You don't look at all well.'

Ear pulsing, cheek burning, eyes weary from the strain of focusing, Mr Devine groped for the chair behind him and sat down once more. He had thrown himself off the cliff; but by some miracle, he was still hanging to a rock on the cliff face. The President was that rock. He had ignored the insults. You could not very well strike an old man who turned the other cheek.

'Mr Heron's niece is the unfortunate victim of malicious, filthy gossip,' the President said. 'So, in large measure, is Mr Devine.'

'He was out all night with her!' the Dean shouted. 'Now look here, Doctor, this girl was carrying on with a married man before she came to Belfast! There's no gossip in that, for Heron told me so himself. I think we're being far too charitable.'

'*Harmp*! Nothing immoral occurred, Father. Although I might add that Mr Heron has wisely decided to send his niece back to Dublin.'

'But it's scandalous, believing the likes of Devine!' the Dean cried. 'A man who insulted your cloth not five minutes ago!'

'Very well, Father,' the President said quietly. 'What would you advise, since you seem so eager to advise me?'

The flat, angry voice replied: 'I would accept Devine's resignation at once.'

'Why, Father?'

'Because a man like that should not be allowed to teach in

a Catholic college. A proven liar, and in my opinion, a possible moral degenerate as well. He stayed out all night with that girl, didn't he?'

'I see. Now, let me ask you a further question, Father. What will we achieve by dismissing Devine?'

'We would clear ourselves of the suspicion that we tolerated vice here.'

'*Harmp*! You are doubtless aware that dismissing Devine is an admission that these rumours are true. That one of our masters is guilty of immoral conduct?'

'All men are human,' the Dean said. 'But that's no reason to show we tolerate it.'

'An interesting point, Father. All men are human. Quite so. Now – '

The President rubbed his stubbled chin and looked at Mr Devine. 'Do you wish to resign?' he asked.

Mr Devine jerked his head back as though menaced by a blow. His eyes, strangely naked without their accustomed glasses, peered uncertainly into the lamplit glare. He felt weak and at their mercy now. But he would not beg. He said, in a hoarse whisper.

'If you wish it, you will have my resignation this afternoon.'

'One moment, Mr Devine. I did not ask for your resignation. I asked if you wished to resign. Are you unwilling to remain here?'

'Do what you want!' Mr Devine heard his own voice scream. 'I'm not going to discuss my private affairs, do you hear? I have been treated like a schoolboy. A schoolboy!'

The President held up his inky hand. 'Mr Devine, wait! I asked if you *wanted* to resign?'

'I have been ten years here, Dr Keogh. Ten years a teacher. Surely that entitles me to a little consideration?'

'Mr Devine, I take it, then that you do not wish to resign. And I have no intention of accepting your resignation. Is that clear?'

The Dean, outraged by this leniency, forgot himself once more. 'You mean you're going to do nothing, Doctor?'

'No, Father. These rumours have not been proved. They are dangerous slanders and it is our duty to put an end to them. It is our word against lavatory gossip.'

He paused, his large head moving in a slow arc, looking at each of his hearers in turn. 'Truth will cast out error, is that not so?'

The Dean crossed his legs. 'If it *is* the truth.'

'Precisely. I have the word of two good Catholic laymen against the gossip of irresponsible schoolboys. I am satisfied. And furthermore, Father McSwiney, there is a simple way to refute these rumours. They arose because of conversations between Heron and Devine. If the rumours were true, these gentlemen would be bitter enemies. They are not true. And the way to prove that is to show these gentlemen are not enemies.

'Not enemies,' he repeated. 'And neither shall they be, from now on. If they are seen together often, if they are frequently engaged in friendly conversation, who would believe that they are other than old friends? And if we are asked about this rumour, what better proof do we have that it is false? Propaganda, Father, propaganda. You, at least, should know where that word originated. Now, Heron – Devine – will you promise me that you will be friends?'

Neither man spoke.

'You must undo the harm that your joint lack of discretion has wrought among the students. Now, Heron, do I have your word?'

'Well, I suppose, for the good of the school . . .'

'Suppose nothing!' The President's voice was shocking in its unexpected truculence. 'It's for your own protection, Heron, and for the protection of your niece. Now – promise!'

'Yes, Doctor.'

'And you, Devine?'

'Yes, Doctor.'

'I shall hold you to it, remember. If we present an appearance of perfect amity, we can give the lie to these untruths. We can ignore them, as they deserve to be ignored.'

'Excuse me, Dr Keogh,' the Dean said, a new accent of triumph evident in his voice. 'You've forgotten that three boys actually heard these two men quarrelling. Not to speak of the class that heard them the other day when they talked in the corridor.'

'Exactly. You took it upon yourself to correct those three boys?'

'Yes.'

'Well, since you did not consider the matter important enough to need my consideration at the time, I fail to see why you raise it now. Those boys are your responsibility, Father McSwiney. I trust that your efforts to keep them discreet will be successful.'

The Dean, with the air of a man goaded beyond all reason, said: 'The Board of Governors might not agree with this laxity on our part. They might hear of it too.' His tone clearly implied that he would make sure they did.

'*Harmp*! Glad you mentioned that, Father. The responsibility is entirely mine. Staff discipline is not, I believe, within your province. I mentioned that to Monsignor Sullivan last night when we were discussing this affair. Apparently, you have already taken it upon *yourself* to discuss this matter with the Monsignor – although you say it is a "minor matter"?'

'Well, yes, I mentioned it, *en passant*.'

'You did indeed. However, the Monsignor and I agreed that this affair must be dealt with discreetly. We feel, and the Board does too, that in these times almost any inconvenience is preferable to losing valuable – I might almost say irreplaceable – staff. You see my point, Father?'

It was evident that the Dean, finally, did. He leaned

forward in his armchair, chin in hand, in the attitude of Rodin's *Penseur*.

'*Harmp!*' The President fumbled in the frayed pocket of his soutane and produced a cheap nickel watch. 'We are all late for classes, I fear. Mr Devine, you had better take the afternoon off. I trust that your wounds will be healed sufficiently to enable you to resume your duties tomorrow morning. I have ordered a taxicab to take you to your lodgings. I believe your spare spectacles have been sent for.'

'Well . . . I . . . ah . . . thank you,' Mr Devine mumbled.

'Not at all. You and Mr Heron should make a point of going home together after school, for the next few days. And be seen chatting between classes. Be seen together, in short. That will be all the thanks I require. Yes, if you follow instructions, it will all blow over.'

He stood up. His hand, ink stained, impersonal, was offered in turn to Mr Devine and to Mr Heron. Then, kicking the ragged hem of his soutane behind him like a bridal train, he linked arms with the Dean, ushering him to the door. There he paused, staring up at the larger man, his mouth forming a small rictus of derision.

'Off you go now, Father,' he said. 'And thank you for your very kind assistance. Your class is waiting.'

Chapter Sixteen

It will all blow over, the President said. Even though he'd shouted at the President, the President had not dismissed him. Even though he'd admitted he spent all night with a girl, the President had taken his word that nothing immoral occurred. His classes would be waiting as usual, tomorrow morning. It was a relief, in a way. But it was also disappointing. After all, for once in his life he had spoken up; for once he had told the lot of them where they got off. He hadn't minced words, either. But they sent him home in a taxi and paid the fare. It will all blow over, the President said.

Mrs Dempsey had been very discreet; she had not asked questions. She sent him down a cup of tea and found some elastoplast for the cut on his ear. The swelling on his cheek was subsiding.

He felt humiliated.

His private life was public now, it was known to several. Old Heron was not discreet, Heron would tell people, it was the sort of story people liked to whisper and joke about.

He would never live it down. He had not even been allowed to disgrace himself, to run off to Australia or Canada or some place, and never be heard of again, a man to be gossiped about, a man who ruined himself. No, he had promised the President he would not resign. He must ignore the whispers and the smiles: he must even pretend to be friends with that lunatic, Tim Heron.

'Mr Devine?'

He started forward in the chair, his hands gripping his knees. In the doorway, Mrs Dempsey's Annie divided her stare impersonally between him and the nearby wall.

'Are you hurt, or somethin'?'

'I fell,' he said. 'What is it?'

'There's a young lady upstairs to see you. Mama put her in the parlour.'

'Who, who?'

'A Miss Clarke, she says her name is.'

'Oh, I'll be up in a moment.'

He went into his bedroom, straightened his tie and wondered if the cut cheek made him uglier. And remembered that it did not matter any more. Not with her. Not with any girl, he thought. I am no longer in the lists. He went upstairs. Mrs Dempsey was sitting at the kitchen table.

'I lit the gas fire in the parlour,' she said. 'I thought it would be nicer in the parlour.'

'Thank you.'

'You're welcome any time you want to use it for a visitor, you know.'

He stared at her. 'That young lady is shortly taking up nursing,' he said.

'Oh, is that so?'

'And she will not be visiting me any more,' he added. 'Not any more.'

Mrs Dempsey watched him cross the kitchen and go into the dark tunnel of the back hall. Why didn't he tell me sooner, she thought, why didn't he tell me he was finished with her? Well, in that case . . . a permanent boarder . . . wouldn't I be daft to lose him? For a moment, she thought of calling him back at once, of telling him that she would not be needing his room after all, of asking him to stay. But he was going to see that girl. Later, she decided. Later. When the girl leaves, I can go into the parlour and turn the gas fire off. I can catch him before he goes back downstairs.

His footsteps were slow as he approached the parlour. He knew why the gas fire had been lit, why the parlour had been offered. Sin must not be given a second chance. But why had Una rung Mrs Dempsey's doorbell instead of his?

Why, for that matter, had she come at all? He paused for a moment before entering the room.

She was standing in front of the gas fire, her shoulders touching the edge of Mrs Dempsey's mantelpiece, her tweed coat faintly steaming as the heat rose to meet its damp surface. She looked as if she had been crying, earlier. She was smoking a cigarette.

'My goodness, Dev, what happened to you? Were you in a fight?'

'In a way.'

'What about?' She came forward as if she would comfort him. 'Uncle Tim came home half an hour ago. He says you told him everything. I wanted to thank you, Dev.'

'That's all right.'

'Sit down,' she said. 'You look awful. You didn't have a fight with Uncle Tim, did you?'

'In a way.'

'But he doesn't look – ' she began. 'Did he hit you – or something?'

'He caned me,' Mr Devine said.

'Oh, no! Why on earth did you let him?'

He made a small useless movement of his hands. He sat down on Mrs Dempsey's flowered sofa and stared at the gas fire.

'What will happen about your mother?' he asked.

'That's what I wanted to tell you about,' she said, sitting down beside him. 'We had a council of war this afternoon and then we phoned Mummy back – at least Aunt Maeve did – and then I spoke to her too. We managed to calm her down, thanks to your efforts with Uncle Tim. She's still upset, of course, but at least she's promised not to come down to Belfast.'

'That's good.'

'But I'm going home,' she said. 'That's one reason Mummy agreed not to come. Don't feel badly about it, Dev; it's just as well I go.'

'But your nursing . . .'

She smiled at him. 'Never mind. I'm going to have a long chat with Mummy when I get back to Dublin. I think I can persuade her to let me go to London to train. We have cousins there, on my father's side. So, it won't be so bad. As a matter of fact, London should be very exciting, I think.'

She stood up, walked to the grate and flicked some ash in it. 'So in a way, it's been a good thing, all this,' she continued. 'Again, I don't know how to thank you for telling Uncle Tim what you did. I know how hard it must have been for you. But imagine him hitting you with a cane! Who does he think he is?'

'A schoolmaster,' Mr Devine said.

'But that's no excuse!'

He stared at the gas fire. He said, in a low voice: 'It's a form of expiation, I suppose. Funny thing – we were reading about it in class today.'

She came over to him quickly. She sat down on Mrs Dempsey's green-and-gold-flowered sofa beside him. 'Expiation?' she asked. 'What do you mean?'

'Nothing. A joke.' He turned from his scrutiny of the fire, the pallor of his face accentuated by the livid weal across his cheek. She saw him fiddle with his ring, a nervous trick she had noticed before.

Then he said: 'I'm going to miss you, you know.'

'Are you, Dev?'

'Yes. I, ah, I don't think I'll ever forget you.'

It was hard to know what to say to him: he was so hopeless – and yet . . . She tried to cover her embarrassment by making light of it. 'Oh, well, London isn't the end of the earth. We'll probably bump into each other sometime.'

She thought he was going to plead with her again: she wished he wouldn't. Poor Dev, she wondered now what she'd ever seen in him. It was the rebound; they said you always ran to the nearest man on the rebound.

But he did not plead. Instead, he stared at the fire, as though she had rebuked him. It was awful, wasn't it, but there was nothing she could say or do. She tried: she tossed her half-smoked cigarette into the fireplace and put her arm around his shoulder, comforting him. 'I'm going to miss you too,' she said. 'I'll always have a special feeling for you, Dev. And now, will you do something for me?'

He wished she would take her arm away. He watched the cigarette butt smoulder in the grate. It was Mrs Dempsey's grate: he must pick the butt up afterwards.

'Yes,' he said. 'What do you want?'

'I told the Herons not to come to the station with me tonight. I'm going to get a taxi and have the man put my luggage aboard the Dublin train. I wondered if you'd like to come down and have a last drink with me, before I go?'

'Yes,' he said.

'Don't you want to? Don't be afraid of hurting my feeling – if you don't want to come, just say so.'

'No, no,' he said quickly. 'I'd like to come very much.'

She removed her arm from his shoulder, stood up and walked to the window, drawing on her gloves. 'It's going to rain,' she said.

In the hall, they shook hands by the opened front door. 'I'll see you at six-thirty, then, under the station clock. All right?'

'Yes. Good-bye, Una.'

''Bye, Dev. See you under the clock.'

He watched her go down the path and open the garden gate. She waved to him, shut the gate and walked down the avenue. In a moment or two, she would be out of sight. He would never see her again. What was the use in going to the station? She was right, he couldn't change. For the rest of his life he'd go on telling people what they wanted to hear. She had wanted to hear him say he would come. He had said it. But in a moment or two, she would turn that corner . . . he would never see her again. In sudden awkward haste, he ran down the steps, opened the gate and ran out onto the pavement.

Beside him, in the avenue, a horse and cart waited idle, as their owner offered wood blocks by the bag at a front door across the way. The horse's head moved like a mine detector along the gutter, reins slack over the strong back. Mr Devine watching as Una turned the corner, absently put out his hand and fondled the horse's neck. The powerful muscles fluttered at his unexpected touch and the horse swung its head up, looking wildly down the avenue in the narrow focus of its blinkers. Horse and man looked down the avenue, and there was no one there. The horse, harnessed, dumb, lowered its head once more. The man went back into the house.

As he passed the parlour door, Mrs Dempsey straightened up and the gas fire died behind her with a sudden cough. Una's lipsticked butt lay like a small sin in the palm of her hand.

'Mr Devine? You've finished in here, I suppose.'

'Yes,' he said.

ALSO BY BRIAN MOORE IN TRIAD/GRANADA
PAPERBACKS

All these books are available at your local bookshop or newsagent, and can be ordered direct from the publisher.

To order direct from the publisher just tick the titles you want and fill in the form below:

Name _____

Address _____

_____

Send to:
Granada Cash Sales
PO Box 11, Falmouth, Cornwall TR10 9EN

Please enclose remittance to the value of the cover price plus:

UK 45p for the first book, 20p for the second book plus 14p per copy for each additional book ordered to a maximum charge of £1.63.

BFPO and Eire 45p for the first book, 20p for the second book plus 14p per copy for the next 7 books, thereafter 8p per book.

Overseas 75p for the first book and 21p for each additional book.

Granada Publishing reserve the right to show new retail prices on covers, which may differ from those previously advertised in the text or elsewhere.